RESISTING THE CEO

IONA ROSE

Resisting The CEO

Publisher: Some Books
ISBN- 978-1-913990-47-3

Hey there!

Thank you for choosing my book. I sure hope that you love it. I'd hate to part ways once you're done though. So how about we stay in touch?

My newsletter is a great way to discover more about me and my books. Where you'll find frequent exclusive giveaways, sneak previews of new releases and be first to see new cover reveals.

And as a HUGE thank you for joining, you'll receive a FREE book on me!

With love,

Iona

Get Your FREE Book Here:

https://dl.bookfunnel.com/v9yit8b3f7

PROLOGUE

Ace

I glance at my watch once more. I know that I'm early but still, Reggie seems to have taken me at my word and won't arrive one minute before four. I have to admit that it's my sheer excitement in seeing this task finally coming to an end that has me here fifteen minutes before the time we agreed on meeting. That's even why I chose to wait on a bench outside rather than a booth inside. After two years I finally have all the answers. Reggie has been keeping close tabs on the target, and this meeting will be the last. It's time for me to step in and take the situation to the next level.

I run a hand through my neatly trimmed hair, pleased that Bobby did a fantastic job as always. As a child I always had a heavy mop of dark brown hair that was always getting into my eyes. It was, of course, out of necessity and an inability to do better at the time. But as I grew, I had vowed that as an adult my hair would never be in my face.

My eyes flick to my watch once more and I rise from the bench I've been sitting on for the past ten minutes and scan the parking lot. Then I see a familiar vehicle and my eyes light up instantly. With a spring in my step I make long strides as fast as my six-foot two-inch height can take me and enter the coffee shop. I head to the corner booth I had reserved earlier and wait.

A few moments later the door opens and several people enter. When the activity at the door clears, I spot the familiar short, plump figure with shocking red hair. I smile as Reggie slides into the booth.

"Well?"

She laughs. "Impatient much?"

I make a face at her. Regina Bernard has been working for me since the day I made my first million. I'm a man who wants the best of everything. So, when I needed a private investigator, Regina Bernard, a retired ex-army officer, came highly recommended. In the years I've known her she has never let me down. And she hasn't this time around either.

She pushes a file across the table to me and my heart skips a beat. This file has it all: two years of surveillance, interviews, transcribed conversations, detailed notes, everything. Regina is very thorough and very good at her job.

She flips it open and points to the picture on top.

"That was taken this morning."

I stare into a pair of green eyes that have haunted me for the better part of ten years. Finally I have something solid. I look up at Regina.

"You have no idea how much I appreciate this."

She laughs and shakes her head. "I know exactly how much you appreciate this, Ace. I have a six-figure check in my account waiting to be cleared that tells me how much."

I grin and she gives me that motherly smile of hers as she continues.

"Ace, I've known you for what, five years? And out of all the jobs I've done for you, this was the simplest. Yet this is the biggest check you've cut for me. I don't know why you needed this information, but clearly it means a lot to you. And based on the subject I can only surmise why."

I point to the picture. "This is one of the reasons I'm here today and have the positions I have in this city. This has been my motivation when I struggled to maintain my college scholarship and balance it with my academics and athletics. When I started with nothing, this was the motivation that made me want to be something. When I had to seek a loan for my first venture, this is what made me determined to get to a position funding myself thereafter and to never need to ask for money again. When I'm at my lowest, this makes me want to get up and brush the dust off and keep going." with every point I make, I jab at the picture for emphasis. I lean back and meet Regina's eyes.

"I have never forgotten the kindness that was shown to me. I'm just trying to show my gratitude."

Regina looks at me carefully and I struggle to maintain my composure, knowing her keen eyes miss nothing. We are thankfully interrupted by a waitress. We order a couple of coffees and sandwiches which come shortly after. I skillfully turn the conversation to other assignments I've had pending the completion of this one. I know Regina is not fooled by my diversion, but she knows to leave well enough alone.

We leave the shop a few minutes before five and head to our respective vehicles. As I drive home, my excitement builds. I can't wait to spread out the contents of the file on my table and go through each detail.

I hasten to my penthouse apartment, and in a few moments, I'm feasting my eyes on every piece of information gathered over the past two years. There are pictures. There are conversations. There are notes about favorite items. Everything is there.

When I've gone through every scrap of paper, I lean back, my mind spinning with the information. I go to the bar and pour a drink before going back to the table. Now what should my next move be in this project?

I skim through the papers once more. There has to be something that I can use to make contact without coming across like a stalker. Then I see it and a thought comes to mind. It's a bit over the top. But when a man has more than nine zeros behind the figures in his various bank accounts, over the top is what he's allowed to be.

I move to my home office, taking the file with me. I turn on my laptop and within a few seconds I'm scouring a company website. I glimpse a few pictures of my target but Regina already has those in the file along with her notations. I sit twiddling my thumbs for a few moments, a tiny smile curving my lips. A man of my means has a variety of investment and business interests. What's one more to add to the collection?

I pick up my phone and call my accountant.

"Yes, Ace?"

"Hey, Anthony. I need to buy a company. It's called McEachron."

There is a slight pause, presumably as he writes. "Anything else?"

"Make it as quick as possible, please."

"I'll get Larry on it first thing in the morning."

"Appreciated."

I disconnect the call and open the file once more. My forefinger traces the picture on top. As I gaze into the green eyes looking up at me, memories of other times when this green-eyed gaze was fixed on me come sneaking up and I feel my heart expand. Those eyes had been the kindest I had ever met, and it had broken my heart to leave them behind. But now that I'm able, I'm going to make good on the promise I made to myself when I turned eighteen. It has taken me nine years to do it. But now, within a few weeks or however long it will take to convince the owners to sell me their company, I will fulfill that promise.

CHAPTER 1

LANA

I feel the warmth of the sun through my closed eyes and I smile. I stretch and slowly allow my eyes to flutter open. Today is going to be a good day. No matter what is thrown at me, my day will not be spoiled. Today I turn twenty-three.

I stretch once more before getting out of bed and opening the drapes in my bedroom. The bright June sun comes streaming in and I smile. I love being a summer baby. It means that there are no snow storms or cold spells to interfere with my big day. My green eyes crinkle with mirth as I think about the celebration my best friend Kyla has already insisted on, no questions asked.

I'm usually the most no-nonsense one in our little group of four. But I will make an exception to my strict rules of no clubbing or drinking during the week. It's my birthday and I'll do whatever I want.

As I get dressed for work, I keep an eye on my phone. By the time I'm heading out the door, my spirit is even lighter having spoken to my parents and siblings. As the youngest in the Gray clan, I expect to be pampered on my special day. And such has always been the case, even when resources were scarce. My family is always making sure that my brother, sister and I enjoy our birthdays and special holidays, no matter the limitations. I remember for my thirteenth birthday we had a few extra people staying in our house and it was more mouths to feed. And so, rather than buying a cake, my mother and sister got creative and made my cake. My brother and his friends used his art supplies to make the decorations, and everyone else chipped in to make my first birthday as a teenager memorable. As the years went on, things got easier and there was a little more money.

I smile as I get to the parking lot. The second-hand sedan had been a graduation and twenty-first birthday gift in one. The entire family had saved for it and revealed they had been saving for it since I entered college at eighteen. And I'm proud of it. I'm also happy to be in a position to do my part in the family. I can't wait for Christmas when we will all be together again. My siblings and I have been hatching a plan for our parents' thirtieth anniversary in December. I can't wait to see the look on their faces when they unwrap *that* gift.

As I drive to work, I can't help the smile that seems to be fixed on my lips. I'm twenty-three! When I think of all my accomplishments in such a short life, I'm thankful. Since I was in elementary school, I set my goals for my dream job. I've always had an interest in writing and journalism, and made it my job to align myself with the necessary entities to fulfill that goal. It came as no surprise to anyone who knew me that I was the editor of our high school newspaper and that I chose to study writing in college. It had been a no-brainer. I loved what I did. And so being one of the editors in a medium-sized publishing company is more of a passion being fulfilled than a job providing a paycheck. I feel blessed to be one of the few of my peers who actually enjoys what I do.

I pull into the parking lot of the twenty story building and find my usual spot. A quick check of my appearance shows my long black hair pinned into a neat bun at my nape. My long lashes need no mascara and only the slightest hint of gloss on my lips to make them shine. I pull out my compact and pat at my nose to reduce the shine. I've never worn much make-up as there is no need. I have to say I have been blessed with good genes. When others look at me they see a pretty face and a well-toned body from years of sports and in recent times my gym regimen. I can't count how many times I've been told to explore a career in modeling. I always make a face and smile out of politeness but nothing will entice me away from spending hours poring over hundreds of thousands of words, with my felt tipped pen making marks as I go on a paper manuscript, or my fingers flying over the keys on an electronic one.

I step out of the car and grab my purse and laptop bag. I straighten my pencil skirt and ensure that my blouse is properly tucked inside. In my heels, my five-foot seven height has been elevated to five-ten. I set off across the lot, the click of my heels creates a tattoo.

I enter the building, smiling and greeting as I make the journey through the lobby to the elevator that will take me to the tenth floor.

As I step off the elevator, I smile broadly at the 'Happy Birthday Lana!' sign on the wall.

"Happy Birthday to you, happy birthday to you, Happy Birthday dear Lana, Happy Birthday to you!"

"Awwww! You guys, thank you!" I smile at the birthday committee.

I allow my bags to be taken as a sash is slipped over my head and a tiara pinned into my hair. This is one of our little office traditions that make us such a tightly-knit company. I know that at lunch time there will be a cake waiting for me in the break room.

I head to my office, smiling and waving as I receive more greetings and well wishes. On my desk, there's a bouquet of flowers and a gift from my department. My smile gets broader as I sniff the pink roses. My birthday has begun.

The day flies by on wings and before I know it, I'm heading home. It's still early and I plan to take a nap before meeting the others later. I strip quickly and hop into the shower. When I get out, I put my hair in hot rollers then slap on a bonnet and climb into bed.

When next I open my eyes, the room is dark and I check the clock to find that it's a quarter past eight. My timing is perfect and I begin to get ready for my night out on the town.

I have to admit that at first I'd been skeptical about Kyla's bold suggestion that I use a sick day tomorrow and live it up with a few drinks tonight. But the more time that passed the more I saw the merit in the suggestion. I'm always the sensible one, but tonight I'm going to throw caution to the wind and live a little. I did have sick days sitting, doing nothing. And what's more, at last month's general staff meeting, Benny and Greg, the company owners, made the shocking announcement that they had sold the company. At first there was unease but we've been assured it is simply a change of ownership and the new owner is not interested in firing anyone so our jobs are secure. So, I consider tonight to be one of my last hurrahs before the new owner takes up residence next Monday. I'm still trying to make up my mind regarding going to work or calling in sick tomorrow, but it all depends on how far tonight goes. And knowing these girls, it may well be that I'll be working off a hangover tomorrow.

I sit in front of the vanity and skillfully apply my make-up. I apply my foundation sparingly and get to work. I do my eyelids in smoky shades, apply a deep red lipstick with hints of gold glitter. I use a swipe of gold mascara on the tips of my lashes as the finishing touch.

I use a body cream that leaves gold undertones all over my skin. I know that the little golden flecks will show up under the strobe lights in the clubs. I slip into a tight red dress that zips at the side. It has rhinestone accents randomly placed and I know these will catch the strobe lights as well. As I twist and turn in the mirror, I begin to look forward to the night out even more. It's been a long time since I let myself go like this. I'm glad Kyla talked me into it.

I pull out the rollers and am pleased with the bounce of the curls. I use my curling iron to further curl a few tendrils around my face. I bob up and down a few times, loving how my hair stays in place. I pull out my jewelry box and find the earrings my sister gave me last year and the necklace my mother gave me for graduation. The little golden balls and necklace are the perfect accessories. Finally, I slip my feet into gold stilettos and buckle them at my ankles.

As I pick up a small evening bag just big enough for my phone, keys and some money, my phone rings.

"I'll be right down!"

I spray a few drops of perfume on my neck, elbows and wrists, pick up my keys and phone and I'm off for a night out with my girls.

I grin broadly as I'm greeted by loud cheers of happy birthday from the mini coupe in the parking lot. Kyla, Megan, Vanessa and I have been friends since junior high. And our bond continues though we went to different colleges. Apart from Vanessa who is an airline hostess, we all live within a few blocks of each other and see each other often. Vanessa, though, always makes it a point to set her schedule to coincide with these celebrations.

I kiss and hug them each in turn and then get into the car. We're off.

Dinner at Broken Plate is everything I expect from a five-star restaurant. And the cherry on top is the birthday cake my friends arranged to be made for me. I know I'll have to hit the gym to work off all the cake I've eaten today, but it's worth it. After dinner it's off to the clubs. The first two don't yield much activity. What else is to be expected on a Wednesday night though? But when we pull into the parking lot at Nirvana a few minutes before midnight, we can hear the music thumping. We park quickly and head inside and are immediately swept into the festive vibe.

We make our way to one of the bars and Kyla alerts the bartender to our celebration. A tequila shot is quickly sent my way, and at the coaxing of my friends and other patrons, I down it in one gulp. I gasp and shudder as the liquid burns its way down my throat and into my stomach. I haven't done shots since college and it feels good to be a little looser than usual.

We head to the dance floor and are instantly taken away by the music and the vibe. We don't care who wants to stare as we throw our hands in the air and move our feet to the beat. A few guys ask us to dance and we oblige from time to time. I have to admit it feels good to relax a little. I can't remember the last time I was not at home before ten on a weeknight. I have to say I'm enjoying my night of rebellion.

We take a break from dancing and head back to the bar. We find four seats and decide to chill and chat for a bit. But talking at a bar is almost impossible. And so, we soon turn to a drinking game of truth or dare.

The first round of shots was easy enough with a little truth. The next round of dares was simple enough as well. Then a round of truth again. I have to admit that after that third shot, I'm feeling quite giddy. I try to remember who is supposed to be driving and end up turning too fast and send my bar stool spinning. I throw my head back and laugh as I spin a few more times.

"Okay guys. This has to be the last shot round. I don't think I can take much more," Vanessa blurts out.

"Let's make it a good one then. Lana, you're up first."

I eye the glass in front of me skeptically.

"Hey! This looks like a double shot!"

"Bigger dares, bigger shots." Megan grins and winks at me. "Now drink!"

I take a deep breath and square my shoulders. I pick up the glass, put it to my lips and lean back. I count to ten as the contents go down. With a triumphant bang, I slam the glass onto the counter.

"There! Now what's my dare?"

"You see that guy over there?" Kyla inclines her head in a direction just over my shoulder and I turn.

"There are many guys over there, Kyla."

"The one in the red shirt at the end of the bar. I dare you to go up and kiss him without saying a word."

Megan laughs. "Good one, Kyla! I've had my eye on that hottie and he's been turning girls away all night. Let's see what he does with Lana. Now remember. Don't talk. Just walk over and kiss him."

"Done!"

I fluff my hair and straighten my dress then take a deep breath. I take a few steps then look back over my shoulder, smirking at my friends. I'll kiss him alright. On the cheek! They can't say that I failed. I turn and continue my journey. I bite my lip to prevent myself from saying anything. When I'm a few feet away, he looks up and our eyes meet. I move quickly before he can react and lean in towards his cheek. My lips are almost at the target when I get the shock of my life. Everything happens so quickly.

At the last second, he turns his head and my lips meet his full on. And before I can try to pull back, he embraces me and pulls me close.

His lips are firm against mine as he kisses me hard. I push against his chest and pull back in shock. I look into his eyes and see the mirth there. Without a second thought, I wriggle out of his embrace and slap him hard across the face.

As I turn to walk away, I hear him laugh. My cheeks are burning by the time I get back to my seat.

"Done!"

My friends high five me and I cover my consternation at what happened with a gulp of water. I'm only half listening to the next dare as I find my eyes turning toward the end of the bar. The man has his eyes fixed on me, a smile on his face. He holds up his glass and nods at me and I spin around to my friends once more. I force myself not to look at the end of the bar for the rest of the night.

CHAPTER 2

ACE

I've learned throughout my life that timing is everything and I can't allow anticipation to make me get ahead of myself. It is one of the strategies I've employed in my approach to investments that have led to my being named as one of the top ten youngest and richest men in the country. I've always kept my cool and am known as a shrewd negotiator. But ever since the meeting with Reggie and the wheels I've set in motion, anxiety has tried to get the best of me. Publicly, I'm still Ace Channing, billionaire investor. But privately I find that I have reverted to the shy and fearful boy, Chester Abrahams. I haven't been Chester in almost ten years. The power of money and a deed poll could have had me changing my name to Tom Thumb for all I cared. As I think about Chester then and Ace now, the difference is striking and goes much further than appearances. My attitude has improved and my mind sharper. I can only hope that she loves Ace as much as she did Chester. There I go, getting ahead of myself again.

It takes a few weeks, but finally, my signature is on the requisite documents and I relax a little. It's been a bit of a haggling back and forth as there was some resistance at first. But ultimately, the all mighty dollar spoke and McEachron is now mine. Now to set phase three in motion.

In the time that remains before I take up my new position as CEO of McEachron, I do some reading on my new company and am impressed. It was started by best friends who had a similar passion for writing and publishing, and has been in operation for almost ten years. Ironically, neither of them is named McEachron. They have won several awards in the field over the years and I do not feel as though my money has been wasted in an effort to get close to my target.

As I continue to read, I know that my management team was a bit shocked at my desire to acquire this company, but they have learned not to question my judgment. After all, hasn't it been my investment decisions that have caused them to be able to live a life of veritable ease and comfort? I continue to let them think this is business. Only I, and possibly Reggie, know it's personal, very personal.

I know it's a further shock to my team when I decide to have a physical office in this company, and I will actually be sitting in the office daily. Let them try to figure it out. I'll keep my cards close to the vest on this one.

The week before I am to occupy my new office is a trying one. I had wanted to occupy the office this week for a particular reason but the old owners had been insistent on finishing out the month. I am not amused, but they were unbending on this point which puts a damper on my spirits.

When I wake up on Wednesday and the realization of being so near yet so far hits me, I take my frustrations out in the gym. I cancel most of my meetings for the day and mope around the apartment. I have dinner delivered, staving off the disappointment I feel in not being able to be out on a date as I had planned. I decide that after sulking at home all day, it's better to sulk by taking myself out for the night. For a man who is accustomed to getting anything he wants, this disappointment is one I have to swallow bitterly.

As I leave home I can't help but drive by my target's home. I get a mild surprise as I find an excursion in progress. I watch as the car with the four girls pulls out of the parking lot, and I do what anyone else in my current state of mind would do, I follow. One restaurant and three bars later, I watch as the group walks into Nirvana. I give them a few minutes to get settled ahead of me before entering. I take up my usual seat at the end of the bar and Paul comes over.

"What'll have tonight, Mr. Channing?"

"The usual."

"Coming right up."

I soon have a drink in front of me. I watch out of the corner of my eye as the group laughs and talks. Cheers erupt as the lady in red downs a shot and I feel something shift inside me as I look at the group. I swallow hard against the lump that has suddenly formed in my throat. I could just walk over and pull her into my arms but I resist the temptation. The anticipation of next week is killing me, but I play it cool.

"Hi there! Would you like to dance?"

I turn to find a pretty little blonde at my shoulder and frown slightly.

"Nope."

I swivel around to the counter once more, not caring whether or not she left.

"Rude!" I hear her mutter underneath her breath. I continue to watch the group of four out of the corner of my eye.

I watch as they go to the dance floor and I feel a sense of possessiveness and jealousy rise up when she dances with several men. I down a few more drinks and turn down a few more invitations to dance.

The group soon returns to the bar and I continue my surveillance. It's all I can do to keep from staring. I notice Paul is spending a little more time at that end of the bar as well as they down round after round of shots.

Then I notice their heads bow together. One of them looks over at me and I turn away quickly, hoping my observation hasn't been noticed. Then I detect a slight movement as the lady in red moves away from the group. I see her look back slightly then she continues her journey in my direction. As she comes closer I feel my heart begin to beat fast. Could she be coming to me? What are they scheming? Have they been watching me as much as I've been watching them? I take another sip of my drink.

I wait until she's close before I look up and look directly at her. For a moment, the bar melts away and the crowd fades and I'm taken back to the first time I saw those green eyes of hers. Will she remember me? I hold her gaze. There is no hint of recognition in her eyes. I glance at her friends who are all watching us.

As she leans forward, I guess her intention and am happy to oblige. I turn and meet her lips, pulling her into an embrace. I am cool outwardly but inside I'm bubbling with excitement. This is not how I pictured our first kiss, but it will do. I have her in my arms and that's enough. I feel the familiarity of her waist and my mind is thrown into a mix of past and present. Has it been a decade since I last saw her, last hugged her? Will there be any familiarity in my embrace for her and any recollection on her part? I want to bury my face in her hair as I did that last morning, but I'm unwilling to relinquish her lips.

I kiss her hard, wishing I could take it further and deeper in an effort to make up for all the lost time. I want to leave the club with her and pour out everything I've held on to all these years and forget about my plan to take it slow and not shock her. I want to forget about allowing her memories to return on their own and just drop the pretense. This first kiss has bowled me over and I feel as if nothing in my life can ever be wrong again. But the peace is not to be.

She pushes against my chest and our lips part. She looks up at me, her eyes glinting angrily. Without a word, she raises her hand and slaps me hard, and my cheek begins to burn. I watch as she walks away and I can't help but laugh. So much for wondering if she remembers me. Clearly, she does not. As I rub my cheek, I remember the fieriness of her personality. Based on what I know is coming, I know I've not seen the last of it either.

She gets back to her group and I see them laugh and high-five each other. Dare completed I suppose. But now that we both have each other's attention, I don't feel awkward about staring. I fix my gaze on her, willing her to look at me. Sure enough, she looks up and our eyes meet across the distance between us. I raise my glass and smile, and she turns back to her friends. I laugh softly at the stiffness in her posture.

My feisty little Lana. It's one of the things I admire most about her. She is strong and determined about her goals. And from the looks of things, some of the things she set for her future have come to pass. I can't wait to be a part of her life.

I beckon to Paul and he comes over.

"The group at the bar with the brunette in the red dress?"

"Yes, Mr. Channing?"

"Put their drinks for the night on my tab."

"Sure thing, Mr. Channing."

I slide a few bills across to him and his eyes widen at the amount.

"They've all been drinking a bit so please see to it that they get home safely."

"Sure thing, Mr. Channing."

I nod and get up. As I make my way to the parking lot, the cool night air hits my face. Who would have thought that my night out to drown my disappointment would have resulted in coming face-to-face with the object of my desire? And kissing her no less! Brief though the kiss had been, it is enough to tell me I made the right decision with finding Lana.

As I drive home, my head is filled with images of her striking green eyes and coal-black hair. She hasn't changed much, maybe a little taller and definitely curvier. I can hardly be surprised that she did not recognize me. I look very different now than I did then.

Now that I've come face to face with her, it's as though every part of my life has shifted to include her. Will she accompany me to my apartment soon? As I enter the elevator, I wonder what our reflections will look like in the mirrored walls. Will she take my hand as we exit and walk down the carpeted corridor to my door?

I head into my penthouse and breathe a sigh of relief at the silence. Over the past few years my life has taken a few unexpected twists and turns, good, bad and in-between. But I can say that I have done quite well for a twenty-seven-year-old man. I look around at the beautiful apartment and smile. If things go as planned, I'll be switching it for a house by next year.

The decorator had given the apartment a masculine tone when I had it redone a few years ago. But I feel as though more colors and softness will be included in my next decorating project. I feel a sense of exhilaration and expectation at the thought. It is amazing how small encounters can change a life.

I sit on the balcony for a while, looking at the city lights twinkling below me. My thoughts are far away, though, as I allow the past to encroach. I rarely think back to those dark times. But now I must if I am to appreciate the present. As the darkness crowds in, I take deep breaths and allow the memories to flood me. But at the end there is a bright spark, a ray of hope. It's the power of that small encounter years ago, and the one less than two hours ago that have made a difference in my life. And it is to this ray I cling as I'm transported back to the present.

I pull a worn picture from my wallet and sigh. So often I've looked at this picture, using it to remind me of the end game. And now everything is within reach. I smile as I return it to its safe place and head inside.

I shower and turn on my laptop. Though it's nearly four in the morning here, I have a meeting halfway across the world where it is now one in the afternoon. I could have flown there but had changed my mind at the last minute.

By the time the meeting ends, the sun is up and pouring in through the floor to ceiling windows. As I log off, I stifle a yawn. I rise and draw the drapes, plunging the room into semi-darkness. I answer a few emails before deciding that I need to get some sleep. But there is one final thing I must do.

I log into the site of the store I had chosen a few days ago and scan the selections. I make my choice and pay, sending delivery instructions in the details. With that being done, I shut down the laptop and head to bed.

My last thought as I drift off is the feel of Lana's lips on mine. I smile into the darkness, anticipating what it will be like to feel her body beside mine and wake up with her. I've made some excellent financial choices over the past five years, choices that have resulted in the billions now in my accounts. But good though those choices are, none of them can compare to my choice to find Lana. And now that I've found her, I'll be damned if I am going to let her go. Lana Gray has no idea what is in store for her.

CHAPTER 3

LANA

I studiously keep my back turned to the man at the end of the bar. The nerve of him! I soon forget all about the encounter, and an hour later, we leave. Megan, Vanessa and I go to the restroom, leaving Kyla to take care of our bill. As we head to the car, Kyla turns to me with a grin.

"It seems we're going to have to let you kiss some more strange men in bars, Lana. The bartender said our bill was paid by Mr. Red-shirt."

"What!" I look at her with a perturbed expression.

"And he even left money for an Uber to get us home if we were too drunk to drive."

"Wow, Lana! That must have been some kiss you planted on him, huh. I wonder what would have happened if you hadn't slapped him." Megan giggles.

I feel my cheeks burn at the remark.

"If I'm to be honest, I was going for his cheek and he turned suddenly. It caught me off-guard."

"Just the same, a few extra dollars in my pocket is not something I'm going to complain about right now. Happy birthday again, sweetie. I hope you had a great time."

"I had a fabulous time. I can't express how much I love and appreciate you guys."

"We'll see how much you love and appreciate us when you wake up in the morning and those drinks come pounding back in your head," Vanessa laughs and we all join her. She is right.

I am the first one to be dropped off, and after kisses and hugs, I make my way upstairs. I slip out of my shoes and my feet wiggle in relief. I head to the bathroom, wipe off my makeup and wash my face. I begin to feel the weariness catching up with me and I slip out of my dress, leaving it in a heap on the floor. I take two aspirin in anticipation of a hangover headache and hope it will stave off the pain when I wake up in a few hours.

I yawn widely as I head to bed. My last thought as I close my eyes is that I need to set my alarm to call in sick tomorrow.

When the alarm goes off, I jump up, startled. My eyes are barely open and my throat feels scratchy. Good. It will convey the impression that I am genuinely ill. I make the call, use the bathroom, and go back to bed.

The next time I wake up my stomach growls. I stretch and turn to look at the clock. It is a little after eleven and I sigh. It has been a while since I've slept this late. Even on weekends I'm up early doing chores and running errands.

I yawn and stretch once more before getting out of bed. I head to the bathroom. Half an hour later, I emerge, somewhat refreshed. I head to the kitchen and fix a bowl of cereal. After breakfast, I set up my laptop on the counter and get cracking on some work.

There are a few emails that I answer in between editing. A few hours later, I stop for a late lunch before plowing on once more. It's nearly four by the time I decide to stop. Just as I'm about to shut down, an email comes in from my supervisor, Charles.

Attention all:

As you are aware, effective Monday July 2, 2021, we will be under new management. As such, there will be a function where we will be bidding adieu to the old and welcoming the new. At the instructions of our incoming CEO, the office will close at midday tomorrow to facilitate a luncheon. This function will serve as a 'meet and greet' as our new CEO seeks to become familiar with the staff. All are expected to be in attendance.

Charles Dunbar

Editor In Chief

Wow! This week is only getting better. This feels like two days off in one week.

As I close the laptop and start thinking about dinner, my thoughts turn to the change of management. Everyone I've spoken to is just as curious as I am regarding the change of personnel. There are no financial issues as far as we know. And the company has been doing well too. The sale is a shock to us all. But we have taken comfort in the fact that our jobs are secure.

I decide on some ramen and prepare it quickly. Before I know it, my evening winds down and I head to bed.

The next morning when I wake up, I'm fully revived and energized, ready to take on the day. I dress carefully, pairing a typical black pencil skirt that I wear for work with a blouse that is a little dressier than my casual Friday oxford shirt. It's a top I've been meaning to wear but have never found the occasion. It's a deep shade of purple and silky. The long sleeves are loose and end in a tight cuff on my wrist. The collar has two ribbons which are tied in a bow at my neck. I put my hair up into a high bun. Feeling a little festive, I slide hairpins topped with rhinestones in on either side. I do my face carefully for the occasion with light foundation and shades of purple on my lids. My lipstick is a deep matte purple to match my top. I contemplate if I should wear pantyhose or not. I decide on the latter and choose a pair of stilettos instead. The six-inch heels are definitely out of place in the office, but for a luncheon of this sort I'm not holding back. One thing my parents always taught me is that first impressions last. I wasn't going to turn up to meet the new CEO in jeans and t-shirt.

Satisfied with my look, I head down to the parking lot and head to work. When I walk into the office, it's clear that I'm not the only one who thinks it wise to dress up a bit. There is a buzz of excitement as the speculation about the new owners gets to a high. Up until now, no one knows who bought the company. There have been rumors about being merged with another of the leading publishers in the city.

There are even speculations that we are now aligned with a foreign entity.

I get to my office and am surprised to find a small package on my desk. I smile at the happy birthday wrapping. I won't turn down any belated gifts. I'm about to open it when there's a knock on my open door. I look up as Charles enters.

"You're here, great! Could you take a quick look at Myra's latest manuscript please? I need a second opinion."

"Sure. Send it over."

"Great."

I slip the package into my purse and turn on my computer. A few minutes later, I receive an email from Charles. Before I know it, I'm buried in the pages of one of our main writers' latest novels. I'm barely half way through when I sense a buzz of activity outside. By the time I look up, Marissa pushes her head into my office.

"It's almost twelve, Lana. Aren't you coming to the luncheon? What kind of stupid question is that, of course you're coming to the luncheon. *Everyone* has to be there. Remember?"

I can't help but grin at Marissa as she asks and answers her own question.

"I didn't realize it was this late. I'll head out in a few. Which restaurant is it by the way?"

"It's that new Japanese affair downtown. Imperial I think is the name." She wrinkles her nose and looks around.

"Justin! What's the name of the restaurant we're going to again?"

"Imperial!"

"Okay! Thanks, Justin!"

"Welcome!"

She turns back to me with a grin. "Imperial. Can I hitch a ride with you, please?"

"Sure. No problem. I'll meet you in the parking lot."

She graces me with one of her stellar smiles that can light up any room. "Thanks, Lana!"

As she leaves, I save what I've done on the manuscript thus far and email it to myself for safekeeping. I make a quick trip to the ladies' room, happy that it's almost empty. But the lingering scents of various perfumes bears evidence of the recent occupants. I redo my lipstick and check my hair before heading back to my office. I grab my purse and head downstairs. The parking lot is buzzing with activity as various carpools head to the restaurant. I find Marissa, Avery and Justin waiting by my car and I frown.

"I hope you don't mind, Lana. I kind of told Avery and Justin they could ride with us." Marissa wrings her hands dramatically.

I give her a tight smile, struggling to remain calm. Justin is no problem. But there is something about Avery that rubs me the wrong way. She is friendly and helpful and everything, but there's something underneath her 'nice' demeanor that doesn't sit well with me. Nevertheless, I open the car and we all pile inside.

"I do hope that you are feeling better, Lana. Charles told me you called in sick yesterday?" Avery's voice is soft as she speaks.

"I'm feeling much better, thank you."

"That's great. It's a good thing you were ill after your birthday and not before. It would have been a shame to ruin your big day."

I glance at her sharply in the rearview mirror. She has an angelic smile painted on her lips. But it doesn't quite reach her eyes.

"Yes. It would have," I respond bluntly.

The rest of the ride is taken up with continued speculation about the new owners and what it means for us. I wisely keep my lips sealed, conscious of my position as a junior middle manager and that I am a senior to Marissa, Avery and Justin who all work in the clerical department.

We soon arrive at the restaurant and are taken upstairs by a hostess. As we step in, I am immediately impressed by the details in the décor. Bistro tables are set up all around the room and there is a buffet running along both sides. There's a bar area at the back.

I mingle with my coworkers, laughing and chatting and accepting belated greetings from those who haven't seen me since my birthday.

As I finish a delicious wrap, I head to the bar.

"What can I get for the lady?" The bartender gives me a wide smile.

"A mimosa, please."

"One mimosa coming right up, beautiful."

I watch as he makes my drink and places it before me. I take a sip as he watches and give him a thumbs up. As I take another sip, I hear a low voice in my ear.

"If a shot gets me a quick kiss, I wonder what a mimosa will get me? Maybe something more?"

I spin around to find the man from the bar at Nirvana. What the hell!? I blink furiously.

"What the hell are *you* doing here? This is a private function. Are you stalking me?"

On the last word, I throw the remains of my drink in his face, not even caring that we have drawn a small crowd.

I hear a collective gasp go up, but I don't care. He fishes out a handkerchief, a mocking smile on his face.

"What a creep." I hiss as I push him in the chest then turn and storm out.

By the time I get to the parking lot, I'm shaking like a leaf. I tear out of the lot as though demons are chasing me. Where on earth did he come from and how did he find me?

I run upstairs and head to my office. Only when I'm behind the closed door do I relax. I take a few deep breaths, forcing myself to calm down.

When I regain some control, I call the deli around the block for lunch, and turn on my computer. By the time my lunch arrives, I'm knee deep in the manuscript once more, all thoughts of this afternoon's incident forgotten. It's after three before I hear any signs of life in the office as people return from the luncheon. There's a knock on my door and it opens before I can give permission.

"Hello, dear." Elaine peeks in and I smile.

"Hi, Mrs. Elaine."

"I noticed that you left rather quickly so I brought you back a little something."

"Thank you, Mrs. Elaine." I smile at the woman as she shuffles into the office and takes a seat. She places a bag on my desk. Mrs. Elaine is the oldest member of the staff in both years of service and age. She's like a mother to everyone and spoils us rotten. But make no mistake, a better secretary cannot be found.

"It's a pity you didn't get to meet Mr. Channing, our new CEO." She nods and smiles. "I have to admit that I had my reservations about this change of management. But we will be fine. Benny and Greg were good, but I think Ace will be better."

"Ace?"

"Oh. That's Mr. Channing. He wants us all to continue being on a first name basis so he asked us to call him Ace. Handsome young fellow too. He might not know a lot about publishing, but he sure knows his way around business. Look him up when you get the chance. Well, I'll be getting along now. Those letters are not going to type themselves you know." She stands and pats the bag she brought.

"Enjoy."

"Thanks again, Mrs. Elaine."

"You're welcome, dear."

She slips out the door and I smile and shake my head. Before I can get back to work, there's another knock on my door. I look up to find Avery's soft blue eyes looking at me, her perfect smile pasted on her face. She pats her blonde hair in a way that I find irritating with her in particular.

"Hi, Lana. I hope everything is okay?"

"It's fine. Why do you ask?"

"Well, you were my ride to the restaurant. I had to find my way back."

"Oh! I'm so sorry about that. Something came up and I had to leave suddenly."

"So I saw." She looks at me keenly and I drop my eyes.

"I'll reimburse your Uber."

She waves me off. "That's okay. Ace saw us looking quite abandoned and offered us a ride back."

"Ace?"

"The new CEO."

"Oh! Okay. Well, I am sorry I left you guys in a difficult spot." I look at her steadily.

"No problem." She returns my steady gaze but I get the distinct feeling that there is something more penetrating in her gaze.

The silence is a tense one and then she shrugs.

"I'll let you get back to work then. Bye."

I look at the spot where she stood and can barely conceal my unease. I pride myself on being a likable person and one who likes almost everyone I meet. But Avery is a different matter altogether. I constantly reject any overtures from her regarding friendship, and go out of my way to work with any of the other clerks when I need their assistance with files. She makes me uneasy.

It's nearly six by the time I turn off my computer. The office has been empty since five and I'm now the last to leave. I visit the restroom before returning to lock up my office. I grab my purse and head to the parking lot. As I pull out, I adjust my rearview mirror. It seems as though I'm not the only one working late as I notice a flashy silver SUV pull out from one of our assigned spots as well. That is the kind of vehicle I can only dream of owning. I will settle with my humble sedan.

As I pull into traffic, my thoughts go back to the scene at Imperial. The nerve of him though! Who does he think he is? More importantly, how had he found me?

As I try to figure out how the stalker had appeared behind me out of nowhere at a private function, all I can think is he probably saw when I entered the restaurant and followed. But why would the hostess have allowed him to enter in the first place? As I recall how he had paid for our drinks and an Uber, I roll my eyes. No one is beyond bribery it seems.

I turn into my complex and find my parking spot. I head upstairs quickly and go through my evening routine of immediately stripping down to my underwear. I grab a bottle of water as I head to the bathroom. It's Friday evening which means it's time for a bubble bath.

I set up my candles and music as I go through my Friday evening unwinding ritual. Two hours later I get out, feeling thoroughly relaxed. I put a robe on and head to the kitchen. I remember the package from Mrs. Elaine and find my purse on the living room floor. As I unwrap the contents, my stomach growls. There is an assortment of wraps, pastry and fruit, quite enough for a dinner for one. I pop the wraps into the microwave and empty my purse. It would need a proper airing out with all that food that had been in it. As I empty it, I see the belated birthday gift I had completely forgotten about.

As I wait for the microwave to beep, I unwrap the gift to find a small box. My interest is now more than piqued. I lift the lid and gasp. There is what appears to be a solid gold bracelet nestled against black velvet. I reach for it with trembling fingers.

As I look closely, I can see that there are diamonds nestled in the creases of the design. The clasp comes open from a spring mechanism. I turn it over to inspect the inside. I frown as I look at the inscription: *L.O.N.G. & C.A.C.A. forever*

My heart races slightly. Those are my initials. But who is C.A.C.A.?

CHAPTER 4

ACE

As I watch Lana run out of the restaurant, there's silence from those around me. I feel the handkerchief plucked from my fingers and look down to find a little older woman with twinkling brown eyes dabbing at my damp shirt.

"I must apologize for our darling Lana. I can't imagine what has gotten into her. She hasn't been well. I do hope it isn't a fever that's gone to her brain." She dabs at me and I can't help but smile genuinely.

When Lana had doused me, I had wanted nothing more than to grab her and shake some sense into her. She has always had a bit of an impulse that needs curbing.

"Perhaps we could get a damp towel somewhere." She looks around and a hostess immediately produces a hot towel. She looks around at the small crowd around us and waves her hand imperiously.

"Go find something to eat and stop your gawking. He's not dead, you know." They disperse at her command and I look at her curiously.

"You are?"

"Elaine Wint. Pleased to make your acquaintance."

"Same here, Elaine. I'm Ace Channing."

"Nice to meet you Mr. Channing. You don't work for McEachron. Are you connected to the new owners perhaps?"

"Something like that."

"Oh dear! Our Lana has really put her foot into it hasn't she. Please forgive her. I'm sure she will apologize for herself when she gets the chance. She's not usually like this. I really don't know what would possess her to behave like this. She will certainly apologize."

"I'm sure she will. Thanks for your assistance, Mrs. Elaine. I can take it from here, I think they are about to begin."

"No problem, Mr. Channing."

I watch as she leaves and takes a seat in the section at one end of the room which has been set up with rows of chairs. I shake my head in amusement at the short conversation. I know *exactly* why Lana did what she did.

I'm directed to the restroom and clean myself up as best as I can. Lana is certainly making things a little rough with our reunion. And I still find it amazing that there is no hint of recognition on her part. Have I changed that much? Or perhaps the impression I thought I had left on her was not as great as I had hoped. The thought that Lana may not roll out the welcome mat has never crossed my mind in all of this. But whether or not she warms up to me, it is already too late.

I want her in my life, and she can either come kicking and screaming or willingly. But come she will.

I head back to the restaurant and stand at the back. Everyone else is now seated and I listen to Benny as he makes his farewell speech to the staff. As I wait to be introduced, I scan the gathering. I've already met Elaine who I already know will be my secretary. Everyone else will be introduced at some point.

I hear my name and walk to the front. There are several gasps and I surmise that these may be the ones who witnessed what transpired between Lana and me. I smile as I step to the podium and silence descends.

"Forgive me for my appearance. No one told me to walk with an umbrella."

There is a scattering of giggles and chuckles and the atmosphere lightens instantly. I continue with my speech.

"As a child, I always loved reading. Unfortunately, it was not something I could do often for one reason or another. As I grew, life took me in other directions and reading was more of a necessity than for enjoyment. I have been blessed, I can't lie. When I got it into my head to acquire a publishing company, I have no idea why McEachron came to mind. My people spoke to McEachron's people and, well, here we are. I look forward to working with all of you and learning about the business as I go. Let me assure everyone here that no jobs will be lost unless you choose to quit. I also want it to be known that I have an open-door policy and can be approached if needed. As a sign of good faith in your welcoming me to the McEachron family, there is a token for each member of staff which may be collected at the end of the luncheon. And one last thing. We are a family here. There'll be no Mr. Channing. My name is Ace. Thank you for having me and I look forward to many years of productivity."

I give a small wave and exit the stage to a round of applause.

The rest of the afternoon is spent with me walking around with Benny being introduced to each member of staff. I immediately place them in categories, especially the ladies. There are a few who are not averse to showing their interest openly. There is a particular blonde with pale blue eyes who places herself in my line of vision quite often. I find her a bit creepy and decide to keep my eye on her.

I feel a tug on my jacket and turn to find Elaine wagging her finger at me.

"You could have told me who you were, you know."

I grin broadly and place my arm around her shoulders. "That would have spoiled the fun, Mrs. Elaine. My humblest apologies. Am I forgiven?"

She looks me up and down briefly before smiling. "You are. For now. But I'm going to be keeping my eye on you."

I bow slightly. "Much obliged, Mrs. Elaine. And I'll be sure to mind my p's and q's with you."

We laugh and I continue to mingle.

At about three, the gathering begins to break up. I watch as the employees collect their personalized packages and leave. I've already instructed the hostess to retrieve the package for Lana Gray and place it in my car.

When the last person leaves, I go to the bar for a final drink. I watch as the efficient staff moves in and begins to clean up and put the room back in order. By the time I leave, the tables and chairs are back in place as the staff prepares for the dinner service.

I look down at my shirt with the stain from Lana's drink and can't wait to get home and shower. As I enter the parking lot, I come to a halt. There, standing in the middle, are two women and a man, all carrying the black and gold bags they have just received. And one of them is the blonde. Shit! And I have to pass them to get to my car.

I slip on my shades and step towards them. As I approach, the blonde speaks loudly.

"I think it's just mean and selfish of her to run off like that after being rude to our new *boss* and leaving us stranded like this."

"I'm sure Lana has a good reason for leaving, Avery. Lay off her," the little red-head responds.

"We can always catch an Uber back, you know." The man pushes his glasses further up his nose.

I take a deep breath and tell myself that it is just for the sake of the other two that I'm about to do what I'm about to do.

"Is everything okay ladies and gent?"

The blonde spins around dramatically. "Oh! Ace! I didn't know you were still here."

"Of course you did, Avery. Remember you said-"

"Shut up, Marissa," Avery bites out through clenched teeth. I ignore what Marissa says and turn to look at Avery with her fake smile pasted on her lips. The little schemer.

"Do you guys need a ride back to the office?"

"We certainly do. You see, we came with Lana, the girl who threw her drink at you, and she left us stranded. She can be pretty high-strung and unreliable, you know." Avery smiles innocently but there is a glint in her eyes. My instincts are right to tell me to watch this one.

"She isn't usually like that. This is unlike her," Marissa chimes in and comes to Lana's defense. Bless her.

"She has a lot to do so maybe she had to head back to the office to meet a deadline or something," the man says.

So far, Avery is the only one trying to malign Lana's character. I open the car with the remote and gesture toward it.

"I can give you a lift to the office if you'd like."

"Oh, thank you, Ace! You're a lifesaver." Avery's voice drips with honey and I shudder inwardly.

Before I can move, she heads to the car and stands by the front passenger door. I'm tempted to leave her waiting there, but the gentleman in me won't allow it. And so, I reluctantly walk over and open the door for her.

"Thank you!" she smiles at me and preens, and I barely smile back.

The young man has already helped Marissa in and I walk around to my seat. I look across at Avery and see that she has Lana's package.

"Let me have that please."

"Oh. I can deliver it to her." I do wish she would stop smiling at me.

"That's okay. I can deliver it myself." I pluck the bag from her fingers and place it in my door.

As we head to the office, we make small talk and I discover the young man is Justin and they all work in the clerical department. I now know which department to avoid since I don't want to run into Avery. Avery talks non-stop, inserting little pieces of information about herself which I studiously ignore. And when she begins to dig for information about me, I'm barely civil. It is with relief when we enter the parking lot and I pull into one of the spaces labeled McEachron. She sits waiting while the others get out. Well, I will be damned if I am going to get out and open her door once more. Thankfully, Justin opens her door and I see her roll her eyes at him angrily. She quickly masks her annoyance and turns to me.

"Thank you so much, Ace. You literally saved us just now."

"No problem."

I watch as they leave and I breathe a sigh of relief. I look around the parking lot and immediately

see that it's a shared space. The ones labeled 'MC' are ours. As I continue my perusal, I

wonder which car belongs to Lana. I check my watch. It's almost four. There's only one way to

find out. I drive around a bit until I find a spot which gives me a full view of the parking lot.

It is close to six by the time I see Lana enter the parking lot. I've watched every other employee, including Avery, depart. She had looked around the lot and I saw her do a double-take when she saw my car. For a moment, I had thought she was going to come over, but then Marissa had distracted her. They had both gotten into a little car and left. I make a mental note to drive the Jaguar on Monday. The last thing I need is for Avery to memorize my car and plates. Hmmm. I wonder what Reggie would turn up on Miss Avery Cartwright if I have her investigated. She seems to have stalker tendencies. I've been with enough to know their type.

I watch as Lana leaves and my heart melts. There's no way I can be angry at her. If only I can get her to calm down and give me a chance. I decide I can't come right out and tell her who I am. Instead, I will woo her. Then I will reveal myself. This way I can be assured she is attracted to the present me and not the past me.

As she drives out, I pull out behind her. As much as we are in city traffic, accidents do happen. I want to ensure that she gets home safely and I follow her to her complex. As I follow her, I decide she needs a new car. This one is looking a little worn. It'll be another birthday gift from me. There are several dealers that I can already think of who would have offerings that would suit what I want for Lana.

When I'm sure she must be safely inside, I leave and head home a few blocks away.

There is a lot I have to get done before Monday, and so, as soon as I shower, I head out once more. My meeting with my friend Edward at his house just outside the city runs longer than planned and I end up staying for dinner and drinks after.

As I sip my drink I look out from his balcony.

"This is a pretty nice setup you have here, Eddie."

"It's pretty sweet. And the wife loves it as well."

I laugh. "I can see that."

I had met Edward a few years ago when I was negotiating a buyout deal and he was one of the company's managers. Somehow, my instinct had kicked in and I had called him into a private meeting afterward. We had clicked and become friends, even after I had bought out his boss. Now he runs the company I bought. He got married a year later and I had been his best man.

"Sophia loves being out of the city. She's always been a country girl. Even though this is not as 'country' as she wants, it is better than skyscrapers and busy streets."

I nod in agreement. "I may look into joining you in another year or two."

He looks at me quizzically. "Oh yeah? Who's the lady?"

I throw my head back and laugh. "Why does there have to be a lady involved?"

"Come on, Ace. The city is where you thrive. You don't strike me as the suburban type much less country. Only a woman could drive you to consider a set up like this. And it would be good if it's true. Don't let one sour experience down the aisle turn you off the right one who is somewhere out there waiting for you."

"Spoken like a true married man." I slap him on the shoulder and he chuckles.

"But it is true. We all get to that stage where we feel the need to settle and start a family."

"You're a little bit further ahead on that journey, my man. I'll be the first to put in my application as godfather."

"You don't have a choice. Try to back out and I'll feed you to Sophia."

I roar with laughter, tears streaming down my face. We talk a little longer before I finally take my leave and make the thirty-minute drive back to the city. As I drive, I reflect on Edward's words. He is right about my love for the city. But I'm not inflexible. It is negotiable. And as I am already contemplating a house, it won't be a hard sell. I'll keep the apartment, of course, for those times when we will need somewhere to stay in the city. It could even be a space for business partners to stay when they come to the city as well. The good thing is that I have the resources to have options. Money is no object.

I pull into my complex and head upstairs. A glance at my watch shows minutes to ten. It's not as late as I thought. Good. I could get an hour's nap before changing and heading out again. The night is still young.

Later that evening as I sit in Corpus, I wonder what Lana is doing on this fine Friday night. Will she walk into the club and make the third time the charm? I doubt it but one can still hope for a miracle. Right?

CHAPTER 5

LANA

All weekend I reflect on the incident at the restaurant. I've always been a bit impulsive, and my temper flares when I'm caught off guard. First with the stranger at the bar kissing me back. Then out of nowhere the stranger shows up again. If I'm honest I don't regret throwing my drink at him. But I do regret that I had done it in front of my coworkers. There is never an excuse for poor conduct to be shown publicly, especially by an adult. And to make matters worse, there is no one at work I can confide in. I'm there to do my job, not make friends. I try to call Kyla but then I remember she and Megan have gone on one of their weird weekend retreats which doesn't allow devices. So, I keep it to myself, not knowing what to expect on Monday morning. I can call in sick again, but that will only raise more suspicion. So I decide to face the music.

I get up early and go through my morning routine. This morning I dress carefully in a dark blue pantsuit with a gold silk blouse. As I look at the bracelet on my vanity, I'm tempted to wear it as it would match my outfit. But I've resolved not to wear it until I find out who gave it to me. Who knows my middle names? I could have asked my family if the engraving had just been my name. But who is C.A.C.A.? And why are we going to be together forever? On top of that, who can afford a trinket from such an exclusive store like Jackson's? It is an expensive piece. And so, with all these questions unanswered, I leave it where it is. I will do some sleuthing today. Perhaps I can ask the building receptionist who had visited the tenth floor, especially delivery people from jewelry stores. I could call or visit the store itself and ask who had commissioned the piece. All of these are possible avenues. But they will have to wait. There are more important hurdles to jump.

I pull into my usual spot and look around the parking lot. The space where Benny always parks is occupied by a sleek black Jaguar. Way to go CEO. I fume a bit as I realize the incident with the bar creep made me miss meeting the CEO as well. He is just not good news at all. I still pondered how he had gotten into the gathering in the first place.

I grab my purse and laptop and head upstairs. Sometimes I don't know why I bother to lug the device around. But it's just a force of habit. I wait patiently on the elevator and am soon being whisked to the tenth floor.

"Good morning, Stacy," I greet the receptionist brightly.

"Hi, Lana. I hope you're feeling better." She returns with a smile.

I give her a puzzled look and answer slowly. "I am. Thanks."

I continue further into the office and receive a few more greetings and enquiries into the state of my health. By the time I get to my office I am truly puzzled. I sit and get ready to begin my day. But before I can even turn on my computer, there's a knock on the door. I look up to find a rather worried-looking Charles in the doorway.

"Good morning, Charles." I smile nervously.

He steps in and closes the door. My anxiety goes into overdrive. Charles has *never* closed my door before. He looks at me with concern.

"Are you okay?"

"What is it with everyone asking me that?"

"Well, with what happened on Friday, we have every right to be concerned. You did something quite out of character, running out of the restaurant the way you did. You were the only member of staff who was not personally introduced to the new boss. So, are you okay now?"

I swallow nervously and nod. "I am."

"Good. The boss said he wants to see you first thing this morning."

"Damn. I feel like I'm being sent to the principal's office."

"Something like that. I suggest you apologize for what happened on Friday. Explain that you weren't feeling well or something."

"Sheesh! All of this just because I was absent, though?"

He gives me a funny look. "Just apologize, okay?"

I shrug. "Okay." I reach over to turn on my machine once again.

"What are you doing?"

I look at him in confusion. “Starting work?”

“The boss says he wants to see you and you’re defying that order? What’s going on, Lana? Do we need to have a little father-daughter moment or something? Are you having relationship issues?”

“What the hell, Charles!? No need for drama. We do not need a ‘father-daughter’ moment as you put it. And there is no relationship with which to have an issue. So calm down, okay? I just didn’t know you meant he wants to see me now-now. That’s all. I’ll go. Okay?”

“Okay.” He mops at his brow nervously then stands.

He goes and opens the door and stands in the doorway watching me. I stand and walk through the door. As I walk through the office to the other end of the floor, I can feel various eyes on me. It seems as if every department is watching me. Somehow the walk to the CEO’s office has never seemed so long before. As I head down the corridor, a feeling of trepidation takes hold of me. The stranger's face comes up before me and I curse him mentally. Had it not been for him, I would not be in this pickle right now.

I wipe a damp palm on my pants before raising my hand and knocking.

“Come in!”

I step into the office. There’s a tall man standing at the window with his back turned.

“You wanted to see me, sir.”

He turns and I feel as if the floor has moved from beneath my feet and I’m left to fall into the gaping hole. Him! I feel my face drain of color and redden alternately. My humiliation is magnified when I detect his smirk.

"Hello, Lana."

I open my mouth to speak, but no words come out.

"Something got your tongue?" I hear the barely concealed amusement in his tone. "Or perhaps it is someone?"

Memories of the kiss come flooding back and my cheeks burn with humiliation.

"I-I-I-" I take a deep breath and close my mouth. There is really nothing I can say. I had thrown my drink in my boss' face. My *boss'* face. And I had called him some names as well. My head is in a whirl as I try to remember how I had dressed him down on Friday. Had I called him a creep or something equally derogatory? And I kissed him too. I kissed *my boss*! My humiliation is complete when I remember what had happened in the bar and how I had slapped him afterward.

He sits and I remain standing where I've frozen just inside the door.

"Close the door."

I turn obediently and close the door then turn to face him. He rocks back in his chair, smiling at me.

"Well? Surprised?"

I remain silent and he laughs.

"I do believe you owe me an apology, Lana."

I look up sharply.

"Oh, come on, Lana. If not for Wednesday night when we were strangers and *you* stepped into *my* personal space and behaved as if you expected me not to react to an attractive woman attempting to kiss me, you need to apologize for Friday."

I look at him as he sits there and I wish I had another drink to throw at him. The smug jackass! Yes. It will be quite satisfying to douse him once again. Then I'll simply clear out my desk and hand in my resignation. But when I think about how hard I've worked to get to this point at this age, I swallow my pride and my temper. There are very few companies who would have been willing to take a chance on a girl fresh out of college. But McEachron had. I had started as a clerk with minimal editing duties. By the end of my six-month probation, I had been made a sub-editor. And after my first year I was promoted to my current position of junior editor. If I resign now, any other company would put me back into the clerical pool by virtue of my age and not my experience. Damn it, bar man! I swallow hard and look at him.

"I am sorry that I threw my drink at you and insulted you, sir."

"You don't even know my name do you." He laughs softly and I realize he is right.

My cheeks grow red and he laughs again.

"My name is Ace Channing, Lana. But please call me Ace."

"I am sorry that I threw my drink at you and insulted you, *Mr. Channing.*"

He laughs once more. "Stubborn as they come. Always was and always will be."

The last part is muttered to himself and I only just catch it. I remain silent and he continues.

"So, do you have any questions for me?"

"No, sir."

"Are you sure? Wouldn't you like to know who I am, where I came from, how I ended up at that bar last Wednesday night and already knew who you were? Nothing?"

My head snaps up. "You knew who I was from the bar?"

"I bought your company, Lana. I make it my business to know my employees."

I gaze at him searchingly, my green eyes peering into his startling grey, almost silver eyes. There is something about his eyes that tug at me. They are an unusual shade and I can't help but think of someone I knew long ago. Instantly I push the painful memory away. I drop my eyes and turn my head away.

"May I go, sir?"

There is silence and all I hear is our breathing and the ticking of the clock. I take a deep breath as I wait for his response.

The chair squeaks as he rises and comes to stand in front of me.

"Look at me, Lana."

The mocking in his tone is gone and is replaced by a gentle persuasion. I look up to find him staring at me intently, an inscrutable expression in his gaze.

"Lana, I like you – a lot."

"You've only just met me."

"I've seen enough to know that I want to get to know you more."

"There can be no getting to know me more, sir. You're my boss."

"Exactly. I am your boss. I can do as I please."

"You can't do anything without my express permission, can you? And, I say that I am not looking to date anyone, especially someone in the office and most especially my boss."

"I was neither seeking your permission nor asking a question. I was making a statement. I am interested in taking things with you further."

"Excuse me, but I do think I get a say in this," I deadpan. "There is nothing to take further."

"I say there is. You can't tell me that you felt nothing when we kissed."

"I most certainly can and will tell you that I felt nothing when we kissed."

"It seems time has dulled your memory. Let me remind you."

And before I can respond, he captures my wrist in one of his hands and pulls me flush against him. I gasp at his intention. But before I can break free, his lips find mine and I'm swept up in an emotion I had put to sleep.

He expertly pries my lips apart with his tongue and surges forward to explore the cavern he has opened. He kisses me deeply and thoroughly. I hear a loud moan and am shocked to find it coming from me. I feel my body quiver as heat floods me. He senses my lack of resistance and releases my hand. He places his hands on my hips and pulls me closer, and there is no doubting his arousal. I find my hands grabbing his shoulders as I begin to kiss him back. It is now his time to groan.

My heart is pounding as I press against him, reveling in the feel of his pulsating manhood against my belly. Had I been wearing a skirt or dress it would have been so easy to.... I grab ahold of my thoughts. What the hell am I thinking? This is my boss!

I stiffen and push at his chest. His embrace loosens and he raises his head.

"Do you still think there is no attraction between us?"

I widen my eyes and stare up at him, allowing my hands to fall to my sides and I step back. Without another word, I turn and grab the door.

"Lana-"

"Nope, not happening!"

I fling the door open and run out. I move quickly, knowing he won't leave his office in pursuit of me. I tear through the various departments until I get back to the privacy of my office. I slam the door behind me and lean against it, my heart pounding. What the hell just happened? Had I pushed myself against my boss? I feel so humiliated by my actions. I press my fist into my mouth to silence my screams as tears pour down my face. I slump to the floor and reach up behind me to engage the lock. I hug my knees to my chest, rocking back and forth as I try to regain a sense of calm. It could have been an hour, it could have been five minutes. But finally, I feel normalcy begin returning to me. I am soon able to stand. I walk on wobbly legs to my desk and sit.

I turn on the computer but don't start work. Oh no. I have some research to do on one Ace Channing. My fingers fly over the keys as I type in his name. My search yields fruit immediately. An hour later, I lean back, numb from the influx of information. Ace Channing is not someone to be taken lightly by all indications.

He has accomplished far more in twenty-seven years than many twice his age. He owns companies, he has investments and charities he supports. Shit, he is loaded! But not only that, he is eligible. There are stories upon stories of his girlfriends and engagement. He seems to go through women as often as he changes his suits. Well, Mr. Ace Channing. Lana Gray is not going to be another notch in your bedpost.

I close the page I'm reading and turn my attention to my work. It's not until I hear an insistent knocking that I remember the locked door and rise to unlock and open it. Charles is there, looking at me intently. I turn away and return to my desk.

"Is everything okay, Lana?"

"It is."

"How did it go with Ace?"

"I apologized." I shrug.

"Okay. Good. I guess he took it in good grace?"

"Maybe he did, maybe he didn't. But for what it's worth, I apologized." I deliberately turn my attention to my computer, ignoring Charles' gaze. Finally, he gets the message.

"Okay. That's good. It would be a shame for him to fire you. You're one of my best editors here. Well, enjoy the rest of your morning."

"Sure. By the way, I sent Myra's manuscript back to you. Take a look and tell me what you think, please."

"Sure, thanks."

He leaves and I take a deep breath. I stare blankly at the screen, trying to recapture my train of thought for the task I had been doing before Charles interrupted. At least I now know the source of his discomfort this morning. And many things now make sense. All the health questions and the silent looks. I had made a royal jackass of myself in front of the entire staff. I'm thankful that Ace didn't demand that I apologize in front of the staff.

But with that hurdle crossed, there still remains the issue of Ace Channing himself, I'm not swayed by his money or his fame. I can't be bought. But I sense that as long as I work here, he is going to be a problem for me. And so, I need to strategize. But how exactly does one avoid one's boss?

CHAPTER 6

ACE

I watch as Lana runs out of my office and I take a deep breath. Wow! If the first kiss ignited my libido, and the second just now was an explosion, I can only wonder what the rest of our lives will hold. The rest of our lives… that has a nice ring to it. It is a pity she is so up in arms about me at the moment, though. Nevertheless, I will just have to bide my time and wear her down slowly. I didn't expect such a difficult task as I was sure her memory would have been jogged by now. But I will still give it time. It is worth it.

I breathe deeply as I remember the hint of her perfume as I held her just now. If I'm to be truthful, if she had been wearing a dress or skirt, the door would be locked for privacy against all the snoopers who have been passing my office constantly this morning. Yes, the door would have been locked and I would be deep inside her. Maybe it's just as well that she ran away. I don't want our first time to be on my office desk. No. Our first sexual encounter will not be a quickie.

My still erect manhood jumps at the thought and I stroke myself absentmindedly. I tighten my grip for a fraction of a second before uttering a sigh of frustration. How long has it been since I have had a woman? Celibate, I am not. But these days I have become a little more picky than usual. And especially with my focus on Lana exclusively, there is now no room for anyone else, not even a one-night stand.

I go back to my desk and turn to look out the window. What a way to start my tenure as CEO. I glimpse the black and gold bag on the shelf and realize that I haven't given Lana her package. I think of taking it to her now. But on second thought, I can use it as yet another reason to call her to my office another day. I smirk at the thought of summoning her once more right now, and the possible heart failure her supervisor might have. This morning when I had asked him to send her to me immediately, he sounded as though he was going to pass out. No, I'll leave well enough alone for today.

I reach into my wallet and pull out the tattered picture. It has become quite worn over the years but I am loathed to relinquish it. A few years ago, I commissioned a blown-up version to be done. I have it carefully wrapped and waiting for the perfect spot to be hung. I trace the familiar features and allow my mind to drift back to the time when it was taken. Those were some rare good days amidst the bleakness that had been my life. I can't help but feel the rush of adrenaline and excitement at the thought that I'm finally able to keep my promise. What I'm doing is proof that my words then were not just spoken in the heat of the moment. I anticipate the moment when it will all come together. But patience is something I must learn to exercise right now, difficult though it is.

With a last, longing look, I put the picture away and turn my attention to the documents on the desk. I've been fully orientated to my function in the company (outside of just being the money behind the name). Though a bit unfamiliar in my usual line of financial business, I am sure I will get the hang of it in no time. I know I don't have to be here either. The managing director is quite a capable woman and I'm a mere figure-head. But my presence is a must if I'm to make any headway with Lana I'm going to see to it that she does not forget me that easily. No. Each day she sees me, she will remember our kisses. I'm going to see to that.

I spend the morning in meetings with Bridgette and Arthur, my managing director and her assistant. They give me more insight into the company and there are a few contracts to be signed. Afterward, I meet two of our new authors and attend a press briefing for a third as we sign yet another contract publicly. I have a late lunch and head back to the office for a meeting with the editorial staff. As they take up their positions around the board room, I notice that Lana sits close to the door. Cheeky little vixen! I stare at her but she refuses to lift her eyes to meet my gaze. So, it's going to be like that, is it, Miss Lana.

The meeting goes without any significant issues being tabled. I thank them for their service and encourage them to keep up the good work and reap the benefits accordingly. As soon as I adjourn, Lana shoots out the door. If Charles and Nadene had not stopped to discuss something further, I would have called her back into the room.

At about three, I decided to call it a day. I pick up my briefcase and head out of the office. I stop at Elaine's desk briefly.

"Mrs. Elaine?"

"Yes, Ace?"

"Do I have any more meetings scheduled today?"

I watch as she checks her diary.

"No. Tomorrow you meet the junior and clerical staff in the morning at ten. Then you have a meeting with Powell Publishers regarding a possible collaboration for our adolescent educational series. There are three other meetings pending with a few authors who want to discuss doing business with McEachron, but none are concrete. So apart from what I mentioned before, that's it for tomorrow."

"Thank you, Mrs. Elaine. I'm off for the rest of the day. See you in the morning."

"Okay, Ace. Drive safely."

I look at her briefly and she smiles gently. "You're looking at me as though your mother never told you to drive safely no matter how old you are."

I smile wryly. "No. She never has. Have a good one."

I pat her shoulder and turn away. As I head to the parking lot, I think about what I would have been doing under normal circumstances. Perhaps I would have been at Skyline having one of my investment lunches. Those are on hold for a week or two until I figure out how to fit them into my schedule. Monica has been given that time off as well. When she returns I'll resume that aspect of my life, I'll have her collaborate with Mrs. Elaine to ensure that I have no clashes with my schedule. Monica and Elaine will work well together to keep my appointments in order. When I had told Monica that I was going to be in a regular physical office space for a few months, she had looked at me as though I had grown another head. I don't like being tied to a physical space. My business can be conducted in my bathroom with me on the toilet for all I care. But Lana is worth it. Lana comes to mind every time my brain goes idle. I feel like someone who has received a gift and each moment I get I want to handle it with care and appreciate it. If anyone could see my mind now, they would find it to be a far cry from what is expected of Ace Channing. I'm known as a shrewd, emotionless man whose only goal is dollar signs. But if only they could see inside my head right now. I feel like a man who's found his muse, his reason for living, his reason for all he does. I chuckle as I get into my car. Fuck the world. If only Lana can see that side of me and understand everything I have accomplished is because of her, I'll be the happiest man on earth.

I don't have a destination in mind when I drive out, but half an hour later I pull into a car dealership. I'm recognized instantly and the manager himself comes to see to my needs. I spend an hour looking through brochures and finally decide on the most recent version of the car Lana now drives. I examine the upgrades and am satisfied. I don't want the one in the showroom and arrange for a new one in dark blue to be allotted for me from a shipment expected in another week or two. I make a down payment and sign the contract. I could have paid in full, but I make it a practice never to finalize payment until I have the goods.

I head back to my car feeling satisfied. I have a good laugh at myself.

"This woman is costing you more than you've ever forked out in your life, Ace my boy. But she is worth every penny. And she deserves it."

I sit thinking briefly. Out of nowhere, I find myself calling Caroline. After a quick conversation I'm heading towards the highway that will take me to the outskirts of the city. Forty-five minutes later, I pull up at a gated community. I give my name at the gate and am let through with no issues. Caroline is waiting in a driveway as I drive inside. She comes to meet me with a grin and I smile.

She hugs me tightly and kisses me soundly on the cheek, leaving the imprint of her trademark red lipstick.

"Look at you, Ace! You're a sight for sore eyes."

"You don't look too bad yourself, Caroline. How are Joshua and the boys?"

"Josh is fine. So are Ted and Bryce. Bryce will complete post graduate next spring. And Ted will be starting college in the fall. Can you believe it?"

"Wow! Empty nesters! Where does the time go?"

"Indeed. I don't know whether to jump for joy or wail in despair."

I shrug. "They are your children. They get on your nerves one minute then can be the sweetest of angels the next."

"Spoken like someone who will have some words of wisdom when he becomes a parent. When will that be, by the way?" she looks up at me, her eyes twinkling.

I chuckle. "I would need to find the woman first, right?"

"Not necessarily. There are so many options for having a child it simply boggles the mind. I wouldn't be surprised if one day I hear that you can plant one in a pot and grow it like tomatoes."

I throw my head back and laugh. "No thank you! I prefer the old and more pleasurable way. The fun is in the trying, you know."

"Indeed, it is." She slips her hand into the crook of my elbow and we begin to walk towards one of the houses. "But I know you didn't call me out of the blue to discuss children and how we get them. What do you think so far?" she waves her hand in the direction of one of the houses.

"Security at the gate is questionable. He should have asked for identification. I could have said I'm the President and I would have gotten in just the same."

"Noted. That's an easy fix. What are your other thoughts?"

I wrinkle my nose and turn to look at her. "Caroline, why are you showing me this piece of crap? You've been my realtor for three years. You know my taste by now."

"I do. Don't judge a book by the cover dear. Let's step inside."

We walk into the foyer and I'm immediately taken aback by the vaulted ceilings in the entryway. The marble floor is polished to a mirror-like shine and reflects the chandelier above. I hold my tongue.

We walk through the house and discuss the amenities and what the property has to offer. An hour later, we're in the driveway once more. She looks up at me.

"Well?"

"You pulled a fast one on me with this one I will confess."

She laughs. "You should know by now to trust me. Admit that it is not a bad selection."

"I have to admit. It isn't. I'm not completely sold yet, though. I would like to look at a couple other places if you don't mind."

"That's not a problem, Ace. Do you have a deadline in mind?"

"Nope. I just know I want something apart from the apartment for now. But I also need to plan for the future."

"Planning for a wife and kids?"

"Been chatting to Eddie lately?"

She waves her hand dismissively. "Not at all. But if Eddie has been talking about your wife and kids, who am I to disagree. It's time you settle down, Ace."

"I'm only twenty-seven."

"But you have the maturity of a forty-year-old. You're ready."

"Gotta find her first."

"Maybe you have, which is why you're house hunting," she shoots back at me.

"Maybe I'm being proactive," I smirk.

"Bullshit. I know you too well, Ace. If you're shopping, you're ready."

"I shopped before, remember?"

"Even an unborn baby could have told you that one would not last. But you live and you learn and you get wiser. And my gut tells me you're on a different path this time. But I won't force the issue."

I smile. "Thank you."

"But I need an introduction as soon as possible."

I shrug casually. We embrace briefly and make plans for other viewings later in the week. By the time I head back to the city, it's already dark. The day seems to have flown by and the kiss with Lana seems so far away and not just this morning. Just thinking of her makes me smile and shake my head. It's amazing how many hundreds of thousands and possible millions of dollars she is costing me. First, I bought the company, then the car and am now contemplating a house. Not to mention all the little trinkets I have lined up for her. I remember the black and gold bag in my drawer. I have to get it to her tomorrow. She needs to begin to understand who I am and who she is to me. I haven't gotten to this point in my life by being careless with my choices and decisions. And even when mistakes are made, I learn from them. I know she's still trying to process the bar, the restaurant and this morning. So, I'll give her a little time to adjust. But soon she will have to understand she's dealing with Ace Channing and I'm a man who gets whatever he wants. This time, though, I don't want a what. I want a who. And that who is Lana Gray and there's not a damn thing she can do about it.

CHAPTER 7

LANA

I dare not allow Ace any leeway to interact with me again, and breathe a sigh of relief when I make it out of the meeting and back to my office. I could feel his eyes boring into me throughout the meeting but refused to give in to my curiosity of being in the same space with him yet at a distance.

As the rest of the afternoon wears on, I begin to seriously process all the incidents with Ace. Not only is he devilishly handsome and sexy as hell, but he's made no bones about the fact he is interested in an intimate relationship with me. This is the part I now have to deal with immediately. I meant what I said, there's no way I am going to be in a relationship with someone at work, especially my boss. It's not that I'm afraid of a relationship as I have had relationships before. But an office romance is something I don't condone. But what am I to do about Ace?

The question stays with me for the rest of the afternoon. Even when I leave for the day and head to the hairdresser to get my hair washed, I wonder if I can wash away the issue. I laugh at myself for thinking the ridiculous.

Three hours later I'm home preparing dinner. I come to the realization that I have allowed Ace to take up too much of my time and headspace. Each option I've processed yields nothing. I'm not going to allow my dream job to slip through my fingers because of him, so I will not quit. I'm not going to become a prisoner in my home so I won't stop working in the office. I'm not going to waste my vacation time by taking it prematurely to get away from him. I'm not going to be a coward so I will not ask for a transfer to any of our partner publishers. Ace Channing is not going to chase me out of my dream job. There is only one clear solution, and that is to avoid him. I retire for the night, forcing away the image of Ace as he kissed me, and the undeniable feelings of arousal it has sparked in me.

The next morning, I put my 'operation avoid Ace' into action. I get to work at my usual time and scan the parking lot. His spot is still vacant. Good. I gather my things quickly and dash inside. I get an elevator immediately and am in my office in no time. I'm happy to see the pile of manuscripts as well as a few emails. It means I have an excuse not to leave the office except to go to the restroom. I order in for lunch most days or take a sandwich to work with me. On the days that I have to go to the cafeteria on the top floor of the building, I'm always on my guard. One afternoon I have a rather close call as I end up leaving the cafeteria at the same time that Ace arrives with Bridgette.

I've heard the talk around the office about how 'cool' he is as a boss, and that he doesn't behave as though he's better than anyone else. I remember one afternoon when Marissa just couldn't stop talking about Ace and how he had treated the clerical department to a pizza lunch the day before. My responses were non-committal and she had smiled at me.

"Come on, Lana. I know you feel badly about what happened that first day. But I don't think Ace is the type to hold a grudge. You did apologize and everything."

I smiled and changed the topic.

But my plan to avoid him is working for the most part. There are one or two times when I spot him in the elevator and duck behind a wall or into the stairwell just in time. I ensure he's not in his vehicle if I pull into the lot and his car is already there. If his spot is vacant, I move like lightning and hustle my behind to my office. Every second always counts.

Successful though my plan has been, it's wearing on my nerves a bit. So when, after two weeks of dodging and hiding, I remember that Friday we will be going out for Kyla's birthday, I breathe a sigh of relief. It will be good to let down my hair and relax for a change.

When Friday comes, I have a very close call with Ace. I decide to leave a little early as I need to pick up Kyla's gift from the jewelry store. As I'm driving out, I drive right past Ace who has just come to the parking lot. He looks straight at me, but before he can react, I'm through the gate. I just narrowly avoid hitting the gate in my bid to escape.

I check my rearview nervously for the first few minutes. Only when I pull into the parking lot of the store do I breathe easily, confident that he hasn't followed me.

Kyla's gift is secure and I head home to get a nap before going out later. Unlike my birthday a few weeks ago, tomorrow is a sleep-in day so anything can happen tonight. And after the weeks I have had, I deserve to be a little carefree. I still haven't told the girls about the man at the bar and the turn that things have taken. Tonight will be the perfect opportunity.

I wake up around eight and dress carefully. I have my hair pulled back into a high ponytail, a hairstyle that accentuates my cheekbones. I add a little blush there for emphasis and use mascara to thicken my already thick lashes. My dress is tiny and black with rhinestones twinkling randomly. I feel like wearing stockings as well and choose a black sheer pair with a seam at the back, running from my ankle all the way up to disappear beneath the hem at my upper thigh. It is tight and hugs my curves. The long sleeves are sheer and end in a rhinestone rimmed cuff. The neckline is square and accentuates my creamy skin. There's just the slightest hint of cleavage. I toy with lipstick and settle on a deep matte red that I blend into a darker tone. I apply a glitter coat and smack my lips. My black purse and black stilettos complete the look. I twirl once in front of the mirror then apply a few drops of perfume to my neck and wrists. I pick up the small package with Kyla's gift and head downstairs.

My timing is perfect as Megan is just pulling into the parking lot. She drives an SUV which gives us a little more leg-room.

"Happy birthday, KyKy. Mwah!" I kiss my friend and hand over my gift.

"Oooooh! Good things come in small packages, you know."

I grin. "I hope you like it."

"It's from you, Lana. If you gave me a rock I'd love it."

We all watch as she opens the little box. In it is a tiny heart-shaped charm with a man and woman nestled in the curve.

"Ohhhhh, Lana! It's beautiful."

"My wish for you this year is love."

The car goes silent as we all think about Kyla and what she has lost in that part of her life. Kyla and Jacob had met in kindergarten and had been childhood sweethearts. They had gone through kindergarten, elementary, middle, junior high and high school together. Their families had loved the relationship between them and had supported them every step of the way. They had planned to get married right after graduation and go to college as a married couple. They had even been accepted to the same college and had made their plans for the couple's housing. Then tragedy struck. Two days before graduation, Jacob was hit as he headed home from his job at a local diner. He died from his injuries on graduation day.

Kyla would have been a basket case had it not been for her support system. We had all pitched in for her birthday gift that year and given her a locket with a picture of her and Jacob. The following year I gave her a charm bracelet, and each year since have given her a charm.

"You are a beautiful person, inside and out, Kyla. And I believe Jacob would want you to share that beauty with someone."

"Awwwww, Lana. You're going to make me cry."

"No, no, no. No tears allowed tonight. It's all about celebration. Three cheers for the birthday girl!"

"Hip, hip, Hooray!"

We laugh and cheer as we leave the parking lot and head to the restaurant. It's an Italian affair and we feast sumptuously on pasta and fine wine. I allow myself to relax completely and feel the stress really begin to melt away. As we wait for dessert, I decide to bring the girls up to date.

"Listen, do you guys remember that guy I kissed at the bar a couple weeks ago?"

Vanessa's eyes twinkle. "How could we forget, tall, dark and broody handsome?"

"Well! Have I got news for you! I ran into him a few days later at a staff luncheon. I was at the bar and he had the audacity to come up to me and remind me what happened the last time I was drinking."

"What!" Kyla squeaks.

"It doesn't end there. I gave him a tongue lashing, threw my drink at him and walked out of the restaurant."

"Good for you, Lana!" Megan cheers.

"Wait. It gets worse."

"Worse?" Vanessa gasps.

"Worse." I nod and look around the table. "My company was bought about a month ago. It turns out he's the new CEO!"

"Oh my goodness! Lana!" Kyla claps her hand over her mouth in shock.

I close my eyes and shake my head. "I've been running around the office like Pacman for the last two weeks. The struggle is real. I can't explain how much I needed to get out tonight." I take a gulp of my wine.

"Wow. Just wow." Megan shakes her head. "That is some drama waiting to happen."

I wonder if I should tell them about the pass he made at me and his desire for a relationship. But I'm interrupted when the waiter comes with our bill. I swipe my card and sign, leaving a reasonable tip.

Megan and Vanessa go to the restroom while Kyla and I wait in the car.

"That's a pretty sticky spot to be in with your boss, Lana. What are you going to do? Did you apologize for dousing him yet?"

"I did. I didn't say this to the others but I'll tell you quickly, KyKy. He called me to his office Monday, but I still didn't know who he was. I got the shock of my life. But that's not the most shocking part. He kissed me again. And I liked it… a lot! He wants us to date but I can't do that Lana. He's my boss."

"Would you date him if he wasn't your boss?"

I look at her sharply and sigh. "I feel so conflicted. On the one hand we got off to a rocky start. But kissing him felt good. But he's my boss. I don't know what to do."

"What is your gut instinct saying?"

"Don't date my boss."

"But what is your heart saying?"

I take a deep breath. "If he wasn't my boss, and maybe if our meeting had not been so antagonistic, I might consider dating him. Honestly, I haven't been kissed like that ever! But

I can't allow that to dictate my actions. The fact is he is my boss."

"But he's also a man, and you're a woman." She looks at the new charm on her bracelet. "Take your own advice, Lana. Find love. It may not come how you think it will, but open your heart to true love, not infatuation."

I have fleeting memories of my crushes and infatuations over the years. Names and faces crowd in, but somehow one stands out a little bit more. I had been thirteen or fourteen at the time, but he had been different. Then there was Stephen who I had dated for a few years.

I push the memories aside and look at my friend.

"I'll just take it one day at a time."

"That's all you can do. And who knows, maybe something can come out of this boss situation. Love works in mischievous ways you know. Maybe the bar was cupid's way of connecting you before so that his position as your boss wouldn't get in the way. Maybe 'Mr. Red-shirt' is your forever love."

"Ace. His name is Ace."

Megan and Vanessa return and we change the conversation. As we head to Quints, another of our favorite clubs across the city, Kyla's words keep coming back. She has forced me to face something I've been trying to avoid, my response to Ace's kiss in his office. It had shocked me. And there's a feeling deep within that warns me it's more than a physical attraction for sex. I wonder if this is how others feel when they connect to someone. But I shake the thoughts away.

There's nothing I can connect to after only two kisses. I'm being ridiculous.

We pull into the parking lot and find a spot. In a few minutes, we're inside. As is our birthday tradition, we make our way to the bar and ask for a birthday shot. Kyla grins as we egg her on to drink her shot which she downs in one gulp.

"There! Now let the party begin!"

We have our first round of drinks then hit the dance floor. It's Friday night and the club is crowded and warm. When we get tired, we head back to the bar for another round. I've taken only a few sips when I feel a tap on my shoulder. I turn to find a guy at my elbow. I look him up and down, quirking my eyebrow questioningly.

"Hi there!" He smiles.

"Hello." I take another sip.

"I couldn't help but notice you out there a few minutes ago. I made my way here as soon as you walked off the dance floor on the off chance that maybe you'd like a partner next time?"

I look at him carefully. He seems safe enough and friendly enough. I finish my drink in one gulp and step away from the bar. He smiles, takes my hand and leads me to the dance floor. The song is an upbeat one and I find my partner quite agile.

"So, does the lovely lady have a name?" He leans in to ask above the volume of the music.

"It's Lana."

He leans in again. "I'm Calvin!"

I smile. "Nice to meet you, Calvin!"

He smiles once more and we continue to dance. The song changes to something slower and I turn to thank Calvin for the dance. My blood runs cold as I look up to find myself looking into Ace's angry eyes. Without taking his eyes off me, he tells Calvin his time has expired. I watch as Calvin looks from me to Ace. There is perhaps something in the way Ace is looking at me and me at him that tells Calvin he'll be safer walking away. He nods and smiles and walks away, leaving me to face Ace.

CHAPTER 8

ACE

It's been two weeks and I feel as if I'm getting the hang of the publishing business. I've had a few meetings of various sorts and feel comfortable with what is expected of me. Additionally, I've fused my other affairs seamlessly with my current state, and conduct my business accordingly. Some days I'm in and out of the office, using the door like a turnstile. Other days I'm in all day or out all day. Regardless of activity and attention required from others, Lana is never far from my thoughts.

It takes me a day or two to realize that she is deliberately avoiding me. It's no coincidence that she dashes around corners and stairs whenever she sees me. I find it very amusing to watch her play her game. And I let her too. Her behavior tells me that I have rattled her. I make her nervous. Good. It means she's thinking about me.

In the two weeks here, I have listened well to what her coworkers say, especially when they don't know I'm listening. Avery seems to be the only one who is not a fan of Lana. I don't have to wonder why for long.

I've been avoiding Avery the same way Lana has been avoiding me. But one afternoon when I return from a meeting in the city, I don't make it back to my office in time to avoid seeing her, and accidentally run into her as she's leaving the photocopy room. She had turned on the charm and batted her baby blue eyes. She had given her blonde hair a toss which I had found quite irritating

"Oh! Ace! I didn't see you there!"

"Hello, Avery. Everything okay?"

She had smiled widely, but it had not reached her eyes.

"Everything's fine. Why wouldn't it be? It's great working here, especially under your leadership. I see myself here for the long haul, and especially because there is room for growth and opportunity for promotions." The flattery rolled off her tongue like water off a duck's back.

I quirked an eyebrow. "Oh?"

"Well, I'm just a mere clerk now, and have been for five years. But I do see myself in the editorial department someday. I look forward to the day when there's a vacancy there and I can fulfill my calling. I do have age and maturity on my side after all."

I had looked at her calculatingly, knowing full well that she was older than Lana. As for maturity, I was sure she was making reference to the incident at the restaurant.

"Age and maturity are not everything needed for a position, you know."

"I'm also working on my Masters."

"A piece of paper is not all that is needed either. There are many walking around with their papers and letters behind their names. Those things carry no weight with me." I had egged her on and had been pleased to see her face get red. Her eyes had glinted angrily but it had been quickly masked and a plastic smile turned on for full effect.

"I'll just have to keep working hard in the hopes that I can make it, I suppose."

"Well, keep on working hard. One day your dream will come true," I had responded noncommittally. The last thing I need to hear through the office grapevine is that I had promised Avery a promotion.

I turned on my heel and headed to my office. When I had gotten to the door and turned to look back, she was standing where I left her, watching me, a curious expression on her face. She smiled and gave a little wave. I went into my office without responding. It didn't take much thinking to do a check with Human Resources and learn that Lana had gotten a position for which Avery had also applied. Avery had been with the company for about two years at the time. Lana as an outsider had been given the nod and Avery's potential promotion had gone up in smoke. Things made sense now. This knowledge strengthened my decision to stay far from Avery. I didn't want to have to fire anyone unnecessarily. And thus, had been the nature of the first two weeks.

As another week comes to an end, I pack up my laptop and head out. Just as I'm closing the door behind me, I catch sight of the black and gold bag once more. I still haven't found the chance to use it to lure Lana to my office again. I turn back and retrieve it, intending to take it to her office. I greet a few colleagues as I make my way there. As I'm about to knock on her door Marissa comes out with a pile of manuscripts.

"Oh! Hi, Ace."

"Hi, Marissa."

I attempt to get by her when she shakes her head.

"Lana left already. You just missed her as a matter of fact. If you hurry you might catch her before she drives out."

"Ok. Thanks."

I hurry to the elevator and catch one immediately. As it crawls downward, I stare at the numbers anxiously. Finally, it's on the ground floor and I make my way to the lobby and hurry out the door. As I enter the parking lot, Lana is driving out. I know she sees me and I'm tempted to force her to stop by stepping into her path. But then again, she may just run me over so I err on the side of caution and stay out of her path. She accelerates and exits, almost hitting the gate as she does. I turn to look at her taillights as the car disappears from view. I stand staring speechlessly for a few moments then look at the bag in my hand. There is no way I'm going back upstairs now. Instead, I head to my car and leave. As I look at the bag a thought crosses my mind. It was just as well that I hadn't handed over the bag as of yet. There's something else I need to add to the trinkets that are in there.

A few hours later I'm pulling out of my complex and heading to meet Lance. He and I go way back to school days. We had been in the trenches struggling together, especially when things were at their worst. When we had managed to make something of our lives, the connection had strengthened.

He's in town for the week and inevitably we meet and catch up over a meal and some drinks.

I find him easily at Cru. We always eat at the same restaurant at the same table. He looks up from his phone and grins as I take a seat.

"Ace! I was just calling you man."

I look at my watch. "I'm not late, am I?"

"You're an hour late, dude."

I look at him wryly. "Did you forget to set your watch back again? You flew across the country. We're an hour behind you."

"Oh shit! You're right!" he laughs.

I watch as he scrambles to reset his watch. Looking at him with his spiky red hair that always looks like it needs a trim, his enormous glasses always perched at a crooked angle on his nose, and his often clueless expression and absent-mindedness, one would not think he's one of the most brilliant computer programmers in the country. When I had made a good return on an investment, he had been the first person I reached out a helping hand to. My investment had helped to get his technology company off the ground. I've never regretted it.

The waitress comes to take our order. As she leaves, I turn to Lance.

"So, what have you been up to these days?"

"Nothing much as usual. Just an app here and a program there. Nothing to write home about, you know."

"Well, that app here and the program there have put quite a hefty amount into my bank account in the last three months according to my accountant. I wouldn't like to see what would happen if you were doing something out of the usual."

Lance had set the world on its ear recently when he had developed a social media app that went viral overnight. To hear him talk about it, he had been bored and fooling around one evening. It had taken him a few hours to put it together. Within forty-eight hours it had become a household name. We were literally raking in billions of dollars for 'nothing much as usual'. If I take a survey of the diners at Cru, I know I would have at least ninety-five percent reporting that they use the app. And they have no idea that the person responsible is sitting a few feet away.

"How about you, Ace? What have you been up to since we last sat here?"

I shrug casually. "I bought a publishing company a few weeks ago. It's not a bad venture I have to say."

He raises his eyebrows. "Publishing? You don't strike me as the type to have that sort of inclination. That's a pretty finicky market you know. The world is going digital. The days of page turning are over. Printed words on a piece of paper will soon be obsolete. I'm working on a little idea in that regard as we speak."

"Oh? Something more than usual? Do tell."

"It's still in the mental space. I haven't put pen to paper yet. But imagine how much space a library takes up with a ton of dusty books. Now imagine all that space and books being in the palm of your hand, literally."

I look at him incredulously and he grins and pushes his glasses up on his nose.

"Like I said, still in the mental state. But I'll figure it out."

"I'm sure you will. And I guess I'll have to figure out where I'm going to put all that money."

"Enjoy it, of course. We only live once, you know. Live the way we've always dreamed."

"But what if the way you've always dreamed just feels as if there is something missing?"

He looks at me shrewdly. "Getting a little philosophical and existential on me? Or are you feeling the need to start your legacy? You always were the one looking to settle down. Remember what happened the last time."

"It's not that serious. Just random thoughts. Nothing major."

"Hmmm." He looks at me skeptically. "If you say so. Back to you and this publishing company. How's that working for you?"

"It's a bit of a change. I go into the office a few times a week."

His mouth drops open. "Does this company have some billion-dollar connection you're not sharing? *You* go into a physical *office*!? I don't believe it."

"Well, I do."

He looks at me over the rim of his glasses. "There's something you're not telling me."

I smile wryly. "Let's just say the company and my presence there is a means to an end for another acquisition I hope to secure before the year ends."

"Ahhh! Now it makes sense although it doesn't. But where there is a means to an end it's all good."

Our meal arrives and we dig in, continuing to converse in spurts. We finish eating and pay the bill. Lance looks at his watch.

"Now that I have the right time, it's not that late after all. Your choice. Drinks on me. Let's try a different bar, though. The last one left a lot to be desired."

I chuckle at the memory of the insipid drinks and cheap décor of the bar we had patronized the last time he had visited.

"Don't worry about that place. They closed."

"They had to! I've never spent my money so foolishly on drinks. Ladies, maybe. Drinks, never."

I laugh as I think about Lance's penchant for strippers. We have always had a standing joke that maybe it's something in his blood that he doesn't know about, and that he needs to trace his ancestry. I have often offered Reggie's services but he has always declined. His love for the ladies on the pole remains.

We head to our cars and get into our respective vehicles. I roll my window down to speak to Lance.

"Just follow me."

We drive through the city, and twenty minutes later I pull into a parking lot. A few minutes later we're at a table in the corner. Lance looks around appreciatively at the vaulted ceilings and sophisticated layout.

"Now this is more like it. Classy."

Our waitress comes and we get our first round of drinks and converse randomly above the pulsing music. We're on our third round when I see them. I have a flashback to two weeks ago with these four ladies. I immediately pick Lana out of the group. She looks stunning tonight. Even from this distance, her beauty stands out. Her porcelain-like features make her look as though she should be gracing the covers of magazines. She has gone goth tonight in all black. From my vantage point, I watch as eyes turn in their direction. They're a striking group but only one can hold my attention.

They seem to be in high spirits tonight. As I watch, the blonde takes a shot and the others cheer. I remember back at the other bar when Lana had taken her shot. So, blondie seems to be the lady of the hour this time around. Lance follows my gaze and whistles softly.

"Now that's a beautiful group of women if I do say so myself. That redhead is a knockout!"

I nod in agreement, relieved that I wouldn't have to put out a hit on him if he had looked at Lana.

We turn back to our drinks and continue to talk for a while. After the fourth drink, Lance decides to call it a night.

"I've got a virtual meeting first thing in the morning. Can't turn up with a hangover you know."

"It's been good as usual, my friend. When do you leave?"

"First thing Sunday morning."

"Let me know when you get back, okay?"

"Sure thing."

He hands me a few bills to cover the drinks, and we do a brotherly type hug. I watch as he leaves before turning my attention back to Lana who has been on the dance floor. I sip my drink as I watch her twist and twirl to the beat of the music. Soon, she goes back to the bar for another drink. I sit up straight when I see a man approach her. The next thing I know, they're on the dance floor. I feel white-hot jealousy shoot through me and I grind my teeth. I watch them closely. The song is an upbeat one so they dance apart for a while. Then I see him lean forward and whisper in her ear. What the fuck!? I watch as she smiles and responds. All I have gotten are slaps, drinks and frowns. And yet this stranger gets to whisper sweet nothings and is graced with her sweet smiles. He's probably inviting her back to his place later. And his lips will be all over her, his hands roaming freely and his body sinking into hers. Well, I'm not going to let any of that happen.

I finish my drink quickly as the song ends and stand. By the time Lana turns to face her partner, I'm standing there. I turn to the puzzled man as he looks from me to Lana and back at me.

"Your time is done. Find a new partner."

He looks at Lana once more before walking away. I step towards Lana, and before she can respond, I pull her into my arms.

"I'm done with these cat and mouse games."

Without another word, I take possession of her mouth. She gasps and I take advantage of the breech to search for and suckle her tongue. I feel her tremble slightly and I hold her waist tight. I pull her against my body, pressing her hips into mine. I want her to feel what she's doing to me. There's a low mewling in her throat and the vibration shoots through me. I have to have her.

I kiss her hungrily, ravaging her lips. My heart leaps when I feel her tongue slide against mine, licking at me and tasting me deeply. I can't silence the groan that seems to rise from the depths of my soul. My body needs her. The pulsing in my groin bears evidence of that. But there's a deep cavern within me that has been unlocked with just one touch from her. She is essential to my soul.

I feel no resistance from her at all now, and I know it's partially because I've caught her off-guard. I'm not stupid though. I can't give her any time to erect her defenses now that I have her where I want her.

I release her just long enough to grab her hand and pull her towards the bar. Her friends look at us speechlessly as I pull out my wallet.

"This should cover the corner table as well as the ladies for the rest of the night." I plop some bills on the bar top then grab her hand once more and walk out with her in tow.

CHAPTER 9

LANA

"Ace!"

He stops momentarily and looks at me, but I get the feeling that he isn't seeing me. His eyes are wild and bright and I feel powerless to stop what I know is about to unfold. Nevertheless, I make a futile attempt.

"We can't-"

The words barely leave my lips before my breath is taken away. He slams me against the nearest vehicle and covers my body with his. I feel every inch of his hardness pressing into my stomach and my knees grow weak at the prospect of feeling him inside me. His tongue probes my mouth once more and my head feels light. His hands are roaming restlessly as if he's trying to touch me everywhere at once.

He raises his head and I take a deep breath. My chest heaves with the effort.

"We both know this is going to happen, Lana. It makes no sense to fight what we feel. And don't fucking deny that you don't want me as much as I want you. Don't give me any no one-night stand and no office romance bullshit either. I made my intention clear that this is going to be a relationship. Now are you going to come with me so we can get this dealt with and move on," he thrusts his body against mine, making it clear what 'this' is. "Or are you going to let me lift the hem of this pretty dress, rip these sexy stockings and just push your panties to the side and bury myself in you right here. Don't dare me, Lana. I'll take you right here, then take you home and take you again, and again, and again."

Each time he says 'again' he punctuates it with a kiss. Kyla's words from earlier come back and I look at him. What if?

He senses my acquiescence and kisses me one more time before taking my hand. We walk through the lot to his car and are soon driving through the city. I barely pay attention to where I'm going as Ace drives like a madman. Nothing is penetrating my consciousness right now apart from the man at my side who has placed my hand on his knee. He reaches down to squeeze my hand often. In my other hand, I have my purse clutched, holding on to it like a lifeline.

With a screech of brakes, we pull into a complex. The trip to the elevator is a blur. As the doors close, he pulls me into his arms once more. His lips don't leave mine until the doors open. We hasten down a corridor and he opens a door at the far end.

As soon as the door closes, I'm pinned against it by his body. My purse falls from my fingers as I give in to the storm of emotions. As he tugs at my dress, I raise my arms. I feel his hands slide it upwards and off over my head and I'm hit by the coolness of the air. I kick off my shoes as he swings down to lift me into his arms. His lips are hard and urgent against mine as he walks through the apartment to the bedroom. He pauses to turn on the lights before he turns towards the bed. As he lowers me, he follows me down.

My hands tug at his shirt, sliding the buttons from their holes as our mouths continue to explore each other. When I have the shirt open, my hands find his skin hot and damp. I rip my mouth from his and press my lips against his heated skin. I nibble and nuzzle around his nipples and am pleased to hear him sigh above me. His hands tangle in my hair and I feel him slide the hair tie away. He fans my hair out around my shoulders. His hands creep down to find the clasp on my bra and my breasts are soon free. He tosses the flimsy scrap of fabric away as he kneads my breasts and flicks at my nipples.

My lips continue their journey down his sternum as my fingers stroke and trace his hardness through his trousers. He hisses softly as I squeeze him gently. I look up at him and find him looking down at me, his eyes burning with desire. I hold his gaze and squeeze again, this time a little firmer. He bites his lip as he reaches down to remove my hand.

"I'm going to lose it in my pants if you keep doing that. I'd rather lose it in you. We need to get this edge off, baby."

He leans down to kiss me once more and I lean back, taking him with me. I fumble with his belt as he rips his shirt off completely. He backs away slightly to loosen his belt and pants. My hands reach out eagerly to push the fabric down his hips and halfway down his muscular thighs. He steps out of reach and finishes the job. Before he rejoins me, my stockings and panties join the pile of clothes scattered around the room.

My pussy feels as though it's an inferno. He holds my gaze as he reaches down to touch me. My chest rises and falls with each breath as I lean up on my elbows and part my legs to give him free access. When he finds me wet, he utters an expletive.

Wordlessly he comes to me, nestling between my legs. His lips find mine once more even as I feel his body slide against mine. I reach down to find him and stroke him. I'm pleased to feel a shudder rush through him as I place him at my core.

With a groan he sinks into me and I gasp at how he fills me. My heart begins to race as I throw my head back and rise to meet him. My clitoris is painful as it throbs with need. I wrap my legs around him, feeling him press urgently into me.

We hold each other tightly as our bodies writhe against each other. My head feels light as I feel my climax rushing upon me. The urgency of his thrusts tells me that I'm not the only one heading to the point of no return. I press up into him, urging him on as I meet him thrust for thrust. I feel that familiar tingle along my spine and I cry out hoarsely as my body convulses.

"Ace!" I can barely gasp and moan as heat floods over me. I feel him grip me as he presses into me. He buries his face in my neck and I feel his body jerk against mine as he bathes me in his release. His stifled groans sound like music to my ears as I hold him close.

It feels like forever as we lie there, trying to catch our breath. I shift restlessly but he holds me even tighter. I stroke his hair as my eyes drift close and I breathe deeply.

My eyes open at the touch of his lips on mine. I think he's finally setting me free. But instead, he rotates his hips slowly, staying deep inside me. And then I feel it: he's stirring again.

He moves slowly as he kisses me and I meet him with kisses of my own. Soon our mouths are mating furiously as our bodies come back to life. When he's at full mast once more, he withdraws slowly and I protest his desertion. He smiles.

"I'm not going anywhere, baby. Roll over."

I obediently roll over and instinctively go up on all fours. I look back over my shoulder to find him staring at me.

"Do you have any idea how sexy you look right now, looking at me like that?"

He places his hand in the middle of my back, pushing my torso down to the bed. I feel him move into place behind me and cry out sharply as he enters me. The new angle touches parts of me that elicit utmost pleasure.

My hands grab the sheets in bunches as I bite my lip to stifle my moans of pleasure. He grips my hips and thrusts into me over and over, taking me over the edge repeatedly. By the time he has brought me to a climax two more times, my body feels like a bowl of jelly.

He kisses down my spine gently as he withdraws. And though I don't feel as if I have enough energy for more, I don't want him to go and mumble a protest. He laughs and leans down to kiss my neck.

"I'm not going anywhere sweetheart. I just want to be face to face with you when I fill you up again."

He gently rolls me over and I reach my arms up to him. He comes to me and I sigh with satisfaction as he enters me once more. He holds me gently as he rocks into me slowly. He showers my face with soft kisses as our fingers intertwine. I press up to meet him, wrapping my legs around him once more. His lips graze my ear.

"I love it when you do that. Wrap me tighter, baby."

I obey by tightening my legs and he chuckles.

"Yeah. just like that. Do you like how I feel inside you?" He kisses my neck gently as his body continues to move.

"Yes," I answer on a soft breath.

"I wish you could feel how good you feel around me: so hot and wet and tight. You drive me crazy, Lana. I can't get enough of you."

I shiver at the raw emotion in his voice as he continues to thrust slowly. His voice is hoarse as he continues to whisper in my ear.

"There is so much I want to do with you. You can't even imagine, sweetheart. So much I want to give you. So much you deserve for what you've done for me. You mean everything to me."

He claims my lips once more as his body begins to move more urgently against mine. I feel the heat building in my core once more, and whereas I thought I had no more left to give, I find myself tapping into a reserve of energy.

There is something about our lovemaking that touches a part of me that no other relationship has ever touched. I can't help but be shaken at how in sync I feel with Ace. I kiss him long and hard as I allow my hands to roam and grip his buttocks. He groans as I squeeze the firm globes and I feel a sense of power in the response I can elicit from him.

I hold nothing back as I rise to meet his every thrust, and before long I feel myself losing control.

"Come with me, Ace! Please come with me," I plead.

He doubles his efforts as I begin to grip him. I gasp and shudder as he stiffens deep within me. As I cry out in ecstasy, his cries join mine as we climax together. I feel white light shoot off behind my eyes and I feel temporarily robbed of every sense as my body goes numb. The only thing I feel is him pulsing deep inside me as he fills me. Our bodies strain and hold as we cling to each other. I'm completely spent and of no use by the time our breathing returns to normal.

My eyes are heavy and I barely register him moving away for a while before returning. I feel a warm rag as he cleans me gently. By the time he turns out the light and returns, I'm half asleep. He slips into bed and pulls me into his arms. He feathers a soft kiss on my brow and whispers.

"Rest well, my love."

I know nothing else after those words as I slip into a deep slumber.

CHAPTER 10

ACE

I lay looking at the ceiling. For the first in a long time, I feel at peace. As I listen to Lana's even breathing as she sleeps, I hold her hand to my heart and cover it with mine. This is one of the most beautiful moments in my life. I think about all the possibilities now that I have Lana. Nothing is impossible. The sky's the limit.

I lean down and kiss her brow gently once more before closing my eyes and allowing sleep to claim me.

The first thing that crosses my mind before I open my eyes is that I'm hard. I feel hornier than I've ever felt in my life and my cock is throbbing like crazy. I groan in my semi-conscious state as I imagine waking up to the warmth of a woman in my bed. I remember Lana and my eyes fly open instantly. She's not beside me! My gasp of shock turns to a groan of pleasure. She's not beside me but she is still in bed with me. I reach one hand down to move her hair away so I can see her face in the dimness of the predawn light.

"Good morning, beautiful."

Lana looks up at me and winks cheekily before turning back to her task of giving me the most stimulating blow job I've ever had. I lean back on one elbow as I watch her work.

Her tongue keeps up a steady pressure underneath my cock as her head bobs up and down. I watch as her mouth devours me while her hand grips me, twisting lightly at the base.

"That feels good, sweetheart. So good."

My voice sounds shaky even to my ears. I continue to run my fingers through her hair as she ministers to me. At intervals, she laps at my dripping slit, drinking the nectar of my precum. I resist the urge to thrust into her mouth, allowing her to pleasure me. But soon I feel the pressure building and I hold her head up and away from me. She looks at me questioningly, her lips wet and pink.

"Ride me."

I lean back and watch as she walks on her knees, straddling my hips. I place my hands behind my head as she positions herself above me. I feel the heat from her pussy as she sinks on to me. I watch as she throws her head back and closes her eyes as her lips part. I lie as still as I can while she gets comfortable.

I watch her face as she rises and falls repeatedly on my body. I move slowly, matching her rhythm. She places her hands on my chest for stability as she bounces agilely above me. I feel every inch of her pussy grip me as she flexes her muscles expertly. I jerk inside her and she squeals. I chuckle and jerk again.

"Like that?"

She nods and leans down to kiss me. I flip her on to her back, and just like that I'm in control. I fuse my mouth to hers, kissing her hard. I withdraw slowly and work my kisses down her neck and between her breasts. Soon I have my face between her legs. I look up to find her watching me. I wink and lower my mouth. Her hips thrust up to meet me as I lick at her swollen nub.

"Fuck! Ace!"

Her fingers grip my hair. I lick and nibble until she screams in ecstasy and floods my tongue with her juices. Only then do I release her.

I move back up her body and find her lips. As we enjoy our combined taste, I enter her once more. I feel her legs creep around me familiarly as I sink into her.

We move in tandem. Sweat pours off our bodies as we press urgently towards the elusive cliff. I feel her tripping before me as her pussy ripples around me. But I'm not far behind. I make one final thrust as I hold her tight. We both shudder as I fill her once more.

I'm loath to leave her and lay half sprawled across her body as we share a pillow. We fall asleep with our legs entwined and our lips mere millimeters apart.

The next time I wake up, the sun is shining brightly in the room. I'm alone in bed and for a split second I panic and wonder if it's all been a dream. Then I hear the shower running.

I sit up and look around the room. My scattered clothing from the night before is on a chair. I look at the clock on the night table. It's a few minutes before ten. As I listen to the shower running, a thought enters my mind, I act on it immediately and spring out of bed. My cock is already at half-mast by the time I enter the bathroom. I stand at the doorway to the shower and look at her as she rinses her body. I step in and grip her hips, lightly thrusting against her. She gasps and straightens then turns around. When she sees me, she attempts to cover herself with her hands. I quirk an eyebrow in amusement.

"It's a little too late for shyness, don't you think?"

"Let me finish showering please."

"No. My shower. My rules. And I rule that we take care of this again." I stroke my now erect cock and I'm pleased to see her blush. I step forward but she puts a hand out to stop me.

"We shouldn't, Ace. Last night was a mistake."

I look at her in disbelief. "A mistake?"

"We allowed our lust to get the better of us and we lost our heads for a moment there. It shouldn't have happened."

"Lust? Is that what you're calling it?"

"It was poor judgment on both our parts, Ace. And it can't happen again. I feel bad enough already that I went back on my word."

"What word?"

"I promised myself I was not going to be that woman who sleeps with the boss and has everyone in the office gossiping about me and thinking that I'm sleeping my way to the top. I've worked hard to get to where I am."

"Well, I don't give a rat's ass what anyone in the office wants to think. I want to be with you, I don't care who knows, and there's nothing you or anyone can do about it."

"That's easy for you to say. You're the boss. I need my job. You don't."

"And you're the boss' girlfriend."

She looks up at me, one hand on her hip. "So, do you think sleeping with you one night means you own me now? I'm not a piece of property."

"I never said you were. But there's no denying there's something between us, Lana. And we can explore that as the relationship grows."

"Well, that's where you're wrong, Ace. It takes two to have a relationship. And I'm not going to be in a relationship with you. Your money doesn't wow me nor does your power. I would rather quit!"

"You'll do no such thing! Calm down, Lana. We can think this through."

"There's nothing to think about. We got caught up in the moment. Let's put it behind us."

"Over my dead body." I reach out to grab her but she slips underneath my arm and I'm left sputtering with a mouthful of hot water. She stands a few feet away wrapping herself in a towel as she watches me.

"I'm serious, Ace."

"So am I, Lana."

"Well, I guess we have to agree to disagree."

We stare each other down for a few moments before her eyes drop.

"I'm going to get dressed and be on my way."

"Don't be silly. Give me a few minutes while I shower. I'll take you home."

"You don't have to. I can catch a cab."

"I'll take you home, Lana."

She looks as though she's going to refuse and I give her a hard look. She sighs.

"Fine."

I watch as she scurries out of the bathroom. She has always been a stubborn one. And I should have known she would begin to overthink as always. It doesn't matter. I'll find other ways to further my goals until she drops this foolhardy thought of us not being in a relationship.

I shower and exit the bathroom to find her fully dressed. She turns away from the mirror as I enter. She's dressed as she was last night with the exception of her stockings. She's left her hair loose. I walk toward the closet, allowing my towel to fall. I see her take a deep breath and avert her eyes. I chuckle.

"Now is not the time for modesty after all that we've done and seen, babe."

"I'll wait in the living room."

She hurries away and I sigh. I should have known she would retreat. As I dress casually in a pair of sweats and t-shirt, I think of ways to keep her here longer. Perhaps if we sat and talked, I could get her to see things my way. And maybe I could wear her down before the truth comes out. I need her to come to me for who I am now and not out of sentiment or pity for who I was.

I go to the living room to find her sitting in one of the armchairs. I head to the kitchen and look at her as she looks up at me.

"I'm making breakfast, if it's okay with you." She shrugs and I continue to move around the kitchen. I look over at her a few times, catching her furtive glances around the apartment. I remember the black and gold bag on the television stand.

"That black and gold bag is yours by the way."

"I don't need any gifts from you, thank you."

"It's not a gift from me to you exclusively. It's a gift to every employee. You weren't at the luncheon so you didn't get to collect yours."

"Oh." She sounds like the steam has been taken out of her sails.

"I came to give it to you yesterday but you were already gone."

"Okay." She rises and retrieves the bag before returning to her seat. I sigh. The wall is clearly up.

I rustle up bacon, eggs and pancakes and plate them. I put them on the island.

"Breakfast, milady."

I watch as she walks over and takes a seat. She refuses to look at me. Silently I hand her a fork. I retrieve a bottle of ketchup from the counter and place it beside her. She looks up at me strangely and I smile and begin eating. I watch as she squeezes three globs of ketchup on her eggs just like she used to do. When she's finished, I take it from her and do the same.

"Don't do it because I did," she cautions me. "It is something of an acquired taste."

I shrug. "It's a taste I acquired some years ago."

I dig in and feel her eyes on me. She watches me carefully while I eat. I look up and catch her eye.

"Eat."

She gives me one more look before turning to her plate. We finish our meal silently and I rise to take her plate and mine to the sink. I begin to wash them.

"How come you're so rich and you do your own dishes? Don't you have a maid or something?"

"Just because I have a few dollars doesn't mean I don't know how to use soap and water. Besides, why would I let a few dishes wait until Monday for Vicky?"

As I continue, she comes to stand beside me. Silently I hand her the plates and she dries them. As we finish up, I feel her staring at me. I turn to lean on the counter and return her look.

"What is it?"

"I thought your hair was black all this time. But it's more like a really dark brown."

"It is a really dark brown."

Then she shocks me by taking my right hand in hers. She turns it over and traces a small scar at the base of my thumb.

"How did you get this?"

My heart lurches at the question. She looks up and holds my gaze. Her eyes search mine as I search for any hint of recollection in hers.

In the distance I hear my phone ring and I go to the bedroom to answer it. It's Reggie with some information on another task I've assigned her. I keep the call short.

CHAPTER 11

LANA

I go back to the living room to wait for Ace. I'm looking through his bookshelf when I hear the front door open. I look up and my mouth drops open as I come face to face with a blonde woman. She looks me up and down, a look of disdain marring her beautiful face.

"Who the hell are you? Is that what maids wear these days?"

"I'm not the maid. I'm Lana."

"Oh. I'm Meredith. Where's Ace?"

I point in the direction of the bedroom.

"He went to take a call."

"So what are you doing in my house at this time of the morning dressed like that?"

I gulp. "Your house?"

She gives me a tight smile. "Yes, dear. Ace is my husband. We have a very open and understanding relationship. I thought you would be gone by now."

Without a word I pick up my things and turn to face her.

"Consider me gone."

I dash out the door and head down the corridor. I don't know how I make it to the elevator, but I do. I don't dare look behind me hoping Ace doesn't follow me. But with Meredith there, I don't think I have anything to worry about. As the elevator doors close, I breathe deeply. I grip my purse and the little gift bag tightly. I have no idea where I am and hope there is an Uber close. But even if there isn't, I am resourceful and can figure things out.

I exit and find myself in a posh lobby. I had barely noticed anything last night. As I stride through the lobby, my heels click on the tiles. I struggle to maintain my composure as I can only imagine the picture I present at this time of the morning attired as I am. I step out of the building and find I'm in one of the richer districts of the city. I hasten out of the building. I stand on the sidewalk and look around. There has to be somewhere I can get off the street and wait for an Uber. I turn in what seems like a promising direction and begin to walk. A fiery red convertible passes me and I'm surprised to catch a glimpse of Meredith. She didn't stay home for long. It does seem like the kind of vehicle someone like her would drive. I think about what she said about the open relationship she and Ace have. Clearly, I've walked into a triangle. My cheeks burn with humiliation. How could I have been so stupid? I waste no time thinking about the situation now as the first order of business is to get home.

About two blocks away, I spot a coffee shop and slip inside. I take a seat at the counter and pay for a cup of coffee. At the same time, I pull up the Uber app and request a ride. I sip my coffee and wait for my ride watching the car move closer to me on the app. I try not to process anything, at least not while I'm in public. The emotions are close to the surface and I can't fall apart right now. The car pulls up at the diner in five minutes. I head outside and as I get into the car, I see a familiar Jaguar heading our way. I duck down in the seat and wait for it to pass. The driver looks at me carefully.

"You're not in any trouble, are you, miss?"

I shake my head. "Trying to avoid trouble is more like it."

The driver takes off and we head toward my home. Whereas last night I had seen nothing, this morning I can admire the scenery. So, this is how the other half lives. I find it amazing how a block separates this exclusive neighborhood from one of the poorest neighborhoods in the city. We soon leave the contrasting neighborhoods behind and enter familiar territory. In another ten minutes of navigating traffic, I'm at my complex. I thank the driver and head upstairs. As I close the door behind me and lock it, it's as though everything I've been holding in comes rushing out.

Angry tears fill my eyes and spill over, flooding my cheeks. I allow a sob or two to escape as I curse my stupidity. Of course, a man like Ace would be married! He is rich and handsome. What woman would not have snagged him?

As I wipe the tears away, I'm further convicted to stick to my decision of not dating anyone in the office.

I slowly undress. As I peel the dress and panties away, my cheeks burn as I recall the last time I had undressed. Every image of the night before and this morning comes flooding back. I cringe at my wanton behavior this morning. I wasn't new to pleasing a man and I just went for it.

I had woken up before him. For a moment, I had been befuddled, not quite sure where I was. Then I turned to find him beside me. I blame it on my groggy state at the time, or how the soft morning light just created an intimate setting for a little early morning loving. But when I saw his cock lying against his thigh, I could not resist. I had to taste him. And I saw where that had led me.

When I had woken up the second time, the enormity of everything had hit me in the light of day. What the fuck had I done by sleeping with my boss? I had intended to shower and be out of the apartment before he woke up, but he had caught me in the shower. It had taken every ounce of willpower not to let him have his way with me in the shower. After all, it would have been another layer added to the experience. It would be like getting totally wasted once and for all knowing that you will probably never go down that road again. As it is now, I won't know what it feels like to make love with Ace in the shower.

I had every intention of requesting an Uber and leaving, but the eggs and bacon had smelled so good, and I was hungry. Besides, if I hadn't decided to leave we would have had something to eat anyway. Who eats their eggs with ketchup though? In my family, I had always been teased because of my weird palate. Only one person had given my concoction a try, and he had loved it and declared he would eat eggs with ketchup for the rest of his life. I push that memory aside forcefully.

As we had done the dishes, I kept casting furtive glances at him. There had been something familiar about him that I could not figure out. When he handed a dish to me, I saw the mark on his right thumb. My heart had skipped a beat. A memory had arisen before me yet again and I had angrily pushed it aside. Lately, those memories have been surfacing at the weirdest times. But I'm careful to keep them at bay. My heart can't stand the strain if I was to release them and allow them to run rampant. But that scar had thrown me for a loop. Then Meredith had shown up.

Meredith. She had looked as though she had just walked off the cover of a fashion magazine. Her blonde hair had the perfect amount of tousle like they do with the fan at a photo shoot. Her clothes were clearly not off the rack. The romper had shown off her long legs to perfection. Her blue eyes had looked at me hatefully as she had spit her venom.

I get up the energy to put some clothes on and begin to move around my apartment to do my Saturday chores. I have a load of laundry in the washer and another in the dryer when the phone rings. It is Kyla.

"Hey."

"When I saw midday pass and I got no call, I knew last night was one for the record books. So, what went down with you and Ace?"

I sigh and flop into a nearby chair.

"You don't want to know."

"Well, we know you didn't sit in the parking lot talking."

"How do you know that?"

"After the shock of watching our friend have the living daylights kissed out of her, and having our bill paid again, we left to come to the rescue. We searched every car. A few couples aren't very happy with us. So, we know you left with him. Did you go to his place or yours?"

"His."

"Ooooohhhh! He lives somewhere fancy I bet."

"Cherry Meadows."

"Shit! Better than fancy. Lana, who is this guy? Cherry Meadows is not for anyone under seven zeros."

I sit and stare for a while. "You make a very good point, Kyla. I've spent so much time stressing myself out with balancing my work and trying to avoid him that I haven't done my homework. Hold on, let me grab my laptop."

I open the device and set it on the coffee table.

"Ace Channing, Ace Channing. Let's just see who you are. Ah. Here we are. Ace Channing."

I skim the biography and my mouth drops open.

"Wow!"

"What is it?" Kyla asks impatiently.

"You were right about those zeros. I mean, I know he's rich. He has to be to buy a whole company. But that seems to be his side hustle. He's really into investments. And wow is he a good one. He's just twenty-seven and listed as one of the top twenty richest men in the world."

"Wow! And you slapped him, flung your drink at him, cussed him out and fucked him. Way to go, Lana. You're set for life you know. He's clearly got a thing for you and you for him."

"But I don't like him like that. And it wouldn't be right to lead him on thinking that I do."

"Lana, I know your nature and I would never in a million years insinuate that you're a gold digger. That's just not you. All I'm saying is there is some chemistry there you might want to examine. You're not a flirt. Yet by your own admission you've enjoyed kissing him. You're not a one-night type of girl. But you went home with him last night. It has to be that your subconscious feels a connection. All I'm saying is don't discount anything."

"There's nothing to examine further, Kyla. Last night was a mistake. And even if I hadn't realized what a mistake it was when I opened my eyes this morning, his wife showing up would have told me in no uncertain terms that it was a mistake."

"Wife!? Damn!"

"Damn indeed."

"He seems to be big on charities, especially orphanages and homeless centers. But in every picture, he's with a different woman. I got a good look at Meredith this morning and not one of these women is her. It gives some credence to her claim that they have an open marriage."

"Wow!"

"Wow indeed. And I guess I was just another notch. I feel so stupid."

"Well, we all make mistakes. But was it worth it?"

I sigh at the memory and mumble.

"It was. But I'm done."

"Well, I'm glad somebody in our group got some!"

"Kyla!" I laugh and feel my cheeks begin to burn at the memories of what I had gotten.

"And I'm sure he gives it as good as he looks too."

"Kyla!" I scream with laughter. "You're incorrigible!"

"I'm just saying. He looks like he can handle his business. That's all."

We talk for a few more minutes before we hang up. I sit looking at the phone for a minute or two as I reflect on the conversation. I turn my attention back to the laptop and read a few more articles on Ace. I skim through several biographies. There is nothing about his early years. It's as though he was born a fully grown man when he popped into the investment scene less than ten years ago. I find one small article that makes reference to his marriage to Meredith.

I can't help but feel like there are some turbulent times ahead. From the looks of things, married or not, Ace is the kind of man who gets what he wants. And he's made it clear that he wants me.

I sigh and go to check on the laundry. I decide to be honest with myself and admit a few truths. Ace is a handsome man, there is no denying that. His thick, dark chocolate hair and striking grey eyes set in his handsome tanned face will always hold anyone's attention. He is tall, lean and muscular. And his voice! That deep baritone of his can wet panties with just a 'hello'. For those who are inclined to snag a rich guy, he is definitely a candidate. But how do I feel about him? I lay my cards on the table.

Am I attracted to him? Yes. Do we have physical chemistry? Hell, yes. As I remember how in sync we were as we made love, I feel my body grow warm. But is there anything between us beyond physical attraction? I do feel an underlying intrigue about him that makes me want to get to know him better. But is it worth the obstacles in our way?

The truth is that if Ace was not my boss and married, I would probably consider his request to be his girlfriend. I laugh. Request. More like his demand that I be his woman. But the facts are he is my boss, he is married, and we have crossed a line. I can't afford for this to get out at the office as it could spell disaster for us both. Well, maybe not both. He is the boss. But it would spell disaster for me. And so, the whole matter is settled in my head. A relationship with Ace is just not going to work.

CHAPTER 12

ACE

I end the call with Reggie as I'm very anxious to get back to Lana. I grab my car keys and head to the living room.

"Are you ready to – what the hell are you doing here?"

I come to a screeching halt as Meredith turns around from the bookshelf. I look around the living room. Lana is nowhere in sight.

"Looking for your little girlfriend, Acey? I sent her on her way."

"What!?"

She flops into a chair, tossing her blonde hair over her shoulder.

"So how have you been darling?"

"I don't know what the hell you're doing here, Meredith, but you have exactly ten seconds to get out of my apartment before I call the police. I don't know how you got in, but someone is about to lose their job. Ten-"

"Ace. Baby. Don't be like that. Please. It's been two years. Haven't you forgiven me by now?"

"Seven-" I reach for the phone on the kitchen wall and she blanches as I start to dial. By the time I get to three, the door closes behind her. I stand in the middle of the living room and look around. It's hard to imagine that less than twelve hours ago, I finally had Lana in my apartment and in my bed. And whereas I could have eventually worn her down as I had started to do in the kitchen, there's no telling the extent of the damage Meredith has caused.

I pick up the landline and call the lobby. They report that a young lady matching Lana's description left about five minutes ago. I shove my feet into a pair of sneakers and head downstairs. I might still be able to find her somehow.

As I drive around the block, I find it hard to believe that I can't catch sight of a woman in a mini dress and stilettos on a Saturday morning. It's not as though it's a common sight. At one point I think I see a woman looking like Lana get into a car, but when I drive by, I see no one. It can't be this fucking hard!

I drive around for another twenty minutes before I give up. I can go to her place, but I think it's wiser to leave her be for now. I have no idea what Meredith may have said to her, so maybe it's just as well I didn't find her. The thought of Meredith irks me considerably and I recall I have the issue of the security in my building to address.

I park in my spot and walk through the lobby and to the manager's office. Fred looks up with a smile which slips when he sees the thunderous expression on my face.

"Mr. Channing! Is everything okay, sir?"

"No, it is not, Fred. Someone needs to explain to me why my ex-wife gained access to my apartment this morning."

"You can't be serious sir! The fault may not be on our end. She may have still had her key perhaps?"

"She does not. It's been two years and I had all the locks changed after we divorced. So that excuse is out of the question. Fred, I pay good money to lease this apartment. I put my safety in the hands of you and your staff. Anything could have happened to me or my guest this morning. Please see to it that the matter is thoroughly investigated and the guilty party dealt with accordingly. I expect a report before the day ends or I will report the matter of unlawful entry to the police. I don't think it will be a good look for Clifton Towers to be recorded as not safe. And imagine if it should get out to the other residents that my penthouse was accessed illegally in broad daylight."

I look at the man's ashen face, but I'm angry. What has happened is carelessness. What if Meredith had come in with a gun?

I bid him good day and leave. I head upstairs, only slightly soothed from the outburst. I meant every word when I said that I want to know who is responsible for the breach. It's a very dangerous situation for an establishment such as this to be so easily accessed. The life of every resident is at risk. We pay heftily to be kept safe.

I get to my apartment and slam the door. I'll need to get a locksmith to have the locks changed again and there's no time like the present.

I make the call then pour myself a stiff drink. They promise to be here first thing in the morning as their job slots for the day are already filled. I brood as I stand at the window and look out at the city skyline. In the past seven to eight years, nothing has ever affected my focus. Nothing has ever ruffled my feathers – until now. As I pour another drink, I wonder what Lana is doing. What is she thinking? What the fuck did Meredith say to her? I itch to call her or jump in my car and head to her apartment and demand that she talk to me. But I err on the side of caution and rein in the impulse. Baby steps and damage control is the order of the day.

Clearly, Meredith said enough to get her to leave. What was it that Meredith had wanted anyway? As I think about Meredith, I think of Reggie. What better way to figure out what was going on with Meredith than to do a little digging? She had only turned up once before since the divorce, but she had accosted me in the parking lot then. What did she want this time?

I call Reggie and brief her on the new assignment and she promises to get on it immediately. I sit contemplating what to do with the rest of my day when my phone rings.

"Hello?"

"Hi, Ace. It's Caroline. Are you busy?"

"No, I'm not. What's up?"

"I have an absolute dream that came on my private listing just as I left the office yesterday. I didn't call before as I went to collect the keys this morning and take a quick look myself. I think it will be worth your while to take a look."

"Ok. Where is it?"

"Norbrook Heights."

"Hmmm. That's not too far from me."

"Exactly. So, are you game?"

"It can't hurt."

"Great."

She gives me the details and hangs up. I finish my drink and grab a light jacket before heading out. The drive is not a long one – a mere ten minutes – but what a change in scenery! As I drive, I admire the view. As I stop beside Caroline's car, I take a deep breath. It is a spectacular view of the city below, and even beyond I can see the highway. Caroline comes over and slips her hand into mine with a big smile.

"Feeling any connection yet?"

I smile back. "The view is worth it, that's for sure. Let's see if the house is as well. Do we need to drive inside?"

"You can if you want to, but I would rather you walk."

"Okay."

We turn and walk and I quirk an eyebrow.

"No security?"

"It's a stand-alone property unlike the last one I showed you which is a gated complex. There's nothing stopping you from putting up a wall, gate and security cameras if you so choose."

"I very well choose."

As we walk up the driveway, I admire the well-manicured lawns on either side of the curving cobblestoned path. The gardens are in full bloom and I smell the mix of sweet fragrances. I'm immediately transported to another time and place where I first experienced the beauty of a floral garden. I shake the memory aside and focus on the task at hand.

There are three steps that lead up to the massive front door. As I enter the foyer my eyes are drawn to the high ceilings and the chandelier hanging above us. I see a low bench and mirror across from what seems to be a door. I peer in and find a powder room.

As we travel deeper, I'm taken in by the high ceilings throughout that give the impression that the house is bigger than it actually is. The four bedrooms have their own en-suites with the master having the added bonus of a jacuzzi tub in addition to the shower and soaker tub which comes standard with the others. The walk-in closet is also a plus. The kitchen, living and dining rooms have an open floor concept and flow seamlessly from one to the other.

As we step outside, I'm speechless. I hear Caroline laugh.

"I trust that this will make up for anything the inside may lack?" She questions with a mischievous tone.

There, in front of me, gleaming with the reflection of the clear blue sky, is an Olympic-size pool. I swallow hard and step forward. I leave Caroline behind as I walk. My mind is teeming with thoughts of the boxes that this house checks. Not only for me, but for what I know Lana wants. It's as though Caroline listened in on those conversations long ago and has delivered the perfect house.

I move to stand on the side of the infinity wall and look over the city. I imagine the evenings Lana and I can spend here doing just that. I imagine the laps we will swim together. I wonder if she still has what it takes. As for me, I'm itching to undress and jump into the pool. I feel a presence and turn to find a smiling Caroline at my elbow.

"Am I good or what?"

"I have to hand it to you, Caroline. You're damn good at what you do."

"Thank you, kind sir."

"How much?"

"Not so fast."

"Huh?"

"Come on, Ace. You know how I operate. I have to make sure you're getting the best that I can find. And this is pretty near perfect. But let me see what else is out there. We can put this on hold."

"But what if someone else grabs this?"

"I've already spoken to the seller and they've agreed to allow me to hold it privately for two weeks before releasing it to the general market. I'll hold it just for you. But my conscience won't allow me to at least look for something that already has a wall and gate."

"Well, get on it this week. If you can't find me something that tops this, I promise you that next week we can stand on this very spot while I sign. Agreed?"

"Agreed. I'm sure the young lady will approve?"

I give her a keen look and she smiles back innocently. I answer as casually as possible.

"I'm sure she will."

"Anyone I know?"

"Someone from my past. I'm surprised you remembered the pool, though, Caroline."

"It's always in the back of my mind. I knew one day you would want a house and to move out of the apartment, so believe me, I've been looking at pools. This is a rare find. The owner's daughter used to swim in the Olympics, so he had this built specially for her to train."

I nod approvingly. We walk around the backyard and examine a few of the trees before re-entering the house. As I stand on the front steps waiting for Caroline to lock up, I look out at the view of the city from this angle. I feel in my gut that this is the place, but I'll allow Caroline to do her due diligence.

She comes out and we make the trek down the driveway to our vehicles. I hug and kiss her before getting into my car. I allow her to go ahead of me and take one last look at the view before beginning my journey back to the city. As I drive, I think. The night I spent with Lana has exceeded my wildest expectations. I'm even more determined to win her over. Now that I've seen what it'll be like for us intimately, the package is complete. I feel a bubble of emotion at the thought of finally having everything I've ever wanted in my life. I have to make it up to Lana somehow.

A thought comes to me and, upon getting back to the city, I drive straight to the jewelry store. I'm greeted with a smile. Half an hour later, I leave, satisfied with my choice and with the instructions I've given.

I stop at a deli and grab something for dinner. I know a couple of people do a double-take now and then. But I'm used to being recognized. I've never allowed my popularity to make me a prisoner. Outside of business, I have a life and will never be hindered from going out in public whenever I choose.

I head back home. It's a rare Saturday evening that I don't have plans to meet anyone. The last twenty-four hours seem to have been the longest ever. Just yesterday at this time I'd been preparing for dinner.

As I enter the lobby, Fred greets me.

"Mr. Channing. Could you step into my office please?"

I follow him down the corridor to the office and take a seat.

"You will be pleased to know, sir, that we tracked down the source of the breach and it has been dealt with accordingly. It seems Mrs. Channing was able to convince one of our temps that she had been away on vacation and inadvertently left her key and you were not home to let her into the apartment. He escorted her to the door with the spare key and opened it for her. I've explained to him the detriment of his actions and he has been removed from his duties here. We do have another apartment complex on the other side of the city so we have re-assigned him there."

I nod in approval. "Good. Thank you."

"You're welcome, sir. And again, I want to express my sincere apologies for the breach."

"Accepted. I have a locksmith coming tomorrow morning."

"Okay, sir."

I leave the office and go up to my apartment. As I enter, I get a sense of emptiness. I remember how it had felt to take Lana up with me the night before. Now I'm alone. I sigh as I slip the meal into the microwave. I sit at the counter eating and all I can feel is Lana's presence at breakfast. I see her sitting across from me then at the sink. Her presence is so real that her absence is painful.

I finish eating and wash the plate before heading into the bedroom. I go to the walk-in closet and look for a wrapped package leaning against the wall. I gently remove the covering and find myself facing a life-sized version of the snapshot in my wallet. I reach out and trace the face of the smiling girl. She had just gotten her braces in and had been reluctant to show her teeth. But I had been telling her a joke and she couldn't help but laugh. The photograph had been snapped at the split second we both looked into the camera, smiling, capturing the moment forever. I sigh heavily as I look at the picture. I remember the house I had seen that afternoon and imagine this hanging in the foyer or some other spot as a constant reminder. Yes. The day is coming when it will be out of its prison. But for now, in the closet it must stay.

I cover it once more and head to the shower. I strip and step underneath the hot, stinging spray, bracing my hands against the wall as I raise my face to the stream. Images of Lana in the shower this morning begin to flood my mind and I feel my body stir, hungry for her. I reach down to grip myself, groaning slightly as I tighten my fist. I want her badly. I wish I had insisted on being with her in the shower. But I had not wanted to push her too hard. But my body aches for her.

I stroke myself expertly, holding an image of Lana in my mind. I imagine her bending over before me as I enter her hot, willing pussy. How she would grip me and tighten around me.

I clench my teeth as my heart begins to race. I know I won't last for long and my hand becomes a blur as my fist twists and strokes, touching all the right places. My legs stiffen as I thrust into my fist one last time. My buttocks clench as I explode and rope after rope of cum shoots out, splattering against the tile. When at last I'm spent, my muscles relax. I lean my forehead against the wall, willing my breathing to return to normal. Finally, I raise my head and finish my shower in record time.

I towel myself dry and head to the bedroom. The sheets from the night before are still there, tangled. I strip them off and replace them with a fresh set. I slip between the cool fabric and reach for the television remote. It's a weird way to spend a Saturday night, that's for sure. But it's as though there is a part of me that now finds my usual activities meaningless if Lana isn't by my side. And if everything goes according to my plans and desires, she will soon be a permanent part of my life.

CHAPTER 13

LANA

I breathe deeply as I finish folding the last load of laundry. It's been a long afternoon and I'm happy to see the end of it. Who would have thought that a couple loads of laundry could have taken so long? I flop onto the couch and pick up the remote control and lose myself in one of the mindless comedies on the television screen. Before I know it, my stomach growls and I'm surprised to find that it's already beginning to get dark outside. I go to the kitchen and rummage through the cabinets. I'll need to go to the supermarket this week as I'm running low. I find a can of soup and put a saucepan on the stove with some water. A few minutes later I'm sipping the warm broth with a few crackers on the side. I almost laugh at how far this is from what I was doing last night. But eating out every night is simply not in my budget. At the thought of last night Ace's face comes up before me as well and I sigh in frustration. I've spent all day avoiding thoughts of him. And just when I think I have conquered them, wham! I push the thoughts aside once more and turn my attention back to the television.

I watch until I feel my eyes begin to close. Only then do I turn off the television and head to the shower. As I shower, I think about what I have planned for tomorrow. I might just go to the supermarket tomorrow. And it would be good to get some ironing done as well. I also have a few items that need to be dry-cleaned. I feel the need to pamper myself a bit as well and decide to make an appointment with my nail tech before I go to bed.

I towel myself dry and put on a nightshirt before crawling between the sheets. I send the text for the appointment and place my phone on the nightstand. My eyes close and I feel myself falling asleep. At the last moment of consciousness, the image of how I'd fallen asleep last night comes up before me but my eyelids are too heavy and my body is already too numb for me to resist. And so, with the image of my cheek pillowed on Ace's chest and my hand gripped in his, I fall asleep.

I wake up, yawning and stretching as I open my eyes. I smile at the sun shining outside and roll out of bed. It looks as though it's going to be a beautiful day. I take care of my morning bathroom needs and have a quick shower before getting dressed. As I'm about to fix myself eggs and bacon, I remember breakfast yesterday morning with Ace. I grumble to myself and choose cereal instead. Will that damn man not stay out of my head? I check my phone and am elated to see that Betty is able to squeeze me in at ten. It's nine right now and the nail salon is just half an hour away.

After breakfast, I wash my bowl and sit at the counter to make my grocery list. At about twenty past nine, I drive out and to the salon in good time. Betty greets me with a broad smile.

"Right on time as usual, Lana. Have a seat and I'll get you set up."

I take my usual seat in the massage chair as she sets up the footbath. Soon my feet are submerged up to the ankles in bubbling hot water. I lean back and allow the massage mechanism to roll up and down my spine. I close my eyes and sigh softly. This was a good decision.

The salon soon gets busy as women come in for various appointments. Betty scrubs my feet expertly and they are soon dry. She removes the foot bath and props my heel up on her knee.

"Your usual color?"

I give it some thought. "Maybe not. What would you recommend?"

Before Betty can answer, a woman next to me jumps into the conversation.

"You're young and hip. You can get away with something really bright, you know. And with that gorgeous black mane of yours and those green eyes, mmm! Neon would look good on you."

Betty holds up a bottle of bright pink beside my foot and nods.

"I think you're right, Caroline."

I look over at the woman and smile. "I think I'll give it a try." She smiles back.

"Try the blue or the green, Betty. That will make her eyes pop for sure."

Betty laughs. "I may have to hire you as my color match consultant, Caroline."

"I don't think you can afford her, Betty," another hairdresser joins in from her station. "She's way too busy selling houses to the rich and famous, you know."

The woman named Caroline laughs. "I'm sure I can take a little time out to pop in now and then. It would be way too easy, especially if they're all as pretty as this little miss right here."

I smile at the compliment and she reaches across.

"Caroline, realtor."

"Lana, editor."

"Betty, nail painter."

We all laugh. Caroline looks at me and smiles.

"Forgive me for staring. But you're just the prettiest thing. And without make-up too. You're just naturally beautiful. But I'm sure you get that a lot, right? I'm sure you could be a model if you wanted to and be splashed across every magazine cover if you wanted. Why would you hide that pretty face behind a manuscript all day?"

"It's my passion. I've always loved writing and anything to do with it."

She nods. "I understand. Just like I've always had a passion to see people living in a home that suits them. As a child, I found I had a knack for choosing the right dwelling for the right person in my family. It got to a point where no one signed any papers unless I approved. When I left college, I decided to get my real estate license. And the rest is history."

"I don't mean to offend you. But I've never thought about real estate in that way… you know, as a skill of matching people and houses."

"No offense taken. Trust me, it is. Take a client I had a viewing with yesterday for instance. I've known him for a few years and got him the place he has now. But I've always known he wants a particular feature when the time comes for something more permanent, so I've always kept an eye out for it. I finally found it, and when he came to view it, I saw the connection he made with the house. It's a feeling I can't explain. It's like putting together a jigsaw puzzle and you see a piece fall into place. He loves the place and wants to sign right away. He's making some changes in his life where relationships are concerned so that house is going to be perfect for him."

I nod. "I kind of get what you're saying. It's the same way I feel when I'm looking at a manuscript and making my notes for the author. And when they interpret and execute it correctly there's just this feeling of rightness about it."

"Yes! That's exactly what I mean. A feeling of rightness." Caroline smiles at me. "You're such a sweet girl. You must have a boyfriend."

Blush slightly and shake my head. "Nope."

"Pretty girl like you? You must be joking! I'd love to have you for a daughter-in-law if my two were old enough. No one showing any interest?" She looks at me curiously.

I laugh. "I have to admit that there is someone who is showing interest but, I'd rather pass. Too many complications there."

She chuckles. "That is the story of our lives. Take my client for instance. He's been there, done that and paid a hefty price. He's a great catch and has a genuine heart, but all women seem to see about him are dollar signs. But I'm sure someone like you might just be the one for him. You seem like a kindred spirit. I can tell. You're a good one. I could maybe hook you up?" She smiles and winks and I laugh out loud and shake my head.

"I think I'll pass. I'm having enough trouble getting rid of this one right now."

"Well maybe if you accept my blind date your fellow will get the message and scram." she reaches into her purse and hands me a card. "I'm serious. I do want to see him happy and you seem like a nice girl."

"Adding to your skill set I see, Caroline. Realtor, nail-polish-color-picker and matchmaker." Betty chuckles as she continues to work on my nails.

The entire salon bursts out laughing. Thankfully, the conversation switches to safer topics. Before I know it, my nails are done in a neon blue. As I look at my toes and fingers, I have to say that it's not a bad choice after all. I tip Betty and leave, waving goodbye to everyone as I do so.

"Call me if you change your mind, Lana!" Caroline calls out after me and I smile and wave.

I'm still smiling at the prospect of Caroline's proposal as I get into my car. The thought of pretending to have a boyfriend to get Ace off my case seems plausible enough. But there is the thought of putting myself in an even worse position if the new one doesn't want to let go either. Then there would be two problems on my hands as I doubt Ace is going to give up that easily. He would be more likely to break up my 'relationship' than let me go.

I pull into the parking lot of the supermarket and shake my head, banishing those meandering thoughts. I fill my cart and make my way to the cashier. I spot a magazine rack and a familiar pair of grey eyes among the other photos on the cover, and my heart begins to race. Before I can stop myself, I add the magazine to my cart. I sit in the parking lot and flip through to find the write-up about Ace. There's a charity to which he's made a donation. I look at him as he smiles at the camera while handing a check to a representative from the charity. The story is a brief one. I place the magazine in the glove compartment and drive out. I remind myself that I'm not going to entertain anything pertaining to Ace as there will be no continuation of anything between us. I refuse to be a third wheel.

I park in my spot, get out my bags and head inside. As I do, the complex manager stops me.

"Oh, Lana! There you are. I have a package for you. Wait right here."

A package? On a Sunday? I watch as she disappears into her office and returns with a small bag. I take it and place it on top of one of my bags.

"Thanks, Miss Dania."

"You're welcome, dear."

I head upstairs with my load, and it's with relief that I close the door behind me. I take a few breaths before tackling the process of putting away my groceries. I place the small bag to the side and only when I'm done with the groceries do I pick it up. There is something familiar about it. Then it dawns on me.

I take the bag with me to the bedroom and reach into a drawer on the vanity. I withdraw the box with the bracelet I had found on my desk a few weeks ago. They are from the same store! My heart begins to beat fast and my fingers tremble slightly as I open the new package. There's a flat box. As I remove the lid my breath catches. My mouth drops open as I stare at the stunning necklace nestled on a bed of velvet. I run my finger along the line of diamonds embedded in the length of gold. I retrieve the bracelet. They are the same design!

I look for a card with the necklace and find nothing. The only source of identification of the sender is from the card which had come with the bracelet: C.A.C.A..

I sit staring in space for a few minutes as I wrack my brain. I think of all the guys I've known but can't come up with any with those initials. The closest I can recall is C.A.. But that was eons ago when I was much younger. I stare at the jewelry once more. Well, clearly this C.A.C.A. knows where I work and also where I live. Whereas I had all but forgotten the bracelet, I can't ignore the necklace. I bite my lips as I think hard. I could call the jewelry store tomorrow, but what reason could I give for wanting to find out who had made these purchases? And besides, would customer information not be deemed confidential? Nevertheless, I can still give it a try.

I place the necklace and bracelet back into their respective boxes and put them back in the drawer and close it. Whoever this C.A.C.A. is, I hope he or she will reveal themselves soon.

Mystery is not my strong suit and an investigator I am not. I laugh softly as I think about making a report to the police.

"Hello? Police? I'd like to report that I have received expensive jewelry."

That would be the joke of the day for sure.

I chuckle and go back to the living room. I move around and fix myself some dinner. After I eat, I turn my attention to the ironing. An hour later when I have everything for the week hung up in the closet, I pick up a novel I started reading a few nights ago. I'm so immersed in the story that I don't realize how late it's gotten until I catch myself yawning. I struggle to finish the chapter I'm on before placing my bookmark. As I look at the flat curved edge of the bookmark, I think about when I had gotten it. It's a simple thing given to a young girl by a good friend. But it is something I have treasured forever. It is, after all, the only thing I have to remind me of that friend. I push the memory aside as less pleasant events begin to surface.

With another yawn I go to the bathroom and brush my teeth. I undress and get into my sleep shirt. I get into bed and snuggle into my pillow. Tomorrow is another day and I'll deal with whatever issues tomorrow and beyond. But for tonight, I'm going to have a good night's rest.

CHAPTER 14

ACE

As the weekend comes to an end, I play out all the possible scenarios for getting to Lana when I get to the office on Monday. But the best laid plans sometimes have hiccups, and when I'm in the process of getting ready on Monday morning, one of these hiccups arise. The next thing I know, I'm calling Elaine to cancel all my appointments for a few days and reschedule what she can for the following week. I make a few more calls to Monica while I'm throwing things into a suitcase. Within the hour, I'm heading to the airport. When I get there, my private jet is fueled and waiting. A few minutes later, I'm in the air and heading half way across the country. This is an opportunistic meeting I've been waiting for. It has taken nearly a year and I'm not about to let it slide.

I spend the next forty-eight hours locked in a hotel board room, emerging only to rest awhile and eat at intervals before the intense negotiations continue where we left off. By the time I'm through, I know my account will be considerably lighter, but it is worth it. This deal will repay the initial investment manifold within a year. On my last night, my new partners take me out for dinner then drinks afterward to celebrate our agreement. Usually, I would have opted to stay for a few more days and enjoy the scenery of this city. But that was before Lana. Now, I'm anxious to return home. And so, the next morning, my jet makes the return trip. I can take the next day off, being Friday, and call it a week. But I'm anxious to see Lana. And so, still slightly jet-lagged, I drag myself to the office on Friday morning.

I wait until mid-morning before I ask Elaine to have Lana sent to my office. A few moments later, the response came. Lana's been out all week on assignment as a client wanted to have an editor sit with her as they make the edits together. I'm not a happy camper and want nothing more than to call it a day now that the reason for my being there no longer exists. I prepare to leave the office and am already in the outer office when my phone rings. Elaine looks up at me with raised eyebrows, her eyes darting to my briefcase.

"Hello?"

"Ace! I hope I haven't caught you at a bad time?"

"Far from it. What's up?"

"I have two places for viewing if you've got the time right now."

"You've actually caught me at a perfect time. I was just about to leave the office for the day."

"Oh! Great! I'm at the first location as we speak. Take this address down."

I grab some paper and a pen from Elaine's desk and scribble down Caroline's instructions.

"Okay. Got it. So, I'll meet you there in under an hour."

"Great."

The call ends and I rip the sheet of paper from the notepad.

"I'm out for the rest of the day, Mrs. Elaine."

"So I see. It seems you popped in just to make sure the building is still here."

I chuckle. "Maybe."

"I couldn't help but overhear your conversation. Buying a house?"

I look at her curiously. "I didn't say anything about buying a house."

"No. But the woman on the other end did say something about properties to be viewed. Your realtor?"

"I thought the older you get the harder it is to hear."

"There's nothing wrong with my ears or my eyes, dear. Have fun with your house hunt. Just one word of advice if I may?"

"Go ahead. I suspect I'm going to hear it whether I want to or not." I grin and take a seat on the edge of her desk. She smiles up at me.

"You're a nice young man. You could be my son. And I just feel the need to mother you from time to time. With this house hunt of yours, is there some sort of futuristic event you have in mind? Like a young lady?"

I shrug nonchalantly, and she continues.

"Well, you're not getting any younger and will soon be looking to settle down with a nice girl. I know you have the money and all, but don't buy a house just for status. Buy a home for the long-term family that I hope you will have one day. Okay, dear?"

I nod solemnly. "Okay, Mrs. Elaine. Thank you. I will keep that piece of advice in mind."

"Be sure you do. And when you meet her, I need an introduction too. You know, just to make sure she passes muster and all."

I throw my head back and laugh. "I'm sure she will. See you on Monday."

"Drive safely!"

I leave the office and head to the parking lot. As I muse on the secretary's words, I wonder what she'll think when she meets the lady in question.

I drive through the city and meet Caroline at yet another fabulous property. As promised, it has a wall, gate and a security post at the entrance. But even with the stunning views and the beautifully laid out rooms, it still doesn't connect with me. Caroline seems to pick up on my vibe and the tour ends shortly after. We drive to another property ten minutes away. This one checks all the boxes, including a reasonably sized swimming pool and backyard. As I walk through, I compare it to the one from the week before.

"This kitchen is fabulous! Don't you think? Can you see yourself in here preparing a meal while looking at the stunning view of the city?"

"It is beautiful. Let's continue."

I feel her eyes on me as we head upstairs. The first three bedrooms are spectacularly laid out, but it's the master that is the crown jewel in this house. It is huge. It could easily hold two more king-sized beds and still leave space. There's a balcony. As I walk out, I get the feeling of being on top of the world. The walk-in closet could be another room altogether there is so much space. I walk through the room and examine the bathroom. It's decorated in marble from ceiling to floor with gold accessories.

"This room is the last one to be redecorated. Gorgeous isn't it?"

I nod in approval. "It is." But even though the house is gorgeous, I can't help but to compare it to the one I had seen last Saturday.

"Do you think your lady will like it? I especially love that it has all this space for a crib or bassinet when the family begins to grow."

I look over at Caroline and she smiles.

"Ace. Give me some credit, okay? I smell something going on with you and I'm ecstatic for you. So, when am I going to meet her? I need to know she at least exists outside of my imagination so I can stop trying to set you up with blind dates, you know."

I frown. "What do you mean, set me up with blind dates?"

"I met the prettiest girl at the hairdresser's last Sunday. She seems like such a darling. I'm sure you would like her too. Pretty but not vain. And quite intelligent too."

"My attention is elsewhere, so I'll pass."

"Aha! So, you do have someone in mind."

"I've never said I don't."

"But you've been so cagey about it, though. So, talk to me!"

I shrug. "There isn't much to say. It's someone from my past as I'm sure I've told you before."

"You're not giving Meredith another chance, are you?"

"Hell no. This is someone from my childhood days, long before you and I even met."

"Okay. Good. Meredith was a failed experiment to say the least. There were many times I wanted to throttle you for marrying her in the first place. We all saw her for what she is, a gold digger. But some things people have to see and learn by experience. It was a relief when I heard you were getting a divorce."

"You and the rest of the world, I'm sure. I was not as clueless about her as people thought, but I guess I thought I could change her. My lesson has been learned, don't accept a substitute, just find the real thing."

"Good boy. So do you love this girl? Is she the real thing?"

"Love? That's such a complicated emotion. I don't want to label anything right now." I know I'm evading the question. But I don't think it's fair for someone else to hear of my love for Lana before Lana herself.

"But you feel strongly enough about her to be thinking about a house."

"Home. I'm thinking about home. Mrs. Elaine schooled me on that point quite clearly just before I left the office."

"Home is right. Good catch, Mrs. Elaine. Is it Mrs. Elaine? I mean, that you're doing all of this for?"

I look at Caroline in disbelief before throwing my head back and roaring with laughter. I laugh until tears are rolling down my cheeks. When I'm sufficiently recovered, I mop at my face with a handkerchief Caroline produces.

"I guess that is a no." She smiles ruefully.

"That is definitely a no. Mrs. Elaine is my office secretary and old enough to be my mother. The last time I checked, I don't have a thing for older women, though heaven knows I should have a mommy complex with the life I've had. But no, it's not Mrs. Elaine."

"Okay."

"The thing is this, it's a bit of a delicate matter right now. We are in the process of reconnecting and she doesn't quite recognize me yet. I'm treading carefully and I don't want anything to rock the boat."

"Understood. But if things don't work out with her, I can always get a number for this sweet girl I met and get you acquainted. You can thank me by naming your firstborn after me."

I shake my head and smile. "I like your confidence in this blind date."

"She's a lovely young lady and deserves a guy like you."

"Spoken like a true matchmaker."

"What can I say? I'm good at what I do. And if you took up my option and it works out, well I guess I could add matchmaker to my skill set."

"That you could. But I'll pass just the same. I think things will work out in due time. And speaking of passing, I think we're wasting time when we both know which house will be my new home."

"The one on Saturday?"

"Bingo!"

She sighs and shrugs. "Let the record reflect that I gave you options."

"And viable ones too. Thank you, Caroline. How soon can you get my offer into the seller?"

"Let me make a call right now. Meet me downstairs."

I walk away and leave her to make the call. I stand by the kitchen sink and look out at the view of the city. The house is a beautiful one. But it doesn't feel like a home. A few minutes later I hear Caroline's footsteps as she walks through the house.

"Kitchen!" I turn and watch as she comes into view.

"They're asking for the valuation cost. I think it's a bit much, though."

"I'll pay full price and throw in a bonus if I can have it within thirty days."

"Full price, Ace? I know that's a hefty commission for me but-"

"Full price. Plus, a finder's bonus for you as well."

"Wow. Okay then. Let me make another call."

I watch and listen as she speaks to the sellers. By her side of the conversation, I deduce that the sellers are shocked at the full price offer being made and they confess that they had deliberately elevated the asking price in anticipation of haggling. They instantly drop the price and declare that they will be out in thirty days.

Caroline hangs up and turns to look at me.

"Congratulations, Ace. I guess you've bought a house."

"Thank you. And no, I haven't bought a house. I've bought a home."

Those words resonate within me as we head back to her office to draft up the relevant documents. Afterwards, I take her to a late lunch to celebrate. We part ways in the parking lot and I head to my apartment. In the privacy of my own space, the enormity of what I've done today hits me. I go to the closet and withdraw the picture. As I uncover it, I smile.

"We have a home, my love."

My heart skips a beat at the four-letter word. Love. Caroline had asked me today and I had evaded. But now, as I face myself, I admit without hesitation that I love Lana. I loved her from the moment I had set eyes on her all those years ago and had vowed to come back and marry her. And now I'm going to fulfill my promise. I can only hope that she returns the sentiment to me, loving me as I am now and not out of loyalty to a memory. As I think about the possibility of Lana rejecting my love, real fear takes hold of me and I feel a panic attack approaching. I've not had a panic attack since I had to leave Lana behind, and all my energy has been focused on making something of myself so I could go back for her. But now, at the thought of all that hard work over the years just to have her walk away, I feel as if the walls are closing in on me. I think about what Meredith may have said to her as well and the damage control I still have to do.

When Caroline had brought up Meredith earlier, she had expressed what I know is no secret among my peers. They had all hated Meredith from the first introduction as someone I was dating. Then when our engagement had come out in the papers, all hell had broken loose with my friends. They had barely shown up for the wedding. The marriage started on the rocks and ended up in pieces when I had learned of her sleeping with Alex, my best friend at the time. The divorce had been a swift one. Admittedly, I had used Meredith to keep other women off my back. After the divorce, my decision to reconnect with Lana was cemented. And now it's within reach. I have to get back into Lana's good graces.

I take a few deep breaths and close my eyes, willing myself to be calm. When the feeling passes, I straighten my shoulders and look at the picture. The foyer is the perfect place for it. I wrap it and return it to its spot in the closet.

Tonight is not a night to stay home. I have an achievement to celebrate. The only thing missing is Lana celebrating with me. But one day, it will not be so. I call and make a reservation at one of my favorite restaurants and get ready for a night out in the city.

CHAPTER 15

LANA

The week has been an intense one being with Mrs. Chambers. I have to admit, though, that I have been glad for the excuse to be out of the office. Which means I'm not within reach of Ace. But Mrs. Chambers is not an easy client. She has an admirable eye for detail but I sometimes have to guide her where to place those details in her novels. Charles or one of the junior editors could do this. But she asks for me specifically. Yay me! But eventually the task is complete and Monday morning finds me donning my professional clothes after a week of jeans and t-shirts at Mrs. Chambers' house. I dress carefully as I have a meeting with a new author this afternoon. I'm wearing one of my favorite navy-blue pin-striped skirt suits with a bright yellow blouse inside. The jacket is fitted and emphasizes my narrow waist while the pencil skirt clings to my hips. I leave my hair in a low ponytail behind me. As I look at the waist-length hair, I mentally decide that I'm due for a trim. Maybe I'll do the unthinkable and cut it all off for Christmas. What a shock that will be!

I moisturize my legs using a cream that has a shimmer. It's the height of summer and I can get away with bare legs today. I slip my feet into low-heeled dark blue pumps. A slight spritz of perfume on my neck and wrists completes my process. I grab my purse and keys. A few moments later, I'm out the door.

The morning goes by and I begin to plow through the mountain on my desk. It is amazing how work piles up in such a short time. I dig in and begin to work on a manuscript that's been pending for a while. I have all but forgotten about Ace until Charles pushes his head into my office.

"Hey, Lana. Ace wants you in his office. He sent for you last week but you weren't here."

"You see how much I have to catch up on, right? I don't have time to jump at every command Ace issues. So tell him I'm busy." I stare at Charles defiantly.

Charles' eyebrows go up. "Lana, this is the CEO we're talking about. This is the man who can fire you. You're a very good employee and you've already had some less than desirable run-ins with him. Please, just go. I'm sure it's nothing. You did square things away with him, right? So it's nothing. Just pause what you're doing, see what he wants, and come right back. Okay?"

If only Charles knew that it isn't as open and shut as he describes. Any interaction with Ace comes with complications. And I'm not going to allow myself to be bullied by those who know nothing about Ace and the extent of our interaction. My eyes flash angrily as I look Charles in the face.

"With all due respect, Charles, I don't know why everyone but me feels the need to kiss Ace Channing's ass. But I am genuinely busy. These manuscripts from last week are not going to edit themselves you know. I'm here taking care of his company's business. I'm not just twiddling my thumbs."

"Lana-"

"Charles. Just tell him I'm busy. At least he'll know you delivered the message so you will be in the clear."

He sighs and leaves the office. I take a deep breath as my bravado of a few moments ago fades. I check my watch. Damn! It's too early to hide in the break room. I get up and close my office door and even contemplate locking it. Almost as soon as I sit at my desk, there's a knock on the door. I jump and my heart begins to race as I watch the knob turn. Marissa pushes her head inside and I breathe deeply in relief.

"Hi, Lana. I have those reprints you asked for this morning."

"Thanks, Marissa. Just leave them on the chair."

"No problem."

I watch as she leaves and I take a deep breath once more. I turn my attention back to the task at hand. A few minutes later, I see a new email come into my inbox. I swear softly as I open it and see *his* name in the sender's line. What part of 'I'm busy' does he not understand?

Come to my office now

I purse my lips as I type a response.

I'm busy

Without a second thought, I press send.

"Take that Ace Channing! You're not going to bully me. You picked the wrong one to mess with when you picked me."

I pick up the manuscript I've been working on all morning and read the same paragraph for the third time. I get lost within the pages, marking with my pen now and then. I'm in the middle of making a note when my office door flies open and hits the wall with a bang. I give a little shriek as I almost jump out of my skin. I look down in dismay at the jagged line across the page. Then I look up to find a furious Ace standing in the doorway. He slams the door and stalks over to my desk.

"My office. Now," he growls in a low voice. He walks back to the door and yanks it open, standing in the doorway and glaring at me.

I suspect I've crossed into dangerous territory and think it wise to drop my stubbornness and obey.

I rise slowly and walk towards him, my eyes not daring to meet his. I hold my breath as I squeeze by him in the doorway, but I still catch a whiff of his cologne and I can't help but remember being with him in his apartment. Now is not the time to have those sorts of memories, and I push them aside. I walk slowly and mechanically, conscious of him behind me. As we go through the office, eyes turn. Some are averted quickly while others stare. I can already hear the whispers. I feel as if I'm walking to the gallows with the executioner dogging my every step. After what feels like an eternity, his office comes into view. I see Mrs. Elaine look up. She greets me with a smile that slips slightly when she looks behind me. I can only imagine the fury he's emanating.

We enter his office and I stand just inside the door. I listen to it close behind me. I stiffen slightly as I feel his arms embrace me from behind.

"Don't be like this, Lana."

"I'll thank you kindly to release me, Mr. Channing."

"Hell no. Not after what we've been through. I missed you so much last week."

He kisses me softly on the neck and I forcefully step out of his embrace, spinning around to face him.

"Ace, I'm serious. Listen to me. We shouldn't have done what we did."

He takes a step towards me, and I step back. He keeps advancing and I keep retreating until I find myself backed up against his desk. He wastes no time in pressing his body against mine and placing his hands on either side of my hips, effectively caging me. I look into his eyes, sparkling with intense emotion, and where I expect to see fury there is something else, something I can't quite understand.

"I say you're wrong, Lana. What should have happened, happened. And there is no way I'm going to let you out of my life. This has been a long time coming."

"It's only been a few weeks, Ace. This is just an infatuation and an obsession that you have with me for now. It will pass."

"This has been far longer than you know. But in due time all will be revealed," he says mysteriously.

"What the hell are you talking-"

The rest of my words are swallowed as, without hesitation, he captures my lips. I raise my hands to push at his chest but he is unmovable. His hands grip my waist and pull me flush against him. His lips continue to plunder mine, begging for a response. As he nibbles softly and moves his hand to caress my thigh, I feel my body begin to respond to his and I sigh softly.

"That's my sweetheart. Let me kiss you, touch you."

As my mouth opens, he invades. His tongue is hot and slick against mine. My hands rise to tangle in his hair as I give in to the wave of emotions. He groans in response and I feel his hand on the hem of my skirt. With some effort, he inches the hemline upward. As he continues to kiss me, I tremble as the cool air hits my thighs. Unerringly, his hand travels upward and I moan once more as his thumb grazes the seat of my panties. I cling to him as he pushes the flimsy fabric aside and strokes my pussy. I lean into his touch and he pushes his hand further to cup me completely. His hand fumbles to find the zipper on the back of my skirt, but it's on the side. I'm not going to tell him though. He compensates by bunching my skirt up around my waist. He pulls my panties aside completely and captures my moan as he plunges a finger deep inside me. I feel his hot, hard length against my thigh and think how easy it would be for him to slide his zipper down and release himself to have his way with me.

Every argument I've come up with to fight my attraction to Ace is defeated at this moment. His touch drives me crazy right now, all I want is to feel him inside me. But something holds me back. Why can't I just stop being hung up on being in a relationship with my married boss and let the chips fall where – married! The reminder is like a slap in the face.

I push against him hard and wrench my mouth away from his.

"No! We can't do this, Ace. You're married and I'm not a homewrecker. You need to respect your marriage. And if you can't, I will!"

I push hard enough to catch him off-guard. As he steps back to gain his balance, I dash around him. I pull my skirt down hastily and head for the door. I yank it open, step out and slam it. I barely look at Mrs. Elaine as I hurry back to my office. I try not to break into a dead run but my heels on the tile make a racket as I speed walk. Heads turn and watch me as I pass by them. But I don't stop until I'm in the safety of my office. I close the door behind me and lean against it, my heart racing. I have to get a grip on myself! It can't be that Ace has so much control over me, insomuch that every resolution to stay away from him vanishes into thin air the moment he appears. I squeeze my thighs together as I feel as though I can still feel his hand there. I take deep gulps of breath as I try to calm myself.

On one point, I know that I'm right, though. It is obvious that Ace is going to stop at nothing until he has his way with me. Isn't that night in his apartment enough for us both? In his eyes it's not. He wants more. But I can't give it, no matter how attracted I am to him. I don't even know anything about him apart from what is printed in magazines and articles. And yes, admittedly we are in sync sexually. But what do I know about him besides that? What is his favorite color? What is his favorite meal? What is his family like? All these questions and more will need to be processed for me to even begin to think of the possibility of anything long-term. But then again, I'm assuming that Ace is looking for something long-term. I feel my face flush with humiliation as scenes from his apartment flash through my mind. I feel more embarrassed at what transpired in his office just now. What if someone had walked in on us? It is as though my worst fears about entanglement with Ace are manifesting. There's no getting past the fact that he has declared and carried through on his declaration that he wants me sexually. I allowed myself to be swept away in the heat of the moment. But the buck stops there. He is married. Even if I can find another job, there is no way I will be the reason for his divorce.

Find another job. The thought crosses my mind again. In the first instance, I hadn't given it a fighting chance. But with things unfolding the way they are, that may just be my best option right now. Can I walk away from my dream job to get away from Ace? That may very well be my last resort at this point.

On slightly shaking legs, I walk to my desk and take a seat. I look at the manuscript once more and see nothing on the page. I bury my head in my hands as I groan in frustration. Escape. Escape. Escape. That is all that's on my mind right now. Perhaps I can work from home for the rest of the week while I try to figure things out. Yes. That will be ideal. I can have Charles email electronic manuscripts as usual and ask the company messenger to deliver the printed ones if need be. But there is no way I'm going to be in the same space as Ace Channing.

I go into my email and compose a message to Charles indicating my work-from-home decision and how things are to be handled. Next, I look around the office for a box into which to pack the current printed manuscripts. There is none. I text Marissa asking her to find one and bring it to my office. As I wait for her response, I begin sorting the material and place them on a chair by the door. When I get them packed, I will ask Justin to take them downstairs for me. I need to take enough work for the rest of the week and possibly into next week. Tears sting at my eyes as I think about the reason for my sudden flight from the office. Damn Ace and his interference. At this rate, I may have to contemplate another job. I keep rummaging through my drawers looking for some specific manuscripts.

CHAPTER 16

ACE

I look at the closed door and wonder how things could have taken such a one-eighty degree turn in a split second. One moment Lana is in my arms once more and I'm about to drop my pants and bury myself in her body, and the next I'm left throbbing with need and no Lana.

Through the fog of shock, her comment about me being married hits home. Damn! That must have been what Meredith told her. I need to clear things up right away and there's no time like the present. But first I need to get myself under control.

It takes me a few minutes but I manage to do so. As I'm about to leave my office when my phone rings. At first, I'm tempted to ignore the call. But I see that it's Reggie.

"Hey, Ace. I hope I haven't caught you at a bad time."

"It's never a bad time to hear from you, Reggie, even when it is. What's up?"

I listen as Reggie updates me on Meredith. As the conversation ends, I'm steaming. So that's what prompted the impromptu visit. Well! She has another thing coming her way.

As I leave my office, I run into Elaine who is about to knock. She opens her mouth to speak and I cut her off immediately.

"Hold my messages. I'll be right back."

She takes one look at me and steps back.

"Okay."

I stride past her and soon find myself walking past the other departments. Eyes turn and I know the gossip mill will be active today regarding these trips to and from Lana's office. But nothing is going to stand in my way. When I get to her door, I find it closed. Without knocking, I open it and find her office in some disarray. It seems as if she is – packing?

"Leave it on the chair please," she says without looking up.

"Where the hell do you think you're going?"

Her head snaps up and our eyes meet. I see the trepidation in her gaze and I feel like a heel that she should feel fear in my presence. I was once her champion. Now I'm her tormentor.

I close the door behind me without taking my eyes off her. I walk across the office and she stands behind her chair, using it as a shield. I hold her eyes as I speak as evenly as possible.

"Why are you packing?"

"I'm going to work from home for the rest of the week."

"The hell you are! And what did you mean in my office by 'I'm a married man'?"

"Just what I said. You have a wife."

I throw my head back and laugh incredulously. I look at her.

"You're serious aren't you?"

"Ace, don't pretend. Please. It's already an embarrassing situation. We can't do this. You're my boss and you're married and-"

I cut her off mid-sentence. "Lana, I'm not married."

"Yes, you are. I saw your wife with my own eyes, heard her with my own ears and spoke to her with my own mouth. You are a very married man who, according to your *wife*, has an open marriage. You know what that means don't you?"

"What!?" I gaze at her incredulously.

"Don't act so surprised, Ace. I guess you simply forgot to tell her that you had someone over so she could stay at her boyfriend's a little longer. The least you can do is wear your ring or admit it now that you've been found out."

"Did you see any hint of the presence of a woman at my apartment, Lana?"

"No. But perhaps her things are in another room locked away or something so you can give the appearance of being single when you lure your targets to the apartment."

"Lure is such a strong and offensive term. It makes me sound like a predator."

"Aren't you though? You've done nothing but hunt me since the first time our paths crossed."

"I'm a man. It's our nature to hunt."

"And I guess I'm supposed to just roll over and allow myself to be caught."

I sigh and look up at the ceiling. I look at Lana as she continues to glare at me.

"Lana, listen to me carefully. I am not married."

"Well clearly your wife didn't get the memo. So what is this? You still want to have your cake and eat it too. Well, you can find some other cake."

"If I didn't know better, I'd say you're jealous."

"Jealous of who? Meredith? Hell no! Your *wife* is very welcome to you, Ace Channing. I'm no third wheel. Please leave my office."

"Technically it's my office. CEO. Remember?"

"How could I forget? Oh, I know. The same way you forgot that you have a wife."

"Meredith is not my wife. We were married. *Were.* We've been divorced for over two years."

"I fail to believe that. Clearly you still have a relationship. How else could she have gotten into your apartment?"

"By lying to one of the security personnel. She has always been good at making up lies."

As I speak, I inch closer to Lana. She watches me warily, but at least she doesn't try to move. I come within touching distance. I sit on the edge of the desk and reach out to cover her hand with mine.

"Lana, I would and will never play with your emotions like that."

"You're always around women. I've seen the pictures in the magazines, Ace."

"You of all people should know that the print media exaggerates when it suits them."

"I don't know anything about you."

I give her a piercing stare. "You know more than you think you do, sweetheart."

"But-"

"You're running out of excuses. We've already settled that Meredith is not an issue. When we split, she got a house and car for her worries. I had no idea what she was doing there that morning. Which reminds me. My investigator called just now and gave me a few possible leads. The bottom line is extortion and blackmail. But that will be dealt with in short order. But believe me, Lana. I am not in nor have been in a serious relationship since my divorce."

"No *serious* relationships. So, I guess I am just another in a string of casual flings then?"

"If you were, would I be here right now considering we've already slept together? I'm here because I want something with you, Lana, not just something from you. Something with *you* that no one else has been able to fill."

"Stop it, Ace. We barely know each other."

"We know each other better than you think we do."

"I agree that we totally connect sexually. But there is more to a relationship than just sex. There has to be conversation."

"We've conversed."

“We have to spend time getting to know each other.”

“We have spent time together.”

“I don’t think a few seconds in a bar when I kissed you on a dare, and another few minutes here and there, and then sleeping at your place for the night can be categorized as ‘spending time together’, Ace.”

“I wasn’t referring to that. But time will reveal that I speak the truth.”

I run my thumb along her hand as I hold her gaze with mine. Slowly I take her hand and pull her around to stand in front of me. I use my foot to push the chair away as I pull her to stand between my legs. I take a deep breath as I look into her eyes. My heart races at being so close to her. I want to pour my heart out, but I restrain myself. There is still damage control to do.

“Lana, I’m glad you came up to me in the bar that night. It saved me the trouble of coming over to you. I noticed you the moment you entered. Your beauty captivated me.”

“I’m more than a pretty face, Ace.”

I place my finger on her lips. “Shhh. Let me finish. Your beauty captivated me. But I knew beyond your face was also a heart of gold. And stop saying I don’t know. You’re going to find I know you better than you know yourself. I’m not the kind of man that begs. I’ve done enough of that in my life and when I became rich, I swore my begging days were behind me. But this is an exception, sweetheart. I’m not too proud to beg you to give me a chance. Please?”

I search her eyes with mine, watching as her emotions change from one to the other in rapid succession. I use my thumb to trace her lips.

"Please?" the word comes out in a whisper as I pull her body closer. I lift her arms and drape them around my neck.

"Please?" My breath feathers against her lips as I claim them.

At first, the kiss is slow and hesitant. But soon I feel her lips relax as she gives herself over to me. I sense the exact moment of her surrender as she opens her mouth beneath mine. My tongue surges forward to find its mate waiting, and with a groan, they are reunited. I find the button on her jacket and tug it open. As my mouth continues to devour hers, my hands roam along her blouse, releasing the buttons from their holes as I do. When my fingers meet the soft satin of her bra, my thumbs travel until they find the stiff peaks of her nipples. I'm pleased to feel her tremble as I pinch and roll them. My hands drift down to this damn tight skirt. In no time, I have it bunched up around her waist once again. My hands find her panties and tug at them slightly until they roll down over her buttocks. I push the scrap of fabric down until her feet move as she steps out of them. My lips have not left hers and I swallow her moans as I caress her hot, wet pussy. My thumb finds her clit, hard and throbbing with need. Touching her sends a signal to my groin as my body hardens once more. I know this desire is more than physical. Each time I touch her it's like the meeting of our souls. With each pass of my finger, she trembles violently. I want to bury myself inside her so badly. But I want to please her first. Her arms are locked around my neck as I keep my mouth fused to hers, our tongues plunging and suckling. I keep circling her clit with my thumb even as I plunge my fingers inside her. She is on fire and so very wet.

I begin to finger-fuck her slowly, loving the feeling of her pussy gripping my fingers with each thrust. She moans in time to the thrusts and I feel her body begin to clench. She rocks back and forth, matching my rhythm. I can tell the moment she is about to come as her pussy tightens like a vice. I thrust once more and hold it there, stroking her clit hard. I swallow her moans of pleasure as I feel her juices bathe my hand. I feel her heart beating fast against mine as I hold her to me. I'm breathing as hard as she is.

Slowly our mouths separate and we stare at each other in wonder. I hold her gaze as I withdraw my hand from her body, slowly. I raise my fingers and watch as her eyes widen as I lick her juices from them. My mouth finds hers once more as I share her taste with her. I find my zipper and the rasp sounds like an explosion as I pull it down. I find my cock, hard and heavy with need. I pull her forward and use the tip to roll over her wet clit. She moans softly. I begin to turn her in my arms so that I can find a better entry angle. I run the tip of my cock up and down her butt crack, inching ever closer to my destination.

"Spread your legs for me, babe."

I sigh as she does. I feel the tip touch her pussy and I'm a goner. I angle myself and slide in, shuddering as her pussy welcomes me. I bend her slightly at the waist as I stand and begin to thrust into her. She bites her lip to stifle her moans. I'm relentless as I thrust deeper and harder. I move faster with each thrust. She peaks once more before I pour myself into her.

"Oh fuck, Lana!" I whisper harshly. "You are exquisite. Do you know that, babe?" I stay buried inside her as I pull her torso up to me. Her back rests against my chest as I find her neck and kiss the tender skin softly. I lick at the pulse beating erratically as she reaches one arm up to drape around my neck.

Suddenly we hear the door opening.

"Lana, Marissa asked me to – oops! Excuse me!"

I turn to find Avery standing in the doorway, her face white. Though my body is shielding Lana's, there is no doubt that we are standing closer than we need to be standing. Lana's hand drops from my neck as she attempts to button her blouse.

"Get out and close the door," I bite at Avery. She stands for a few more seconds, a look of hate turned on Lana, before she does what I say. Only when the door closes behind her do I move swiftly. I hasten to the door and turn the lock.

CHAPTER 17

LANA

My head feels as if it's fuzzy and I'm not quite in my right mind as I begin to process the implications of all that has just happened. As Ace locks the door, I dig into my purse for a wet wipe and begin to clean myself. He comes to me and kisses me gently, taking the wipe from my hand.

"Let me."

He holds my gaze as he wipes away the evidence of our illicit behavior. Tears come to my eyes. How could I have allowed this to happen?

"Lana. It's okay."

"That's easy for you to say, isn't it? You're the boss. But me? It's not okay. Now I'm going to be labeled as the office whore."

"Lana-"

I hold up my hand and stop him mid-sentence. "Please, Ace. I've made my bed. I'll lie in it."

"I'm not going to leave you to handle this on your own, Lana. We're in this together and I don't have a problem making it known that we're in a relationship."

"But I do, Ace. I don't do office relationships."

"There's always a first time for everything."

"Not this."

He takes my chin gently between his fingers. "Lana, it will be okay. With the way things have been between us, it was bound to come out sooner or later."

I bite my lip and nod nervously. "I still have to face the music. It's me they're going to talk about, not you."

"I dare anyone to say anything."

"What are you going to do? Fire the whole company?"

"If I have to." His lips twitch and I sigh.

"Ace, this is serious. Avery doesn't like me very much. I'm sure that by the end of lunchtime it will be all over not just this floor, but the building."

"You give her more credit than she deserves. Avery is smart and will keep her mouth shut."

"How can you be so sure?" I look at him carefully. "Unless-"

"Unless what?"

"Unless you have something going on with her as well so you're sure she will keep quiet."

"Hell, no. Avery does not interest me in any way. You are my focus, Lana. Believe me. And I don't care who knows. I own the damn company. I can do as I fucking please with whomever I choose, and I dare anyone to tell me otherwise. Relax. One day at a time."

He kisses me softly and strokes my cheek. "Just relax, sweetheart. It will be fine. You'll see."

And with one last kiss, he walks out of the office, closing the door behind him. I sit staring at the closed door, my mind in a whirl. I move like a robot as I put the manuscripts back into the cabinets. I guess working from home is no longer an option.

It's a struggle to get through the rest of the afternoon. I send for take-out for lunch as I dare not show my face outside of the office. I also end up working pretty late. When I leave the office at seven, thankfully, it's empty.

I have a quick meal and shower and hop into bed. Just as I'm about to fall asleep, a text message comes in and I sit up. It's from a strange number and I'm tempted to ignore it. But the message begins with my name.

Lana, thanks for giving me a chance. Rest well, sweetheart.

Ace. I save the number and turn off the light.

The next morning, I arrive early and slip into the office. Again, I keep out of the way. It's not until Wednesday that I venture out to the photocopy room and walk through the other departments. I'm tense and hold my breath. But no one looks at me weirdly, nor do I perceive any whispered conversations. I relax a little. As the rest of the week goes by, the atmosphere feels normal enough. Whenever I see Ace, we greet each other casually. It seems he is right and Avery has held her tongue. But there is something niggling at me that wants to know the reason behind her silence. It isn't revealed until the following weeks.

The summer days have been beautiful and on Monday I decided to take advantage of the fast-disappearing days of being able to be outside. At lunchtime, I head to the elevator, intending to walk to the deli on the next block. As the doors begin to close, I hear a shout.

"Wait!"

I place a hand in the opening and the door slides back. I watch as Marissa comes running. I smile. But then my smile slips when I see Avery as well.

"Thanks, Lana," Marissa breathes dramatically with a hand over her heart. "I don't know when we would have caught another."

"No problem."

I turn my attention to the numbers as the doors close and we begin to descend.

"I was just telling Marissa that having Ace as CEO is one of the best things that could have ever happened to us. What do you think, Lana?"

My heart thuds in my chest as I turn to meet Avery's stare. She smiles slightly but I feel the malice in it.

"Oh, Avery. Leave Lana alone about Ace. You know they have their issues and haven't been on good terms from the beginning."

"Well, things do change, Marissa. Sometimes those who were the worst of enemies become the best of *bed*fellows. Don't you agree, Lana? Maybe the day will come when you and Ace can put your differences aside and let bygones be bygones. Turn over a new *sheet* so to speak?"

"I think you mean a new page, Avery," Marissa chimes in cluelessly.

Avery giggles, but it's a bitter and empty sound. "Oh, dear me! You are right. Sheets belong on beds after all and it's not like we're talking about anyone sleeping with anyone."

I feel my cheeks grow warm as Avery holds my gaze. Though my tongue feels as if it's cleaving to the roof of my mouth I respond as calmly as possible.

"Everyone deserves a second chance to make a first impression."

"And I'm sure you know how to impress, right?"

I try to think of another response, but thankfully the elevator gets to the ground floor. I hurry out as if I'm being chased.

"Enjoy your lunch, Lana!" Marissa calls after me.

"Thanks, Marissa." I wave without looking behind me.

"Don't have any rendezvous we wouldn't!" Avery chimes in tauntingly. I begin to walk faster. As they head towards the parking lot I head to the street. I hope they don't head in my direction and it is with relief that I look behind me and see them go the other way.

I order a sandwich and iced tea from the deli at the corner and take it with me to a nearby park. I find a bench with some shade and have my lunch. As I eat, Avery's words play over and over in my head. I should have known not to trust her! The little snitch is probably waiting for the right time to use the information to her advantage. I wonder if I should let

Ace know. He's taken to texting me every morning and night, and we have spoken a few times. On Saturday evening when he called, I was in the middle of watching a movie. Immediately he wanted to know which movie and had switched channels. Then he video called me, and we watched the movie together. It has been only a week, but with each conversation, I become more relaxed. There is something about him that is familiar but it eludes me. Sometimes he says things that jog my memories of a childhood friend. But Ace is nothing like Chester. Chester had been shy and like a giant teddy bear. And my thirteen-year-old heart had been smitten by the quiet seventeen-year old. He had been my first and last crush, for as soon as he had come, he had gone and I had been heartbroken. No. Ace is nothing like Chester. Ace embraces the spotlight and is confident in who he is. Chester was so shy he hardly spoke to anyone except me. And boy did we talk! He had been a very good listener, especially when I had told him of my dreams of writing. He hadn't scoffed as others had, but had encouraged me to go for it. Not for the first time I wonder what has become of him. I should call my mother this weekend and see if she knows although it has been a few years.

My phone chimes and I look down to find a message from Ace.

Where are you, dear? I wanted to surprise you with lunch but your office is empty.

I'm already out.

My bad. I should have remembered that you're not very big on surprises. We'll talk later then.

Okay.

I frown slightly. I think hard, but I can't remember at what point I would have told Ace that I don't like surprises. Only those close to me know that. I shrug and figure that I must have said it but just can't recall doing so.

As I finish my meal I think about Ace. Having given myself a chance to get to know him, I realize that I do like him. The main selling point is how easily we converse. We flow from topic to topic, following each other's train of thought and picking up nuances. I find him to be quite intelligent and well-learned as well. Little by little he shares snippets of his past and I do likewise. I can't help but feel as though we are nibbling on the edges and that a time is coming when the serious conversations will begin.

I think, also, that though Avery has kept her mouth shut, I have to prepare for the possibility that one day our relationship will get out. I think about the gossip and that I may be labeled as a gold-digger. I can't ignore the fact he is rolling in money. But in my heart I know if he was as poor as a church mouse it would not make a difference to me. I see beyond the pocket. I know Ace has a good heart. I can't help but feel a tingle of excitement at the prospect of getting to know Ace some more. I'm still wary of being out in public being who he is. But for now, I'm enjoying texting and talking on the phone.

I finish my lunch and head back to the office. The week runs by without any further run-in with Avery. I'm still gauging the vibe in the office as well. No one seems to know anything. Good.

I have an unexpected attack of allergies and end up leaving work early on Friday. When Ace calls me that night, I'm hoarse. He keeps me company for a while before I decide that I can't take the stuffiness anymore and take an antihistamine. The last thing I remember hearing is his soft kiss as he tells me to sleep well.

I'm enjoying my drug-induced rest when I'm awakened by a persistent buzz. I finally figure out that it's my phone. I take a deep, sleepy breath and answer.

"Hello?"

"Hi, Lana. It's Dania. I'm sorry to wake you. I know how residents treasure their Saturday mornings. But could you come downstairs, please? There's a delivery here that I can't sign for on your behalf."

I sigh. "Okay. I'll be right down."

I roll out of bed and pull on a robe over my nightshirt. I push my feet into my rubber slippers by the door and head downstairs. I find a small gathering in the parking lot, and for good reason. There, with a brightly colored bow adorning the hood, is a brand-new car. Dania pulls me forward and I find myself with a clipboard in my hand. I scan the documents and sign as I'm told. The driver smiles.

"We've been instructed to tow the old one, Miss Gray."

I stifle a yawn.

"I need to go get the keys and take some stuff out."

"We'll wait."

I head upstairs in a daze, retrieve my car keys, then head back downstairs. I clean out the glove compartment and remove a few personal items before handing the keys over. I dump my stuff on the back seat of the new car. I clutch the bag that he hands me with the keys, car papers and manual as

I shuffle back to my apartment. I barely get my robe off before my head hits the pillow and I'm asleep once more.

It's nearly midday when I wake up. I'm still a bit hoarse but feel much better than last night. I frown as I find myself tangled in my robe. I must have been really out of it last night to fall asleep in my robe. I shuffle to the bathroom and wash my face. It revives me somewhat. I go to the kitchen and put on the kettle to make some tea. I'm waiting for the water to boil when I catch sight of a bag on the counter. What is that and how did it get there?

I open the bag and stare in puzzlement at car papers, a manual and car keys. Somewhere in the fuzz of my brain I recall what must have been a dream. Or was it. There is only one way to find out.

I grab my robe once more and head downstairs to the parking lot. I blink once. Then twice. But no matter how many times I blink, there is no doubt that the shiny new car with the obnoxious ribbon is sitting in my parking spot. And there's only one person who could have done this. Ace. Damn, I hate surprises!

CHAPTER 18

ACE

"I guarantee that in a year this is a company that is going to be making headlines. They're nobody right now but they have a cutting-edge approach that can't fail, especially with the direction in which the world is going right now."

I look around the table, reading the contemplative expressions of the men sitting there. It's one of our monthly Saturday lunches where we toss ideas around for investment opportunities. I take a sip of my drink. William is the first to speak.

"I have to admit, Ace, you've never steered me wrong yet. That foot in the door with Leeway two years ago was money in the bank. I'm in for as much as I can get."

There are nods of agreement around the table and I smile. The importance of networking is something I discovered early in my rise to wealth and fortune. And of the group here only William hasn't been with me for the past five or so years when I really got serious about making money and decided on strategic partners to take with me. We have learned from each other and made our mistakes along the way.

I look around the sports bar and wonder if the other diners understand the power and wealth sitting at table nine. We all have a minimum of seven figures in at least three accounts. And we are all young, all under thirty-two. I smile and raise my glass.

"To another quite lucrative lunch meeting."

We all laugh and clink our glasses. The conversation trickles down as we finish our meal. As the waitress comes with the bill, William reaches for his wallet.

"Today is on me, gentlemen."

"No problem," Darren chimes in while pulling his wallet out as well. "I'll do the tip."

We finish off our last round of drinks while we wait for Sally to finish with the bill. As we wait, my phone vibrates in my pocket and I take it out. I smile.

"Give me a second, fellas. I have to take this call."

I stand and walk away from the table. I lean over the balcony which is a few feet away and connect the call. As I look out over the street below my heart races as I wait to hear Lana's voice.

"Hello beautiful."

"Don't you 'hello beautiful' me, Ace. What did-"

"Would you prefer? Hello gorgeous, hello sweetheart, hello love, or all of the above?" I chuckle softly at her indignant tone.

"Ace! I'm serious."

I laugh as I imagine Lana's green eyes flashing with animation.

"So am I, darling."

"I can't take it. It's too much."

"Can't take what, dearest?"

"You know what."

"Do I?"

"Ace," she growls warningly. "I'm already on edge about what people will think in the office."

"So now they'll have something else to talk about."

"You know what they'll think."

"I don't. What will they think?"

"They will think that these are gifts in exchange for sexual favors, Ace."

"Well, it isn't. You can check with the dealer if you like. I bought it for you almost two months ago. I was just waiting for it to get into the country."

"You did what!? But we didn't even know each other then."

"Exactly.

"But-"

"But nothing, love. Enjoy your gift. You still sound a bit hoarse. How are you feeling now?"

We speak briefly about her being under the weather before we hang up. I go back to my table where the others are waiting.

"Everything okay?" Darren asks.

I smile. "Great. So, gentlemen, next month, same place, same time?"

There is agreement all around and we head to the parking lot. We run into some random photographers who take our pictures without permission as usual. They are always hanging around places like this trying to spot who they can. We get into our respective vehicles and leave.

On the way home, I have an idea and stop at a restaurant. I place an order and give some instructions. My next stop is a pharmacy where I place another order and give more instructions. I head home to get some paperwork done and catch a quick nap before a business dinner this evening. I would rather spend it nursing Lana, but I'm still making up for the meetings I missed when I was away.

While I'm getting ready to leave home a few hours later a text comes in from Lana telling me thanks for the soup and the medication. I text her back a smiley face and heart.

I go to the meeting with my mind elsewhere and several times I have to ask for questions to be repeated. Finally, I excuse myself briefly.

"Give me a few minutes please. I need to check on a sick friend."

I step outside and dial. The phone rings three times before she answers.

"Hello?"

"Hey, babe. How are you feeling now? Did the soup help? Have you taken the pills? Are you sure it's just your allergies?"

She laughs softly and I feel my heart beat just a little bit faster.

"I'm feeling fine. The soup helped a lot. I've taken the pills. It's just my allergies so it'll blow over by tomorrow."

"Just the same, if you don't feel well enough on Monday, stay home."

"I'll be better by then, Ace."

"I'm just saying."

"You're just fussing."

I chuckle. "I'm going to fuss and there's nothing you can do about it. But now that I know you're okay, I can get back to my meeting."

"Meeting? On a Saturday night?"

"Yes, dear. I missed a few when I was away so I'm catching up."

"Oh. Okay."

"If I wasn't here, I would be there, you know."

"Oh?"

"Lana, I'm serious when I say I'm serious about you. Hopefully you believe me. This is not a short-term relationship.

Now go get some rest and I'll catch up with you later or tomorrow."

"Okay."

I wait for her to hang up and I stand looking at the phone for a few moments before heading back inside.

"Is your girlfriend okay?"

I look up sharply at Mrs. Wentworth's question. The others look at me, waiting for me to answer. I open my mouth to respond then close it just as suddenly. Julia Wentworth is a known gossip and I know if I respond in the affirmative my business will be all over the city in the morning. I choose my words carefully.

"My *family friend* is okay."

"Jeez, Ace. Take a joke."

"Sorry. It's been a hellish week."

"It shows. Besides, we know after the number Meredith did on you there's no way you're going down that road again. Now where were we?"

We finish dining and discussing our business and a few hours later I'm heading home. As soon as I step inside and close the door behind me, I text Lana.

I'm home. Are you awake?

I head to the bar and fix myself a drink, looking at the phone on the counter anxiously. It vibrates and I lunge for it.

"Hello. Did I wake you?"

"Nah. I was up reading. I feel much better. Thanks again for the soup and tablets. They worked wonderfully well."

"Not a problem, sweetheart. What are you reading?"

"A Johnny Crenshaw novel."

"Ah, yes. You always were an old soul." I mutter the last to myself.

"What was that?"

"Nothing. Crenshaw is a good writer."

"An acquired taste. I've been reading his novels since elementary school."

An image comes before me as I remember the first time I saw her. She was sitting on the porch all arms and legs and hair with her head buried in a tattered novel. She had looked up at me with those bright green eyes and time had stood still. I had become even more tongue-tied than usual and had barely been able to stutter out my name.

"That's a pretty long time to be a fan." Even as I speak, the seed of an idea pops into my head. And when an idea comes to me, I become like a bulldog. Whereas before I couldn't wait to talk to her, now I couldn't wait to get off the phone to start my research. If this can materialize, it will knock her socks off her dainty feet.

We talk a little longer before I send her to bed with a promise to call her in the morning. As soon as she hangs up, I take what's left of my drink into the bedroom. I turn on the laptop and watch as it boots up while I undress. I type in a few words and have a few false starts. Then finally I find something that makes me smile. This is going to be even better than I thought. I copy a few links and send them to Monica with instructions. I look forward to a positive response by Monday.

I shut down and prepare for bed. As I slip between the covers and sigh. For the first in a long time, I am truly, blissfully happy. And if things continue to go as I have them planned, there is more happiness in store for me. I can hardly wait.

With a smile on my face and Lana filling my mind, I fall asleep.

When I wake up the next morning, I waste no time showering and getting dressed. I head to the supermarket then straight to Lana's. I get a few weird looks when my Jaguar pulls into the parking lot and I find a spot in the visitor's section. I put on my dark glasses and hurry into the building before anyone can wonder if I am who I am. I've never been here but with Reggie's details etched in my mind I find her apartment easily. I knock and wait then knock again. Finally, on the third try, I hear movement from within. Only belatedly do I realize that she may still be in a medication-induced sleep and I've disturbed her. Way to go Ace.

When she yanks the door open, it takes her a few seconds to register that I'm on her doorstep. But by that time, I've stepped past her and am standing in the middle of her living room with grocery bags in my hands.

"Kitchen?"

She stands at the door gaping. Then she slowly points. By the time I place the bags on the counter, I turn to find her in the alcove watching me as I move around. I walk over to her.

"Good morning. I heard a personal chef was needed today so here I am. Go take a shower while I fix breakfast."

I drop a quick kiss on her forehead and turn her around. I swat her on the behind and push her gently in the direction of what I think is her bedroom. She casts one look over her shoulder before ambling off to do as instructed. I watch her go. She turns at the door and I smile. She smiles back.

As soon as she disappears, I get busy. By the time she returns to the kitchen, I have scrambled eggs, hash browns, bacon, pancakes and waffles ready. I make just enough for two as I don't believe in wasting food. Her eyes widen as she takes her seat. I've set the table to look like a diner, vase and all. I have a single daisy there and she smiles as I pull out her chair.

"I love daisies."

I bite my tongue as I almost say 'I know'. Instead, I serve her as a waiter would before serving a plate for myself and taking a seat. I sit to her right rather than across from her. She giggles as I hook her ankle with mine.

"Where did you learn to cook like this?"

"I wasn't born with a silver spoon. I've had to fend for myself a time or two. In some parts of my previous life, I've been a waiter."

"Really? What else have you been in your previous life?"

"A carpenter, a pharmacy delivery boy, a windshield washer, a bellman, should I go on with my list of former occupations?"

"Wow! How old are you again?"

"Twenty-eight in December."

"December? What date?"

"Eighteenth." I shield my face with a glass of orange juice as her gaze fixes on me. She searches my face and I quirk an eyebrow. She shakes her head and turns her attention back to her plate. I wait for her to say something else. Surely my birthday must have jarred her memory, but she remains silent.

I change the subject and we talk about things that she's done over the past few years. We do the dishes and then retreat to the couch. I make myself comfortable in a corner of the couch and beckon for her to curl up next to me. I turn on the television while she buries her nose in her novel. I stroke her hair gently as we just enjoy being in each other's company. She shifts and I look at her. She smiles up at me.

"Nature calls. Be right back."

I release her and she gets to her feet. She places her book on the couch and heads to the bathroom. I pick up her book and look at the cover. But then something makes me freeze. I trace the smooth metal hook holding her place in the novel. I can't believe she kept it all these years. I hear the toilet flush and I put the book back where she left it. She soon appears and I stretch a hand up. She takes it and sits beside me once more. This time, she places her head in my lap and looks up at me. She smiles and I smile back.

"What's on your mind?"

"I'm just thinking that I could never imagine being here with you like this from kissing you on a dare in a bar."

"Oh? I could."

"You say that with so much confidence."

"Because I am confident. And I am serious about you."

She searches my face and I hold her gaze. I lean forward and brush her lips with mine briefly before leaning back and smiling.

"Read your book. I'm going to get lunch started."

She sits up and allows me to stand.

As I work in the kitchen on sandwiches while putting some chicken to marinate for dinner, I feel her eyes on me now and then. I feel a sense of exhilaration at the prospects for the future with Lana. Is this what it will be like to be with her for the rest of my life? I certainly hope so.

CHAPTER 19

LANA

When I wake up on Monday, I feel as good as new. How can I not with the way Ace has taken care of me all weekend? Yesterday was a huge surprise but a welcome one.

While he had worked on lunch and dinner, I had watched him. All morning there had been something at the back of my thoughts. There is a familiarity about Ace that I can't fathom. It's as though I knew him in a previous life. And more and more memories of *that* year surface. I had brushed the feeling aside as there is no possibility of a connection. But I firmly resolve to not let the week end without my reaching out to my mother to see if she knows what became of Chester.

As I head down to the parking lot I smile. Ace had left late last night. After dinner we played a game of scrabble and for the first time, I feel as though I have a worthy opponent. We both won an equal number of games and we have a rematch planned with an odd number of games. I had been tempted to ask him to sleep over and it was as if he had read my mind.

He had said he would have stayed if he had brought a suit for work. But with a wink he promised to think ahead the next time. The next time: that has a nice ring to it.

I carefully remove the bow which has sat on the vehicle all weekend and stuff it into the trunk. I'll dispose of it later. It purrs to life and I have to admit that it drives like a dream. I feel better about accepting it as a gift as Ace had said it is a birthday gift. I didn't bother to try to figure out how he knew my birthday had been a few weeks ago. It's the same way I won't try to figure out how he found a daisy in the city close to autumn.

I enjoy the drive to work and the feel of the vehicle. My only trepidation comes when I turn into the parking lot and the old reservations arise. I make it to my parking spot safely and breathe a sigh of relief. I get out and am in the process of grabbing my purse from the back seat when my worst fears are realized. Of all the mornings for Avery and Marissa to drive in at the same time as me, it has to be this morning. And to make matters worse, they park next to me. Marissa has her window down and smiles at me brightly.

"Nice wheels, Lana!"

I smile back. "Thanks."

"Very nice. Where did you get it?" Avery smiles tightly at me.

"Avery! That's a bit rude and nosey don't you think?"

I'm saved from answering as Marissa parks her vehicle. As much as I want to walk away, it would be rude to do so. So, I wait for them to exit their cars. Marissa comes over and rubs her hand over the hood.

"This looks like it's brand new off the lot. Is this the first time you're driving it?" she trails a finger on the shiny mirror.

"I got it on Saturday but just got the chance to drive it this morning. It's a birthday gift."

"Wasn't your birthday in July, though? A bit late for a birthday gift don't you think?" Avery sneers at me.

"It's a *belated* gift."

I step away and they fall into step beside me.

"Some gift though. Your boyfriend must be loaded to buy that. And I can only imagine what one has to put out to get a gift like that!" Avery is making no attempt to mask the maliciousness in her tone. Marissa gasps and laughs awkwardly as she tries to cover her friend's anger.

"Don't listen to Avery, Lana. Bitter grapes if you ask me seeing as she can't even catch a cold much less a guy. But maybe your millionaire sweetie has a brother or a good friend and you can hook a girl up?" Marissa digs me with her elbow. "I'm a nice girl just looking for a nice guy and his having a few dollars will definitely not hurt."

"Don't be a gold digger, Marissa. Have some class and standards. Not every woman should be after a man just for his money you know," Avery chimes in hotly.

"I'm sure Lana is no gold digger, Avery. She's a very nice girl who happens to have attracted a very nice guy with a few dollars. A nice guy, I might add, who might have a brother or friend for one of her equally nice friends?" Marissa smiles at me hopefully.

I can't help but chuckle and shake my head. "I don't know about any brothers or friends."

"So, you do have a rich boyfriend!" Marissa squeals and I see how I walked into that trap.

"You've got it all wrong, Marissa," Avery chimes in yet again. "Lana's guy is more of a *billionaire* than a dumpy old millionaire. Right, Lana?"

I stare at Avery hard and she smiles spitefully. We enter the building and walk towards the elevators. Suddenly, I spot someone at the receptionist's desk and think fast.

"You ladies go ahead. I need to have a quick word with Jack."

I whirl on my heel and walk away. As soon as I turn the corner, I breathe deeply. I give the elevator enough time to be sure that they are no longer there before I head back to catch another upstairs.

I speed walk through the office, saying good morning as I do. I breathe a sigh of relief when I get to my office and close the door behind me. The conversation in the parking lot replays in my thoughts. Avery is a sore point and it makes me wonder about her motives for not spreading what she saw with Ace and me. She isn't that nice a person and I can't help but feel that she's going to find some way to use the information against me somehow.

It is often said the things we fear the most come to pass. A few hours later, there's a knock on my door.

"Come in!"

I look up expectantly. But instead of Marissa coming with the manuscripts I've requested, it's Avery. I take a deep breath as she steps into the office.

"You may leave them on the chair. Thank you, Avery."

I watch as she places the manuscripts carefully on the chair as instructed. As I wait for her to leave, she closes the door instead. My heart begins to race as she approaches my desk. I try to appear as calm as possible, not knowing what she has up her sleeve. I watch as she takes a seat on my desk.

"I've always thought that this is a very nice office. It's a good space, has a nice view of the park across the street, everything. I do wish I had an office like this."

I remain silent, waiting for her to get to the point.

"But come to think of it. I should have had this office. I applied for this position, and it would have been mine. But they gave you the job instead. And I'm still stuck in the clerical department."

She gets off the desk and walks around to the window. I turn my chair, not trusting to have my back turned to her.

"It's not a nice feeling to work hard for something, only to have someone else scoop it up from under your nose. But that seems to be your trademark… taking what belongs to others. So first it was this office…" her voice trails off and I continue to keep my eyes on her. She turns and our eyes meet. I have never seen so much hatred in someone's eyes. She purses her lips.

"I don't have to ask where you got the car. I guess that's a gift from Ace for 'favors'? Maybe that's how you got this office in the first place. You just know how to get to the CEOs, don't you? I would have thought that after the way you embarrassed Ace at the restaurant that you would be mortal enemies. But that goes to show what I know, huh."

"What's your point, Avery?"

"What's going on between you and Ace?"

"That is none of your business."

"When he's your boss and I saw what I saw, it's my business and can become the office business too, don't you think?"

"Is that a threat?"

"I don't threaten. I promise. And I promise you this, Miss Lana Gray, if you don't end whatever it is you have with Ace, the whole office will know what took place in here."

"What exactly do you think took place in here, Avery?"

"Oh, come on, Lana! Give me some credit. I walk in here and he's got his arms around you, your arms around him, your blouse undone and your skirt bunched up around your waist, and you looking like you've just gotten the sweetest fuck of your life," she bites out between clenched teeth. "Your window has a reflection you know."

I glance at the window and go pale. She is right. She stalks over to me and places her hands on the arms of my chair.

"Get out of my space, Avery."

"It is you who needs to get out of my space, Lana."

"Why are you doing this?"

"Because I'm tired of watching you take things that belong to me."

"Are you saying Ace belongs to you?"

"I'm saying he should be with someone like me and not someone like you. And you're in my way. What you two are doing is against company policy. If you don't end it, I will report you both to the board. And with someone like Ace, I'm sure the press will have a field day with this bit of scandal on the illustrious Ace Channing."

I gasp as Avery stands and smirks.

"You wouldn't!"

"Try me."

I stare hard at her and she stares back. I stand suddenly, drawing myself up to my full height. I'm not going to allow the likes of Avery to think she can bully me. I step towards her and am pleased to see her step back.

"I got this job fair and square and there is nothing you can do about it. What Ace and I do is none of your business and I'm not going to let your little brat's ass dictate who I should or should not see. If you want an office with a view and a man who pays you some attention, I suggest you fix your attitude and maybe, just maybe, you can experience some measure of happiness. You're very unhappy and very bitter and I don't want you in my space any longer. Leave my office. Now!"

Her face reddens at my words. But she goes to the door. She places her hand on the doorknob and turns to me.

"You can't say I didn't warn you, Lana."

She goes out and closes the door and I sit. My heart is racing as I think about what Avery has said. I know she hates me but I didn't think it was so deeply rooted and goes back to when I was first employed here. Wow! I take a deep breath. Nevertheless, all the cards are now on the table and I guess I need to prepare for the proverbial shit to hit the fan. I think of texting Ace to let him know about the conversation with Avery, but just then, my office extension rings and I get caught up in talking to clients.

The morning goes by and I order out for lunch to make up for the lost time. At around three I take a break and head to the ladies' room as nature calls. I'm in a cubicle and about to exit when I hear voices outside.

"Did you hear about Lana?"

My heart races as I hear my name. I look through the door joint and see Shelby and Trisha from marketing.

"Hear what?" Shelby responds.

"Where have you been today? Under a rock? It's all over the office about her and Ace."

"I've been out at meetings all morning. What about her and Ace?"

"Well, don't say I said, but I heard that she was in her office giving him a blow job!"

I clap my hand over my mouth to stifle any sound as my eyes widen in shock.

"What!? Are you sure it's Lana? She doesn't strike me as the type to sleep her way to the top."

Trisha fans her hands dramatically. "I know! Right? But it's those quiet ones who get down and dirty. And I hear that it's not the first time either. How do you think she even got the job here in the first place? We all know she's an outsider and they overlooked everyone from inside and gave it to her."

"Now that you mention it, that is kind of weird. But I would have never thought she would sink so low, though."

"No one did. Did you see that new car in the parking lot? The royal blue sedan?"

"I didn't. But I'll surely look out for it on my way out."

"He bought it for her."

"Wow! I would never peg Lana as that type in a million years. That is so sad. I always thought she was a nice girl."

"I'm sure that's how we all felt about her."

"But are you sure this is true, though? Suppose someone is out to get her so they're making stuff up."

"That's a possibility. But who would want to make up so many details and base them on lies? I think there's some truth there. But you know even if it's not the whole truth, it's pretty darn close. And if you think about how she threw her drink at him at the luncheon but she still has a job, it makes sense. All those trips to and from his office. And him going to her office. Who knows what goes on behind closed doors, right?"

The women wash their hands and leave the restroom. I give them a good half a minute before exiting the stall. I look at my face and I'm pale. My ears are burning with humiliation. What I have dreaded all these weeks has materialized.

I wash my hands quickly and leave. As I head back to my office, I'm acutely aware of gazes following me, followed by bowed heads and whispered conversation. I feel my cheeks burn as I speed up my steps. Finally, I'm in the safety of my office. I sink into my chair, trembling at what I just heard. Avery has thrown her blow, and what a blow!

CHAPTER 20

ACE

I'm caught up in more meetings all day and find myself in and out of the office. At one point I glimpse Lana's new car in the parking lot and smile. I feel pleased that I'm able to do these things for her. It's not until around four that I get back to the office. I breeze through, greeting as usual and head to my office. I sit and relax for the first time all day. As I gaze out the window at the trees in the park across the street, I see that they are already beginning to change color. My mind wanders as I think about the months ahead. Now that my goal of attaining Lana is partially accomplished, I will soon give up this office. I'm already assessing possible replacements, and whereas I will retain ownership of the company, I will step down as CEO before the end of the year. I know Lana will want to continue working even though she will be financially stable. But when children come along, that may have to be revisited.

I smile at the turn my thoughts have taken. I see a bright future for Lana and me.

I turn my attention to some paperwork and it's close to seven before I leave the office. I head home and have a shower while I reheat something in the oven for dinner. I have just stepped out of the shower when the phone rings. My face lights up.

"Hello, sweetheart. I'm sorry I haven't been in touch all day. It's been a busy one. But how was your day?"

I hear her sigh on the other end. "It's not been a very good one. If you've been so busy, I guess you haven't heard?"

"Haven't heard what?"

"The entire office knows we had sex."

"Hmmm. Avery?"

"Avery. She confronted me in my office this morning."

"I guess she has stewed long enough."

"Or it could be the brand-new car I happened to drive in just as she and Marissa drove in this morning. She did her math and deduced the source of my new gift. Needless to say, she made some rather distasteful remarks about the favors women give in exchange for gifts."

I put the phone on speaker while I pulled on a pair of sweat-pants. I pick up the phone and head to the kitchen. Lana continues to speak.

"She seems to have had it in for me since I was first hired. She wanted my position."

"Ahhh! Now it makes sense."

"What does?"

"Just some comments she's made to me in relation to jobs and positions that she thinks she should have. I've known from the beginning that Avery is not your biggest fan."

"She seems to think that you and she should be an item as well."

"Really? I wonder what would have given her that impression. Trust me, Lana. I've not had any such conversation with Avery nor led her on in any way."

"I know. Avery is just that sort of person. Who knows why she thinks the way she does? But, suffice it to say, we're now the talk of the office. A part of me knows it was just a matter of time. But now that it is out, I will have to figure out how to navigate-"

"What's this 'I' you're talking about? It's *we* Lana. As in you *and* me. Okay? *We* will face this together. How are you feeling about it though?"

She takes a deep breath. "It's very awkward. But what can I do short of resigning?"

"Which you won't."

"Which I won't. It's what I was scared would happen. And now that it has, I just have to roll with the punches. The talk will soon stop."

"As long as you're not breaking up with me."

"I'm not."

"Good. I was serious when I told you we're in this for the long haul. And if I have to fire a few folks I will."

"Can't fire folks for telling the truth, scandalous though it may be. And speaking of scandals, she threatened to report us to the board as well as leak it to the press."

I sit up straighter. "Oh? Did she now? Miss Avery likes to play rough, I see. I hope she can take what she's dishing out."

"Ace. What are you thinking?"

"Nothing, sweetheart. I'm just saying spreading rumors in the office is one thing. But when she's going to go out of her way to get other entities involved, then I may just have to have a little meeting with Miss Avery. I do hope for her sake that she has no secrets and skeletons in the closet. But we've wasted enough time on Avery."

We switch the conversation to other things and chat for a while longer before bidding each other good night. Before I go to bed, though, I make a quick call to Reggie. She promises to get to it first thing in the morning.

The next morning when I step into the office, the tension is palpable. I smile and greet as usual, but I detect an undertone of fear in the responses of those who are not fans of Lana. Avery's eyes can't meet mine as I pass her at the filing cabinet, and her response is muffled.

"Everything okay, Avery? You sound like you're coming down with a cold."

I'm acutely aware that I can hear a pin drop in the clerical department.

"I'm fine, Ace." Her response is mumbled and I raise my eyebrows.

"Oh. Okay."

I continue to my office.

"Good morning, Mrs. Elaine. Any meetings this morning?"

"None on my records, Ace."

"Okay."

I disappear into my office and get ready to start my day. As I wait for the computer to boot up, I make myself a cup of coffee. I'm halfway through answering emails when there's a knock on my door.

"Come in!"

I look up waiting. Mrs. Elaine pushes her head around and steps inside.

"Yes, Mrs. Elaine?"

She closes the door behind her and comes to my desk. I lean back and indicate that she can take a seat. As she sits, she smiles at me in her kindly, motherly way. I smile back.

"Ace, I'm a very forthright woman. So, I won't beat about any bushes. I've heard some things going around about you and Lana. Is it true?"

I look at her for several moments before responding.

"Well, that depends on what you've heard."

"I've heard that you two were seen in a very compromising position in her office and the week where you were both away from the office you were actually on vacation together. You've bought her a new car and she lives with you."

I throw my head back and laugh. "It's amazing how fertile the imaginations of people can be and what stories can be cooked up in the space of twenty-four hours. I guess it comes with the territory of working in publishing."

"So, they're all lies?"

"Not all. I did have obligations out of the city and I'm sure the client Lana was with can verify that she was with her. I did get her a car as a belated birthday gift. But she's not living with me – yet."

I chuckle as Mrs. Elaine's eyebrows go up on the last part. I lean forward on my elbows.

"I'm a very forthright man, Mrs. Elaine and appreciate your directness rather than add to the rumor mill. So, I won't lie. Yes, Lana and I were seen in a questionable manner in her office. I am very attracted to her and interested in a serious relationship with her. It's just a coincidence that I happen to be her boss. I'm sure if I worked on the ninth floor there would be no cause for concern."

"True." She takes a deep breath and sighs. "Since we're being honest here, can I talk to you like a mother to a son?"

"When have you ever done otherwise?"

She laughs. "You've got me there. Lana is a very nice girl. I love her like a daughter. She has all the qualities I would want in a daughter-in-law if my boys weren't already taken. I'm happy to hear you say that you're interested in a serious relationship. If she feels the same way you do, I wish you all the happiness in the world. My only distress is these nasty things they're saying about you two in the office."

"We do admit that discretion at that moment was not at the forefront of our thoughts."

“If I could find out who started these stories, I’d wring their neck!”

“Don’t worry. We know who it is. They will be dealt with properly.”

“Good. Two wrongs don’t make a right. You and Lana should have kept your business private. But no one has the right to blab about it.”

I nod in agreement. “Mrs. Elaine, I really appreciate this conversation.”

She smiles and stands. “I just had to get it off my chest. Take care of Lana and she will take care of you.”

“I intend to do just that.”

I watch as she leaves. At least someone is on our side. Just then, the phone rings.

“Ace? Where on earth do you find these crazy women?”

“Don’t tell me you have some information already.”

“Do I ever!”

I listen as Reggie gives me a veritable chapter and verse on Avery and her misdemeanors. This is her third job in six years. She was dismissed from her first two jobs for vandalism of her coworkers’ property. It turns out that they were women with whom she felt she was in contention for varying positions. When she came to McEachron, she cooled her heels and decided to use other means to secure her spot. Enter her flirtation with a member of the board who she is now blackmailing. He made a pass at her and she’s holding it over him. No wonder she’s so confident in her mention of reporting us to Human Resources. How Reggie gets her information, I don't know. But she can find the needle in the haystack, of that, I am sure. Avery had seen to it that her application would be looked on favorably but hadn't counted on the board choosing Lana as the best candidate. She had been up the proverbial creek without a paddle until I took over the company. And given Lana's publicly embarrassing me, Avery must have thought that if she plays her cards right, she could get Lana out and finally get the position she wants. Reggie's report has filled in several blanks. I know how to handle Avery now.

I thank Reggie for her usual thorough work and hang up. I sit for a few moments and consider how to approach the matter discreetly. I want Avery to know that I have her ticket and I can fight as dirty as she can. But I've learned that revenge is a dish best served cold, so I let it sit for a few days.

As Lana has said, rumors do become yesterday's news. And though there are still a few weird looks, the atmosphere is noticeably less tense.

On Thursday afternoon I return from a lunch meeting. As I leave the parking lot and stand waiting for the elevator, Avery joins me to wait. I feel her eyes on me but I force myself to face forward. The elevator arrives and I'm tempted to let her board it alone as I do not want to be in the same space with her. As soon as the door closes, she speaks.

"Ace, I'm really sorry-"

I look up in surprise at her apology.

"-that you got mixed up with the likes of someone like Lana."

My jaw clenches. "What do you mean, someone like Lana?"

"Come on, Ace. What kind of woman has sex in her office with her boss? Doesn't that strike you as someone who is a bit loose in their sexual exploits? Who knows who else she's been with! I'm just so sorry that you got caught in the little gold digger's web."

"Suppose I wanted to be caught?"

She laughs hollowly. "So, you're just in it for kicks and feels. I knew it! This little fling will soon be over. And when it is, a real woman will be here waiting."

She bats her eyes and reaches for my hand. I back away.

"A real woman? Where?" I look around the elevator in surprise before looking her in the face. "Surely, you can't mean you?"

I'm pleased to see the color drain from her face and I smirk.

"Let's get something straight, Avery. Lana is a hundred times the person that you can only hope to be. There is no way on earth I could give her up for the likes of you. A pretty face cannot hide an ugly heart. And your heart is as black as midnight. Why would I want to be with you? I don't have a death wish. So, tell all the lies and exaggerated truths you want, it won't break Lana and me apart. If you were the only woman on this earth, I wouldn't touch you with a ten-foot pole. Stay out of my way and Lana's if you know what's good for you."

"Is that a threat?" She hisses.

"No. It's a promise."

"You're going to be sorry you ever crossed me, Ace Channing."

"I wait to see who has the bigger guns."

The elevator doors slide open and I'm through before they open completely. I stride through the office, not once looking behind me.

I'm furious at Avery's audacity. That night, I talk to Lana about the encounter in the elevator and tell her to watch her step with Avery. I bear in mind Avery's previous jobs and tell Lana to report any form of physical aggression from Avery immediately.

The next morning, I'm barely at my desk before Mrs. Elaine sends a message that the board has called an emergency meeting in an hour. I barely get through answering my emails before heading to the board room.

I take my seat as we wait for the other members to arrive. I look at one gentleman in particular who used to be the friendly sort but now can barely look me in the eye. Aha! I have a eureka moment as I remember his name. This must be Avery's poor sap. The chairman arrives and he wastes no time in calling the meeting to order.

"Thank you all for coming at such short notice, but I only got wind of a very delicate matter late last night. I'm due to leave the city tomorrow and won't be back for a month, so I thought it prudent to deal with this matter today." He turns to look at me.

"Ace, I won't beat around the bush. It's been brought to my attention that you and an employee are in an intimate relationship. Is this true?"

I look him in the face. "Yes, it is true."

Shocked gasps go up all around the room and whispered conversations begin. The chairman mops at his brow and frowns.

"Well, this simply can't be allowed to continue! You must break off your relationship at once. It is against company policy."

"Show me the clause which speaks explicitly to this."

"Well, there is nothing in writing. It's just common sense and principle that would tell adults not to have office relationships."

"There is nothing in writing therefore there is no company policy."

"You must step down as CEO!" the sap blurts out.

There is a muttering of agreement around the room. I fix my gaze on the idiot Avery is manipulating.

"I would not be so hasty to make such a statement as requiring my resignation. I'm sure there are skeletons that some of us have that we prefer to keep in the closet, don't you think?"

I'm pleased to see him go pale as he clamps his lips together. I turn back to the chairman.

"You seem to forget, sir, that I am not only the CEO but also the majority share owner in this company. I do as I please. And it pleases me to pursue my relationship *and* remain as CEO. And if anyone has any further issues with that you are free to tender your resignation. I also demand to know the identity of the person who informed you of my relationship as I do not tolerate underhanded and sneaky behavior and they will be dealt with accordingly.

"Well, that information is strictly confidential. I received an email from a board member who in turn says he received an anonymous message detailing the matter."

"I highly doubt it was anonymous," I again look at the idiot. He looks at me and looks away quickly. I stand and look around the room.

"Is that all? Are you done wasting my time?"

"Mr. Channing, please reconsider your stance. Imagine if this should hit the media."

"I imagine it may. And then what? Another day another scandalous celebrity story. Story of my life. You have done a very good job of wasting a good portion of my morning. I bid you all a good day."

With that being said, I stride out of the room, every step heavy with anger. There is no doubt that Avery is again up to mischief. So, she wants to play dirty. I'm up to the task. But unlike her, I will not lower myself to blackmail. A simple call to Human resources to look at her evaluations will suffice. She wants to cite company policy? Company policy it shall be. She won't know what's going on by the time her citations for negligence of any form of duty begin to add up. And since clearly the staff has been informed informally, I'll inform them formally of my relationship with Lana and my intentions to remain in said relationship, and to hell with what they want to think.

By the time I get back to my office, I'm chomping at the bit. I stop briefly at Mrs. Elaine's desk.

"I want a meeting with the staff in the main area in an hour."

"Okay, Ace." She makes a note. "What is the purpose of the meeting?"

"I'm going to quash the rumors once and for all and officially announce my relationship with Lana."

"You'll do no such thing!"

Mrs. Elaine shocks me by taking me by the arm and pulling me into my office and closing the door behind us.

"Are you crazy? Why would you do such a thing?"

"The emergency board meeting was to discuss my relationship and ask me to break it off or resign."

"Oh no!"

"Oh yes! I reminded them that I own the company and can do as I damn well please. But I'm a tad annoyed by all the rumors flying around as well as the instigator of said rumor reporting me to the board."

"So, you know who started it?"

"I've always known who knows even before the rumors began, Mrs. Elaine."

"Oh dear!"

"Indeed. Anyway, inform the staff of the meeting please."

"About that. Ace, I know you're angry. But I don't think an announcement to the staff is best. Even if it will clear the air for you, think about Lana. You're not here every day. She is. You're not out of your office and interacting with staff. She is. It's one thing to hear rumors and not know if it's true. But it's another thing to know the truth and have that cemented. Unknown to you, there may be many who will try to use this against Lana. The less they know the better. So, if I were you, I would relax, calm down and let things remain as they are."

I look at Mrs. Elaine and take a deep breath. I nod slowly.

"I know you're right. I'm just angry right now and it is never good to do things in the heat of anger."

"Good. So, no meeting?"

"No meeting. However, I would like to see the director of HR. Could you have him come to my office immediately please?"

"Now that I will do."

"Thank you, Mrs. Elaine. And thank you as usual for your wisdom. I don't know what I would have done without you since I've taken office."

She smiles and nods.

"Just doing my job."

As she leaves, I begin to process the board meeting. The audacity of them all! I'm tempted to put the idiot on Reggie's radar. But I refuse to fight dirty. I decided that after the meeting with HR regarding Avery I'll have a meeting with him outside the office. He needs to understand a few things about how to deal with blackmailers like Avery. And I will be happy to teach him.

CHAPTER 21

LANA

On Monday morning, I sit in my car for a few minutes longer after parking. Last week at this time when I had driven into the lot, I had not envisioned by the end of the week I would be the target of the thriving company grapevine. I sigh and get out of the car. I paste a smile on my face as I stride through the parking lot, greeting the few people there. I see eyes turn towards the car then back to me. Then heads bow to whisper. By the time I reach the elevator, my cheeks are burning from the forced smile, but I keep it going. The elevator is filled with people bound for the tenth floor. But rather than the usual conversation, there's an eerie silence. I feel their eyes on me and I keep my gaze fixed on the numbers as we pass the other floors. Finally, we are on the tenth floor. I hang back a bit and allow a few people to exit ahead of me.

As I walk through the main area, the buzz of conversation lessens. It is obvious. They can't even pretend to hide the fact that they are talking about me. I want to get on top of a desk and scream at the top of my lungs that yes Ace and I had sex and are in a relationship. But then I remember what Ace said he had to go through in the board meeting and how he had felt afterwards. If I allowed my emotions to get the better of me and make a public spectacle of myself, it would have been just as well that he had the meeting and made the announcement after all.

Instead, I bite my lip and hold my head up, looking straight ahead. This has to pass.

I get to my office and close the door behind me. This has become my haven. I stay in here all day, ordering out for lunch. I don't leave until after six when I'm sure that everyone has left. This is the pattern of my days. And to add to this, Ace is now away for two weeks on business. It feels like forever as those two weeks crawl by like molasses.

The day he is due to return, I decide a visit to the salon is in order for the weekend and decide to leave work a little early on Friday to beat the rush. I send a message to the clerical department to have two manuscripts printed and delivered within the hour. There are some things I need to look at on the weekend in order to have them ready for Charles on Monday. As I pack my things, there's a knock on the door.

"Come in!"

Marissa pushes her head inside. Ever since my run-in with Avery, only the other clerks have been delivering my manuscripts. I hear that Avery has been assigned specifically to Ursula. Ursula is a demanding slave-driver of an editor and a stickler for detail. Nothing will pass her. Avery has her hands full. The few times I have seen her even from a distance, her smugness is no more. She looks as though she has aged a few years as well.

"Thanks Marissa. Leave them on the desk please."

She comes to the desk and places them on the corner. She walks to the door and I continue to pack. Suddenly she turns back and I look up.

"Lana, can I ask you something?"

I brace myself and swallow. "Sure."

She comes back to my desk and pulls up a chair.

"Well, it's not really a question. I just want to say that you've been doing a pretty good job of keeping your head up with all of what's going on right now. I just want you to know that a lot of us, and by us, I mean us clerks, really like you and like working for you. Things happen and you don't choose who you fall in love with and where. But I'm glad you're hanging in there. It will soon blow over. I know a thing or two about being the center of nasty rumors. And it always gets forgotten sooner or later."

I stare at Marissa, not sure what to say and she smiles.

"For what it's worth, Ace is a pretty good catch if you ask me. And if I were in your shoes, I wouldn't have been able to resist a little hanky-panky either."

"Marissa!" I feel my cheeks turn red and she laughs.

"I'm still serious about getting a hookup with a friend or brother, by the way."

I can't help but laugh now and she reaches over to pat my hand.

"Now that's the Lana I know. What Avery did was wrong. But I think she regrets it now."

"Avery doesn't strike me as the type to regret anything."

"I wouldn't be so sure about that. A lot of stuff she's done over the years has been coming to light. Her hands are not clean and she's reaping the rewards of her past actions. With the pressure HR has under her now with evaluations every month plus being assigned to 'Dragula', she has to dot every I and cross every T. She has no time to shirk her duties and laud over the other clerks as if she's some supervisor. Even her desk has been moved to the hallway outside 'Dragula's' office." Marissa laughs then continues.

"And to top it off, we've all kind of cold-shouldered her as well. She's not very happy right now, that's for sure."

No wonder Avery looked like a shell of herself these days.

"Don't be surprised if she's gone by the end of the year. HR has her on a tightrope and she's bound to fall."

"I wouldn't want to be responsible for someone losing their job. Everyone needs to have a means of earning an honest salary."

"You see! That's why I love you! Avery was not thinking about saving your job when she went and blabbed about you and Ace. She said explicitly to me one day that she wants you fired so that she can have what is rightfully hers. She seems to believe you have her job and her man. Poor deluded woman." Marissa shakes her head and sighs. She stands and looks at me and smiles.

"Anyway, I won't take up any more of your time. I just wanted you to know that we don't all think poorly of you. Things happen. You just have to brush yourself off and move on with life."

"Thanks, Marissa. I really appreciate this little chat."

"You're welcome, Lana. Have a great weekend."

"Same to you."

I look at the door for a few minutes after she exits. Wow. That conversation has comforted me somehow, and I find myself holding my head a little higher and smiling a little brighter as I leave the office and wish everyone a good weekend.

I head to the salon and get there a few minutes before my set appointment. I relax under the expert hands of Neil who does my shampoo. On a whim, I decided to have a manicure and pedicure as well. While I'm under the dryer, my phone rings. I use my wet fingers to awkwardly stuff my earpiece in then answer the call.

"Hello."

"Hello, sweetheart. Did you miss me as much as I missed you this week?"

I can't help the way my lips curve into a smile. Ace and I have spoken every morning and evening in his absence, and to be honest, I did miss seeing him.

"Well?"

"I did."

"I can remedy that tonight. Have dinner with me."

I squawk in surprise. "Tonight? I can't!"

"Why not? It's Friday so you don't have any work tomorrow if we stay out late. And I realize we really haven't spent much time together physically since that weekend you had allergy issues. I want to do more than just talk on the phone, Lana. I want to see you tonight, sweetheart."

"Can't we do it tomorrow night? I took work home."

"Dinner tonight. Work tomorrow night. I want to see you. Tonight. Gotta go. The jet's landing right now. Please?"

That please being tagged on to the end was just a charade to make the command seem like a request. I sigh, knowing that I want to see him as badly as he wants to see me.

"Okay. Fine. What time?"

"I'll make the reservations for nine. I'll pick you up at about eight-thirty."

"I'll be ready."

"Great."

With a click, he disconnects the call and I sigh. I look at my nails and shake my head at the smudges.

"We're going to have to fix these, Betty. I can't go on my date with these."

"I've got you covered, honey."

An hour later, I leave wearing a pair of plastic push toe slippers to prevent my toes being smudged, and have my hair wound and pinned around my head. As per Neil's instructions, once I take the pins down and give it a shake, it will fall into place.

A few hours later, I sit in front of the mirror carefully applying my make-up. Tonight, I have a gold dress selected and decide to do my makeup to match my choice. When I'm finished, I carefully take the pins down and give my hair a shake. I smile at my reflection. Neil is right about my hair falling into place. I slip into the dress and twirl slightly. It's a dress that I wore to a dinner party a few months ago but the cut is not really suited for the club so it has remained in my closet waiting for a just-dinner occasion such as this. It is an off-the-shoulder affair and cinches at the waist before flowing out in an A-line over my hips. I like the feel of the fabric as it floats around my body. I pick up a matching shawl and slip my feet into gold stilettos. As I am buckling the straps, the phone rings.

"I'll be right down."

"You will do no such thing. I'm at your door picking you up the way a proper date should."

I giggle. "Oh! I'll be right there."

I stand and check my reflection once more before picking up my clutch. I walk into the living room and take a deep breath before opening the door. As I catch sight of Ace my heart thuds heavily in my chest. I stare at him hungrily. He seems even more handsome than the last time I saw him. He steps inside and closes the door behind him. Without hesitation he pulls me into his arms and I go without protest.

As he kisses me, I melt into him, kissing him back fervently. When at last he raises his head, his eyes are sparkling. He stares at me.

"If you keep looking at me like that, we won't make it to dinner, sweetheart."

I blush and duck my head. "Looking at you like what?"

He grasps my hips and pulls me flush against his groin where he has the beginnings of an erection. "Looking at me as though you want us to forget about dinner and skip straight to bed where we can put this to use." He grinds against me slightly and I laugh and pull back.

"You promised me dinner and I'm hungry!"

"And I'm a man who likes to fulfill his promises. Your chariot awaits. Shall we?"

He steps back and bows slightly as he offers me his arm. I curtsy and take it.

"We shall."

As we head downstairs, my heart is the lightest it's felt in weeks. No one and nothing else matters when I'm with Ace.

CHAPTER 22

ACE

As we leave Lana's house, I feel a sense of euphoria sweep over me. I realize that the adage 'absence makes the heart grow fonder' is true. I want to hold Lana and never let go. It's not until I see her standing at the door I realize just how much I've missed her these past weeks. We've both been so caught up in work and trying to keep our distance in the office we forget we have a life outside of the office. I open the passenger door and seat her before going to my side. I sit and look at her for a few moments, a silly smile on my face. She looks at me and smiles back.

"What is it?"

"Do you realize this is our first official date?"

Her smile grows wider. "It is, isn't it?"

I reach across and take her hand in mine. I hold her gaze as I bring her fingers to my lips.

"Here's to a million and one more."

She smiles and reaches her free hand up to caress my cheek. Our eyes meet and hold and I lean across to place a soft kiss on her lips. It's the barest touch but it sends a fire roaring through me. I lean back.

"If we don't leave now, we'll never leave."

I put the car in gear and head out. I reach for her hand and place it on my knee as we drive. Just that connection comforts me. I pull into the parking lot of Broken Plate, one of the most exclusive restaurants in the city. I have a private booth reserved. Heads turn in our wake as the hostess escorts us to the VIP section. Once or twice, I catch the murmur of my name, but I have no attention for anyone except the woman at my side.

The VIP booths are set up like small rooms with doors for privacy. They range in size from dinner for two to a meeting space for ten and everything in between. I've asked for a room with a banquette as chairs can be quite uncomfortable sometimes. The room is also decorated with bouquets of daisies and I see Lana's eyes light up. Champagne is waiting as instructed. The hostess smiles and leaves us with the tablet to order. I allow Lana to slide into the banquette before joining her. I pour two glasses of champagne and hand her a glass.

"What are we celebrating?"

"The official beginning of us."

She smiles and I smile back. I slide close enough to place my arm around her shoulders. She looks at me before leaning her head against my shoulder.

"Thank you for insisting that I come to dinner, Ace. I missed you."

My heart skips a beat at her admission. I brush my lips against her temple.

"I bet I missed you more."

She laughs and straightens up.

"We're not going to spend the whole night debating, are we?"

"Nope." I reach for the tablet.

After a few minutes of perusing the menu, we place our order. A few seconds later we receive a confirmation notification that our order has been received by the kitchen. I turn to face her.

"Now where were we?"

I enjoy the feel of her head on my shoulder as I breathe in the delicate scent of her perfume. I run my fingers lightly along her arm and smile when she places her hand on my thigh.

She recounts all that's happened since I've been gone, ending with her conversation with Marissa. In turn, I bring her up to date with things on my end. While I was away, the chairman had reached out to me with an olive branch so to speak. I'm not sure why he had second thoughts, but ultimately, I've been let off with a warning and a caution to keep the affair out of the office space.

At this juncture, there's a discreet knock and a good twenty-second pause before the door opens. The waitress comes in with our appetizers and a message that our main course will be brought in another twenty minutes. Lana and I tackle the dainty crab meat crepes with spinach dip. We had contemplated ordering separate items but nothing else had sparked any interest.

We laugh and continue to chat, and I take pleasure in feeding her a bite or two. At intervals, I steal little kisses.

When the waitress returns to clear the table, I order mixed drinks to go with the main course. A few minutes later, we are feasting on steak and duck with an assortment of sides. I watch as Lana consumes her meal.

"What is it?"

"I love to see a woman who knows her way around her plate."

She shrugs and laughs. "I don't have time to waste pretending to watch my figure. There's a time to eat and a time to work off what I've eaten."

"Good girl."

We polish off our meal and the waitress soon returns to clear the table. Our desserts are next. I have a tiramisu while Lana has cheesecake. I look longingly at her plate and she smiles.

"I told you to order cheesecake. Don't be looking at mine like you want to inhale it."

"Just a little taste. I'll trade you some of my tiramisu."

"If I wanted tiramisu, I would have ordered tiramisu. But I'll give you a taste."

I watch as she uses her fork to cut a sliver of cake. She raises the morsel to my lips and I lean forward. At the last moment, she whisks the fork away and places the cake between her lips. She winks and smiles as widely as her lips will allow her. I don't think twice.

I lean forward and place my lips on her, trapping the cake. As the succulent dessert melts between our lips, my tongue delves deep and I'm rewarded with a low moan which rumbles in her throat. My hands grip her waist and I maneuver her into my lap. I use my foot to push the table away a few inches to give us more room. Our desserts are forgotten as her arms come up around my neck and our mouths fuse hungrily. My hand travels to the hem of her dress and slides up her leg.

She leans back slightly and whispers. "The waitress-"

"-won't be back until I indicate that we're ready for the bill."

She smiles and places her lips on mine once more. It's all over after that.

My hand continues its journey and I'm pleased to feel her tremble in my arms as I touch her pussy. She is hot and even through the scrap of fabric I can feel that she's wet. I feel as if all the blood in my body has rushed straight to my cock. As my fingers stroke her, she rolls her hips to meet them. I shift the crotch of her panties and insert my forefinger as deep as it can go. She leans back and shakes her head. I frown as she stands. My frown turns to a smile as she reaches underneath her dress and pulls her panties down. She steps out of them and picks them up. I take them from her and stuff them into my pocket as she unzips my pants. I help her by unbuckling and unbuttoning to give her more freedom for her goal. As she touches me, I lean back and sigh. She straddles me and leans down to kiss me. I feel her pussy hover over me before I'm engulfed in her heat. My groans are lost in her kiss as she begins to ride me.

I reach under her dress to caress her naked ass, kneading the firm flesh and digging my fingers in when the feeling gets to be too much to bear. As she rides me, her pussy grips me hard and I'm powerless to hold back. I thrust up into her as much as our position and any attempts at discretion can allow and I'm pleased to feel her shudder as she clamps down on me. I feel her body grow slick as she climaxes and stifles a scream. I feel her heart racing against mine. I push her body down on mine as I thrust up once more. And it's my turn to tremble.

We remain locked in each other's arms as we struggle to breathe. There's a sheen of sweat over our brows and I can feel perspiration trickle from her arms around my neck. She places her lips against the pulse beating in my throat, kissing me softly. Her chest rises and falls against mine as I continue to hold her.

When we seem to have regained some measure of consciousness, we part reluctantly. I watch as she sits slightly slumped. She looks at me with a dazed smile.

"I've never done that before."

I reach across to stroke her cheek. "There's a first time for everything. I look forward to more first-time experiences."

We clean ourselves up as best as we can and rearrange our clothing before asking for the check. The waitress arrives shortly after and I settle the bill. We leave the booth and I'm surprised to find that the restaurant is still quite busy at minutes to midnight. We head to the parking lot but I'm not ready to take her home.

"Would you like to go for a drive?"

"Sure."

We get into the car and ten minutes later we're heading to the hills. I know exactly where I'm going. I have the keys but tonight is not the night I wish to introduce Lana to her new home. I park at a look out spot and switch off the engine. I pull her into my arms as we look out over the city. She giggles.

"This is the sort of thing teenagers should be doing."

"We can pretend that we are."

"Shouldn't we be making out then?"

I laugh. "You seem to have a one-track mind tonight."

"Sometimes you don't know what you're missing until you've had it then had to do without it for a while. You can't introduce a girl to good lovin' then have her go without for almost a month you know."

"True. I have been depriving you. I think I need to remedy that somehow. Let's head back to your place."

I drive as safely as I can with Lana's hand in my pants stroking me. When we get back to her apartment, we barely make it in the door before we are all over each other. As soon as the last piece of clothing falls, I lift her into my arms and brace her against the wall. Right there, in the living room, I thrust deep into her. She wraps her legs around my waist as our eyes lock and hold. The restaurant has only wetted our appetites for more of each other, and now that we don't need to be silent, our groans ring out around the room. I feel as if I can't go deep enough, I can't hold her tightly enough, I can't kiss her hard enough, to satisfy the need boiling within me. I want more.

I hold her to me as I whirl away from the wall. I lift her off me and turn her back to me. I bend her over the couch and spread her legs as I enter her from behind. She grips the couch hard as I begin to pound into her once more. I feel an intensity rise within me as the new angle makes her shriek.

"That's it babe. Scream for me," I bite out between gritted teeth.

"Oh fuck! Ace. That feels so good! So good! Right there! Oh yes! Right there!"

I keep up my assault as she pushes back to meet every thrust. Finally, I feel her body tighten around me as she pants. She goes up on her toes and throws her head back, rolling her hips as she climaxes.

"Ahhhhhh!"

I'm not far behind her. With one more thrust, I lay myself on her back and hug her tightly, burying my face in her hair.

"Oh fuck! Lanaaaaaaa! Babe! Fuck!"

My legs tremble as I shoot my juices deep into her womb. I'm a trembling mass and I feel slightly faint as my body sags. I don't want to move, but if we don't, we will both collapse. Reluctantly I withdraw and watch with hooded eyes as our collective juices run down her inner thigh. She turns to me and drops to her knees. Without hesitation she takes me into her mouth and I cry out.

"Fuck!"

She just holds me there as I'm too sensitive for much stimulation. Then I feel her tongue slowly roll around me and I sigh with pleasure. Slowly I bend and pull her to her feet. I hug and kiss her gently, swaying against her. She raises her arms and places them around my neck as she kisses me back.

Somehow, we make it to the bedroom and collapse in a tangle of limbs. She snuggles into my side as I stroke her breast.

"Making love with you is the most amazing feeling on earth." I nuzzle her temple and she sighs.

"I love the way you touch me. You just seem to know what buttons to press."

I laugh. "Or maybe it's trial and error and I keep getting lucky with my button pressing." I shift my body so that we are sharing a pillow. I smooth her hair away from her brow.

"Lana?"

"Hmmm?"

"I want you to go away with me for the long holiday weekend."

"What do you mean go away with you?"

"I'm flying out to a resort and I want you to come with me. Will you?"

I hold my breath as she's silent.

"Please?" I use the back of one hand to caress her cheek.

She turns her lips to kiss my fingers. "I will."

I smile. "Great."

“What will I need?”

We discuss the weather and clothing needs as well as some plans I have for while we are there. Little does she know that I have a surprise for her that will only be topped by the moment I ask her to marry me. Yes. There is no doubt that I love Lana and want to spend the rest of my life with her. It is simply a matter of choosing the right time to pop the question.

CHAPTER 23

LANA

If anyone had asked me six months ago if I believed in fairytales and happily ever after, I would've had to give it some thought. But the last few months since I met Ace have been the most magical time of my life. All my reservations about a relationship with him seem to have melted into thin air. Sometimes I have to pinch myself as I realize I have a boyfriend. A boyfriend. I'm not new to relationships and have had my share of dalliances in the past. But there is something at the back of my mind that tells me that Ace is the real deal. I feel my heart opening up to him more and more each day. I know I'm falling in love with him and I'm powerless to stop it.

As planned, we went away for the holiday weekend. Imagine my surprise to find he had found a resort close to where Crenshaw was having a book signing. As if that wasn't enough, he had ordered an autographed copy of every Crenshaw novel. Every time I walk through my living room and look at them, I can't help but smile.

As for things at the office, the nine-day wonder is over. Avery seems to have disappeared in the wake of it all. I mention her low profile to Ace one day at lunch and he laughs.

"She has other things to tend to apart from meddling in business that doesn't concern her I guess." He takes a sip of his drink with a mischievous twinkle in his eyes.

"I would have thought that since the threat with the board didn't work, she would have followed through on her threat to leak it to the media."

"Well, when you have other scandals that are potentially more damaging to you than the one you want to spread, you might want to think twice."

"What did you do?"

"Me? I did nothing. It's what she did that she thought was buried deep. Reggie did some more digging even beyond what I had requested and found some very useful information. I just fight fire with fire. And although holding someone's past over them is not my thing, sometimes you just have to do what you have to do."

I lean on my elbow and look him in the face.

"So did you have Reggie investigate my background as well?"

"Maybe. Maybe not. Do you have something to hide?"

"Not that I know of as I've tried to live without looking over my shoulder. But maybe I have a library book I didn't return or something."

"Or maybe a childhood sweetheart who's going to come blasting back from the past and turn things upside down."

I look at him with my mouth open and he smiles and looks at his plate. I say nothing else on the matter.

The office is busy as everyone has to buckle down as we head towards the end of the year. The workload triples with authors trying to get novels published by Christmas and New Year.

But in spite of our busy schedules, we still manage to find time to be with each other. Sometimes it's as simple as grabbing a cup of coffee on the way home from the office. Other times it's a planned activity like a movie, a play or dinner. Thus far it's been just the two of us. But I know the time will come when we have to begin integrating our families and friends.

I've been out with my girls a few times as well, but only Kyla knows what's going on between Ace and me. Thankfully she's not the kind of friend who pries unnecessarily. But I know we are overdue for a proper conversation and so I set a lunch date with her one Saturday afternoon.

As I sit waiting, I'm texting Ace. He too is out with a friend. As Kyla comes into view I end the conversation and tell him I'll see him later.

"Lana!"

"Kyla!"

We hug and a waitress comes and takes our order and we soon have appetizers and drinks in hand.

Kyla looks at me and smiles. "I don't have to ask if you're happy, you know. You're glowing like a freaking stadium bulb."

I laugh and blush. Kyla doesn't know the art of subtle conversation. But it breaks the ice. She stirs her drink.

"So how long has it been?"

"Since we met or since we've been seeing each other?"

"Both."

"Well you know we met on my birthday. Then two weeks later we started seeing each other. So that makes it what? Nearly four months?"

"Wow! Somehow it seems longer."

I sigh. "And to me, it feels like yesterday, I have to admit."

"How do you feel about it though?"

I blink a few times as I process the question. "Strangely enough, Ky, I feel as if I'm where I'm supposed to be with who I'm supposed to be. Does that make any sense?"

"It makes complete sense. The heart knows."

"The heart?"

"You do know that you're in love with him, right?"

"In love?" My heart begins to pound as I hear the words coming from someone else's mouth. "Is it that obvious?"

"Lana, you are *glo-wing*. If that isn't love then I don't know what is. There's just an aura about you that you've never had before. You're in love with him. But how does he feel about you?"

"I think he feels the same."

"Has he said it?"

"No. But he sure acts like it."

"But has he said it? Remember, hon, that's always their loophole. If they haven't said it, it doesn't matter what they do. Those three words are important to hear from their lips."

"I know. If it's any assurance, I'm still trying to navigate my feelings but they are leaning in that direction. But I haven't said it either."

"Good. He needs to say it first. Yours is a given."

Our conversation is interrupted briefly as our main course arrives. As we eat as we continue to converse.

"So, what have you learned about him in these four months?"

"Surprisingly? Not more than what I've read online."

"What! You're sleeping together for heaven's sake Lana. You can't be depending on gossip rags to fill you in about your boyfriend. What about his family? His friends? His life before getting rich?"

"I ask but he's a little bit closed on the subject. He says one day when the time is right, we'll sit and we can have a full discussion about his life."

"That's a red flag if you ask me."

"Strangely it doesn't feel like one. It almost feels as though I know his life. He reminds me so much of Chester, though."

"Chunky chocolate Chester? That guy who lived with you guys for a year or so? Ace is nothing like him. They are complete opposites."

"I know. But there are just a few memories now and then. That's all."

"Still, though, Lana, I'm happy that you're happy. *I* would want to know a little more about my pillow buddy by now. But you and I are two different people. For your sake I do hope he has no past issues that will affect your relationship."

"So do I. But enough about me. What's going on with you? It seems like ages since we've actually sat down like this. I know we talk on the phone and all but it's so good to sit and *talk*. You know what I mean?"

She laughs and we continue to talk way past our main course and dessert. By the time we part, the restaurant has already started preparing for the dinner service. I drop Kyla home then head to my apartment to grab a box. A few minutes later I'm on my way to Ace's place.

As I walk through the lobby, I greet the doorman by name. He smiles and nods as I enter the elevator. I hum a happy tune as I watch the numbers climb up. Finally, I'm in the corridor. I fumble for the key Ace gave me and let myself into the apartment. As soon as I enter, I'm greeted by the scent of food. I sniff appreciatively and my stomach rumbles in response.

"Honey? Are you home?" Ace calls out from the kitchen and I begin to giggle.

"That's my line, isn't it?"

"Well, you were taking a little too long to say it so consider that a prompt. Now step out and come back in and try again."

"Ace!"

"Go on."

"Ugh!" I sigh in exasperation. I step back into the corridor then re-enter the apartment.

"Honey!!! I'm *hoooo-ooooome*!!!" I shriek at the top of my lungs.

"I'm not deaf, you know. Do it again, this time with a little less shouting."

"I swear, if I step back into that corridor, I'll be getting into the elevator to go back to the parking lot and my apartment."

He laughs and comes over to scoop me into a hug. "Can't you take a little joke sweetheart?" he brushes his lips against my temple.

"Sometimes you take a joke a little too far." I pout playfully.

"I'm sorry. How about I make it up to you with what I've been slaving over since I got home."

"What is it though? It smells delicious."

"Go freshen up and meet me on the balcony in half an hour or so. No peeking and sniffing around. It's a surprise."

I raise my eyebrows and he rolls his eyes.

"I know, you don't like surprises. But be honest. Have any of my surprises been bad?"

I have to admit, they have not. I shake my head.

"Exactly. So be a good girl, freshen up, and be at the balcony in thirty." He kisses my nose and turns me in the direction of the bedroom. I move obediently, turning only once to look back. I find him standing where I left him, a small smile as he watches me. He fans at me with his hand, indicating for me to continue. I do as I'm told.

A few hours later I'm rendered speechless. I sit looking at the feast we have just devoured. I look at him in amazement.

"I can't believe you cooked all of this."

"Most. I cooked most of it. Scratch that. I followed the instructions I was given on how to combine the ingredients and shove it into the oven. I follow instructions very well." He smirks as he refills our wine glasses. "And the best is yet to come."

My mouth drops open. "You mean there's more? I don't think I can take another morsel."

"I wouldn't be so sure. I guarantee you will find space for this dessert. You always did."

Before I can respond, he heads inside. I always did? What does he mean by that?

I turn as he comes back to the balcony. He's carrying a covered tray and I raise my eyebrows.

"Is this the surprise?"

"You take a look and tell me."

He places the tray in front of me and slowly removes the cover. I smile when I see a chocolate lava cake. I look at him and laugh.

"What's surprising about a chocolate lava cake?"

He smiles and winks. He hands me a fork. "Dig in, sweetheart."

I shrug and take the fork and do as I'm told. At first, there's nothing but cake and a bit of oozing chocolate. I look at him and he smiles. I take a second forkful. By the time I take a third, my mouth drops open. I look down at the cake, then at him then back at the cake. As my eyes fill with tears, the multi-colored specks of candy become a blur. How the hell did he know I love this candy in my chocolate lava cake?

CHAPTER 24

ACE

I pull my coat a little closer around me as I hurry down the sidewalk. The early November air is chilly although the sun is shining brightly this morning. Winter is definitely on its way. I duck into my destination and breathe a sigh of relief to feel the warmth inside. I'm greeted familiarly.

"Mr. Channing! We have your package ready sir."

"Awesome. May I see them?"

"They're in the vault for safekeeping. Follow me."

The manager beckons for me to come around the counter and I follow him to his office. I take a seat while he opens the vault in his office. He withdraws two boxes and reseals the hole in the wall. He sits and pushes the bigger box across the desk. I open it and look down at the pair of earrings, a small smile on my lips. They are perfect. After I had bought the bracelet and necklace, I had commissioned matching earrings. There will be no delivery this time around. I will deliver them to Lana myself and finally tell her who I am.

I close the box and the manager pushes the smaller box towards me. I reach for this one slowly, my heart beginning to race. As I flip the top open, I feel as though time stands still as I stare at the piece nestled in the black velvet.

"It took us some time to find the right shades and cuts according to your specifications. I hope it is what you wanted, sir?"

I pluck the ring from the box and hold it up. The jade sparkles in the light as I turn it from side to side. The diamond clusters surrounding it shine brilliantly, enhancing the polished platinum of the ring itself. I examine the engraved initials inside and smile: *To LONG from CACA.*

"It's perfect." I pull out my wallet and hand him a card. He leaves me to run the transaction and I sit looking at the ring. The green jade matches her eyes and the diamonds match mine. I sit contemplating if I will commission a different set or simply add his and hers bands for the wedding rings. I'll let Lana decide. I replace the ring in the box and close it.

I smile at the thought of her. Things have been going great and I feel as though I can now reveal my identity without fearing a fallout. I just have to pick the right time to give her the earrings as those will be a dead giveaway. As for proposing, I already know when and how it will be done. Almost as though she knows I'm thinking of her, my phone rings with the special tone I've assigned to her number.

"Hello, sweetheart."

"Hi!"

I smile as I hear the joy in her voice.

"What's going on in that pretty little head of yours?"

"I was just wondering if you wanted to come over for dinner tonight. You've been doing most of the cooking so I just wanted to return the favor."

"I'd love to have dinner tonight. And maybe we can finish that game of chess we started last weekend as well."

"Ummm. About that-"

"What about it?"

"This morning when I was grabbing my purse, I accidentally bounced the table and the pieces fell."

"Uh huh. A likely story."

"It's true!" she giggles.

"That is as true as pigs flying. It's just as well that I took a picture of the table with how I left the pieces. So, we can pick up where we left off and I can finish beating you fair and square."

"You did *what*!?"

I throw my head back and laugh. "You never like to lose and I was not taking any chances. Anyway, what time should I get there?"

"I'm leaving the office around three. Six should be good."

"Okay, sweetheart. See you at six."

There's a pause as we both go silent. The words "I love you" hover on my lips. But I bite my tongue. I'm waiting for the perfect time to say those words and now is not it.

"See you at six, Ace. Bye-bye."

The call disconnects and I sit looking at the phone. I look up as the manager returns.

"All done, Mr. Channing." He hands the card back to me then places the boxes in a bag. "Nice doing business with you as usual, sir."

"Likewise." I stand and take the bag and shake his hand.

As I step out of the store, I pull my coat close again. I check my watch and find that it's almost eleven. I need to get back to the office for a meeting at eleven-thirty. I hurry to my car and head back.

It's almost five before I call it a day and pack up to leave the office. I have just enough time to get home and grab a bottle of wine before heading to Lana's. Just as I get to the parking lot, my phone rings. It's Monica. I brace myself.

"Hi, Ace. Do you have any plans for tonight?"

"As a matter of fact, I do."

"Well, you will have to put them on hold. I finally got hold of Devonish and set up a meeting. He's willing to do dinner at seven. I've called ahead and reserved your usual table at Crompton."

"Sure. No problem. I'll reschedule my other plans."

"Great."

As she hangs up, I dial Lana's number. I pace as I wait for her to answer.

"Hello?"

"Lana, sweetheart. I have bad news. I just got a call from Monica to meet an investor I've been trying to track down for months. I'll have to take a rain check this evening. But I'll make it up to you tomorrow night."

"Oh." I can hear the disappointment in her voice. "Okay. Tomorrow night then?"

"Tomorrow night. Thanks for understanding."

The call disconnects and I jump into my car. I dash home to shower and change and make it to the restaurant in record time. A few hours later, I leave on cloud nine. Everton Devonish is just the kind of ally I like to have in this business, and he has given his word that he will partner with me for future projects.

When I get home, it's almost ten. As I fix myself a drink and undress, I dial Lana's number.

"Hello?"

"I hope I didn't wake you?"

She laughs. "Ace, it's barely ten on a Friday night. I'm twenty-three, not ninety-three."

"Just checking."

"Besides, I would be out with my girls if we had an occasion, or be at a bar or club or something. So I'm more than wide awake."

"You know, you're right. That's where I would be as well. We're young. We're hip. What the hell are we doing at home on a Friday night?"

"Being a pair of old biddies. That's what."

I throw my head back and laugh. "Tell you what, let me grab a pizza or something and come over. We can be old, home-bound biddies on a Friday night together."

"That sounds like a plan. See you in a few."

I disconnect the call and call a pizza parlor. Half an hour later I'm on my way to Lana's with a pizza and a couple of sodas. I also have a suit bag with an outfit or two for dinner the next night as I've decided to take her out to make up for missing tonight. Her talk of being out at a bar or club gives me an idea to take her out for dinner then for dancing and drinks afterward. At the bottom of the bag, I have the box with the earrings. I know exactly how I'll present them tomorrow night.

We spend the night watching television and feasting on pizza. It's almost three before we stumble to bed. As she curves into my body, I place my arm across her torso. We both fall into a deep sleep. I've grown to love the feeling of her skin against mine, the last thing before I fall asleep and the first thing when I wake up. If I have things my way, it will be a permanent thing before the year ends.

The next day, we wake up late and have a late brunch. I give her a hand with a few chores. She runs out to the cleaners to drop off some suits while I relax and watch television. My phone rings just as I'm about to take a nap.

"Hello?"

"Ace! How are you doing?"

"Hey, Eddie. Not bad. What's up?"

"I'm just wondering if you wanted to come over for dinner tonight. It's been a minute."

I groan softly. "I'm going to have to decline, Eddie. I already have plans. And I already disappointed Lana last night when I had to cancel our plans. Tonight was to make up for that."

"Bring her."

"What?"

"Bring her. I'd love to meet the girl who's turning your world upside down."

I look up as the door opens. Lana enters with a few bags and I rise to help her.

"Hold on, Eddie."

I take the bags from her and place them on the kitchen counter.

"Sweetheart, I have a proposition for you."

"What's that?"

"I wanted to go out tonight to make up for last night. My friend Eddie is inviting us to his place for dinner instead."

"Okay."

"Okay? As in, you don't mind?"

"Why would I? We're still going out and we're still going to eat, aren't we?"

I laugh and kiss her softly. "Indeed, we are."

I pick up the phone. "Eddie? You there?"

"Yup."

"What time should we be there?"

"Seven is good. She sounds like a trooper. Nothing like you know who. I can't wait to meet her."

"Seven it is."

I disconnect the call and walk over to Lana in the kitchen. I pull her into an embrace from behind and she leans her head back automatically as I nuzzle her cheek.

"Thanks for being so understanding."

"It's okay. I need to meet your friends sooner or later."

"Likewise. When will you introduce me to yours?"

"Well, there's always Christmas. Then there's my family," she hesitates slightly, "And yours."

I stiffen and sigh. "I'd love to meet your family. Can't say the same for mine. We'll talk about that one day. But for now. Let's get through dinner with Eddie. I promise things will get clearer after that."

She turns in my arms and slips her arms around my neck. She holds my gaze for a few moments before stretching up to brush a kiss across my lips.

"What time are we leaving?"

"Around six. It's a bit of a drive. He lives in the hills."

"Okay."

I hold her close and smile. "Wear the gold dress, please."

"Okay."

Later that evening as we get ready, I watch as she gets dressed. As I sit on the edge of the bed, she skillfully applies her make-up. Her hair is pinned in a bun atop her head, leaving her neck exposed. I wait until she's about to choose her accessories. I stand and go to the suit bag and retrieve the box.

"I think these will go beautifully with what you're wearing. And maybe you have something that will match them perhaps?"

I hand her the box and stand with my hands in my pockets. I watch her carefully as my heart begins to beat faster. She looks at the box, a slight frown creasing her brow. Then she looks up at me.

"Go on. Open it."

She bows her head to the task and does as I ask. I hear her gasp and my heart goes into overdrive as she looks up at me, confusion marring her face. I swallow hard as I speak softly.

"Do you have something that will match them? A bracelet or necklace perhaps?"

Wordlessly she opens a drawer and retrieves two similar boxes. She turns to me.

"It was you all along?"

I step towards her and take the earrings out of the box.

"Let me help you."

She stands and I avoid her eyes as I focus on slipping the earrings into her ears. I can feel her gaze boring into me and my fingers tremble slightly. I turn and reach for one of the boxes and find the necklace. I move around her as I fasten it at her throat. The final piece is the bracelet. As I place it on her right wrist, I take a deep breath and finally meet her eyes. She looks at me questioningly.

"Ace? What's going on? Why did you send me these gifts? CACA?"

I cup her cheeks with my palms and feather a soft kiss across her lips. I place my forehead against hers.

"We will definitely talk after we come back from Eddie's. Okay? It's a conversation that is long overdue. Please, trust me."

I step back and she grabs my shoulders. Before I can react, she presses her lips hard against mine, then steps back.

"I trust you."

The words send a shiver down my spine and exhilaration races through me.

We leave her apartment and head to Eddie's for dinner. As we drive, her hand creeps across to find mine and our fingers intertwine. I've never felt a more comforting feeling in the world.

CHAPTER 25

LANA

As we drive to his friend's house, my heart feels as though it's pounding out of my chest. The last thing I expected tonight is this bombshell revelation. Ace is CACA!? What the hell!

I barely pay attention to anything except the feeling of his fingers intertwined with mine. I don't know how I'm going to get through dinner tonight.

His friend Eddie is the jovial sort and I immediately take to him and his wife. I can see he's sizing me up and clearly I pass muster. The evening passes well and before we know it, we're heading back to the city. My anxiety which has been at bay all evening comes racing back with a vengeance. With each turn of the wheels, my heart beats faster and faster. It seems as if every stoplight has conspired to delay us as I can't recall seeing so many red lights in succession in my life. My fingers grip his tightly as we sit at yet another light.

He looks over at me and squeezes my hand. "Relax, sweetheart."

I take a deep breath and try, but the journey seems so long. Finally, we pull into my complex.

As we enter the apartment, I fumble with the lights and rush to the bathroom as nerves make my bladder go weak. When I come out, Ace is standing by the door.

He takes a deep breath and takes my hand. Wordlessly, he leads me to the living room and we sit on the couch. He turns at an angle to face me.

"Lana? It's me. Chester."

I feel as if my world shifts on its axis as my mind goes blank for a split second.

"Do you remember me, Lana?"

I nod mutely, not trusting my voice. Chester? But it can't be!

"I've never forgotten you, Lana. When the home placed me with your family for that last year, it was the best year of my life. I only wished I had been placed with you guys years earlier rather than end up moving from foster home to foster home. Lana, believe me when I say that the twelve months I spent with your family have kept me going all these years. I made promises and I like to keep my promises. Do you remember those conversations we used to have, Lana?"

In an instant, I'm thirteen again with a huge crush on this seventeen-year-old foster kid. I look at him carefully, struggling to find a resemblance. Now all the memories I've been having of Chester make sense. And even though physically he looks nothing like he did then, it seems as if my spirit knew. I reach out to touch his hair.

"It used to be so long and shaggy and always hiding your eyes."

"I've learned to hold my head up with confidence and look people in the eye. Lana, back then I know you were just a kid and a kid who I should have considered as a little sister. But you were the only one who saw past my weight, my acne, my untidiness, my shyness, my stutter and saw a person. Your family treated me like family. All the others treated me like a government check. I've never forgotten your family. And I've never forgotten you."

"I don't know what to say, Ace, I mean Chester, I mean. Shit. I don't even know what I mean. CACA?"

"Chester 'Ace Channing' Abrahams. I changed my name when I changed Chester."

"My heart was broken when you left."

"I turned eighteen. I didn't have a choice. I was out of the system. Besides, I didn't want to be a bother although I know your parents would have allowed me to stay."

"It's like you disappeared into thin air."

"I did for a while. I was depressed for a bit. But when I remembered some of the promises I made to you, I had to pull myself together. You promised to pursue your dreams in the writing industry only if I promised to find something I was really good at and stick to it. Do you remember some of the things we talked about? Did you know you were the only one who believed I would make something of my life?"

"We talked about so many things. We were just kids with fanciful imaginations."

"Well, I vowed to make those fanciful imaginations a reality. I gave myself five years to make something of my life and find you. By then you would be eighteen and it wouldn't be a crime to love you."

"To love me?" I gaze up at him with my eyes wide.

He slides closer to me on the couch. "Lana-Banana, I love you. I've loved you from the moment I laid my eyes on you on that porch with your nose buried in that Crenshaw novel."

So many things made sense now. "That's how you knew I loved Crenshaw, and the lava cake, and the daisies, and-"

"I told you I know you better than you know yourself, my love."

I reach out to cradle his cheek. "Chester? I don't know what to say. How could I not know it was you?"

"Well, I lost a lot of weight for one. I started taking better care of myself as well. And with the motivation of promising to give you the life you've always dreamed of, I worked hard. I had so many odd jobs before I finally struck some luck. All it took was one good investment and I haven't stopped since. You'll notice that you can hardly find anything on me prior to my twenty-second birthday which is when I made my first million. It was full steam ahead after that. A good orthodontist got my teeth straight. A good optometrist lasered my eyes. A good dermatologist got my skin clear. I've been keeping tabs on you for a while now, but I decided to speed things up this year."

"So, my kissing you in the bar-?"

"-made me move a little faster. You do remember my telling you that if you had not approached me, I would have approached you? I knew it was your birthday and I was at your apartment when you drove out with your friends. I followed you."

"You did *what*!?"

"I wanted to see you. I had no idea how I would reintroduce myself. So much had changed about me. I followed you to the restaurant and then the bar. I was contemplating how to get you away from your friends when you came over."

"You knew it was my birthday and sent this the next day." I hold up my wrist with the bracelet.

"Since I'm confessing, I might as well confess everything. I bought the company just to be with you."

"You did *what*!?" I'm beginning to feel like a broken record.

"I didn't know how else to keep you near me."

"You could have just asked me out on a date like a regular man. Or better yet, told me who you were."

"About that. I felt as though I didn't want you to love me because of a memory. I wanted you to love the person I had become."

"And I do, Ace. I do love you."

His eyes darken as he reaches for my hand. "Say that again."

"I love you, Ace Channing. I love you as much as I love Chester Abrahams. I love you with all my heart."

He reaches out to caress my cheek with the back of his hand.

"Lana, I've waited ten years to hear you say those words again. Not a day has gone by that I don't think of you. Do you remember this?" he reaches into his wallet and retrieves a scrap of paper and hands it to me.

I look at the faded picture. I can still make out the boy in baggy clothes and shaggy hair covering half his face as he smiles down at the girl beside him. Beside him is a knobby-kneed girl staring wide-eyed into the camera. The photographer caught the moment I smiled and I can see my new braces. Chester had known I hated them and had told me a joke to get me to smile at that moment. I look at us as we were then. We had become fast friends and best friends. My young heart had fallen for the shy, awkward boy. And it had been broken when he left.

He brushes his fingers against my cheek once more.

"I love you, Lana."

Tears fill my eyes as I feel the enormity of his words. "Ace, I love you."

Without another word, he pulls me into his arms. As his lips find mine, the photo falls to the floor.

He pulls me across his lap as he kisses me hungrily. He presses his forehead to mine as he whispers.

"My sweet Lana. Words cannot express how much I love you. But I can certainly show you."

He holds me tightly as he gets to his feet. I wrap my arms around his neck as my lips seek his once more. He holds me securely behind the knees. There's a lightness in my spirit as he walks with me to the bedroom. I feel as if we are about to consummate our marriage. There's such a feeling of newness and rightness about it.

He places me gently on the bed and turns on the light. I lie looking up at him as he stares down at me. I watch as he kneels and pulls my shoes off. My breath catches as he kisses my toes and instep. He feathers soft kisses along my calf and strokes the back of my knee, making me shiver slightly. As he continues his journey upward, his hands grasp the hem of my dress and push it up. My head rolls back and I bite my lip as he nibbles my inner thigh, his lips a whisper away from my pussy. Then I feel him kiss me there through the scrap of fabric and I moan slightly. He kisses me again. Then his fingers hook into the elastic waist and pulls them down and off my legs. He leans forward and kisses me once more, using the tip of his tongue to trail along my labia. He nips at the plump flesh and I jump slightly at the sensation. His hands brace my thighs apart and I open to him willingly.

My fingers grip the sheets tightly as my back arches. His tongue touches me and I feel as if a flame shoots through me. He licks along my slit and I squeeze my eyes shut. As he dips his head to taste me fully, I give myself over to him. His hands slip underneath me as he raises me up to meet his mouth. I plant my feet as I lift my hips. I bite my lip as I feel my clit throb with need. As though he reads my mind. He takes it into his mouth, suckling it. I cry out as my hips buck upward. I feel my juices flow as he stimulates me and I can't help but thrash helplessly. He fastens his mouth on my pussy once more, plunging his tongue as deep as it can go and I fall apart.

I jerk and shudder as I climax. My body feels hot and cold all at once. I feel dizzy and faint. My heart feels as though it will jump out of my chest at any moment. I vaguely feel him move away from me. His fingers find the side zipper of my dress and he pulls it over my head. My bra is next. Then I hear the rustle of his clothing as he undresses.

When I feel his body cover mine, I reach for him blindly. He kisses me and I taste myself on his lips. I reach down to take him in my hand and he groans at my touch. I'm impatient. I want, no, need him inside me.

I place him at my core and he presses forward, our lips still fused. He takes my hands as I wrap my legs around his waist. Our fingers intertwine as our tongues dance and our bodies press urgently against each other.

I feel my blood boil once again as our bodies find their rhythm. I press up to meet him as he thrusts deeper and harder into me. He's slick with my juices and I feel nothing but heat as he thrusts into me repeatedly. Our tongues dance to the rhythm our bodies have created as perspiration bathes us and makes the sheets damp. Where our words fail, our actions do not. It feels like forever and it feels like a second all at once. As I feel that familiar tingle lick along my spine, I move faster and harder. He meets me with his own urgent thrusts. And when I reach my peak, he is there with me. I feel liquid heat fill my body as he pours himself into me, filling me with his essence.

We lie shuddering as we fight for air, but we are loathed to allow our mouths to separate. I cling to him and he to me as we lay with our limbs entwined. I keep my legs wrapped around him, as I want us to stay joined as one. He buries his face in my neck and I can feel him take deep gulps of air.

"I love you. I love you. I love you..." He punctuates each word with a kiss. And I kiss him back, chanting my own litany of love.

Over and over, we reach for each other throughout the night. When we are finally worn and completely sated, the sky is tinged with pink heralding the approaching dawn. As I lie with my body filled with his, I feel complete. It's as though nothing before and nothing after matters. And it doesn't. This is my life, lying in Ace's arms.

CHAPTER 26

ACE

I take a sip of my coffee as I look out at the beauty of the fall foliage. My heart is light and I can't help but smile. I never knew how much of a burden my unknown identity was until I revealed myself to Lana and felt that sense of release. And she loves me! I feel as though my life is complete.

There's a shift in the atmosphere of our relationship and it's a wonder we haven't burned the office down with the radiance of our countenances. Several times I've caught Mrs. Elaine looking at me with a tiny smile. But I can't help it if my happiness radiates. Lana has told me that she gets some of those secret looks from others as well.

After that night, there's no doubt she will be wearing my ring before the end of the year. We've both decided that I will go home with her for Christmas. What a surprise that's going to be!

I check my watch and take another sip of coffee as I wait for Caroline. There are some details regarding the house that I need to go over with her. As I pick up my phone to call her, she appears in the doorway. She hurries over and a waitress is at her elbow instantly. She places her order as she removes her jacket.

"Sorry to be late, I had a call from a client just as I was rushing out the door. It's getting a bit nippy, isn't it?"

"I was about to call. It is going to be a chilly winter, for sure."

The waitress returns with Caroline's coffee and I order a second cup along with a plate of cinnamon danish which we split.

She looks at me over the rim of her cup. "So, what's so important that we have to go to the house on this chilly Saturday morning?"

"I haven't seen it since I told you how I wanted it renovated in some areas. I just thought we could take a look at it together to see if there's anything else I want to change. I want to move in within a week or two."

"Finally!" She gulps down the rest of her coffee. "For a moment there I was wondering if you bought it only to slap some paint on it, change a few appliances and fixtures and put it back on the market. Do you still plan to keep the apartment?"

"For now. I may give it up later."

"Or – rent it. It's in a prime spot and I'm sure I would have no problem finding renters."

"That's another option." I point to her empty cup. "Are you finished?"

"I'll maybe have another to go. If it's this cold down here I can't imagine what it'll be like there. And the central heat isn't on as of yet either."

We get extra coffees, pay the bill and head to the parking lot. We take my vehicle and half an hour later we're standing in the foyer. After completing the purchase, I had seen the house only one other time after the previous owners had removed their belongings. I had walked through with Caroline and given instructions for changes to be made. I haven't seen it since.

As soon as I walk deeper into the house, I feel a sense of peace sweep over me. The freshly painted rooms gleam brightly. As I walk from room to room, I mentally check the list I had given Caroline. Everything has been covered and I'm pleased. All that now remains is to get Lana up here. I'm already enjoying the prospect of decorating our home together. I turn to Caroline with a smile.

"This is excellent, Caroline."

"Is there anything else that needs to be done? I have the furniture store on speed dial if you're ready to move on to that phase."

"As for that, I'll take care of myself with my soon-to-be wife."

She raises her eyebrows. "Wow! Is it the mystery lady?"

"It is."

"I never thought that things were getting that serious."

"I have been serious about her for a long time. I know the buck stops with her and she is the one I want to be with for the rest of my life."

"Do you love her?"

"Of course! That's a given. And she loves me too." I smile broadly. "I can't explain the feeling I have inside, Caroline. But it's as though my world feels balanced. I feel as if nothing can go wrong."

"Ace, anyone who looks at you can't help but know that you're happy. Now I can't wait to meet her."

"And I can't wait for you to meet her either. Are you free now? I could ask her to meet us at the coffee shop when we head back. There's no time like the present."

"I am. And even if I wasn't, there's no way I would miss meeting the future Mrs. Channing." She reaches over to squeeze my shoulder. "I really am happy for you Ace. You are such a sweet person. You deserve to be happy. For your sake, I hope she meets my standard."

I throw my head back and laugh. "I'm sure she will. Let me make that call."

I step into the next room and dial Lana's number.

"Hello?"

"Hello, my love. Are you busy?"

"Ummm, I'm just doing some laundry."

"Can you meet me by Solay in about half an hour? I won't keep you for very long. There's someone I want you to meet."

"Okay. No problem."

"See you in a few."

I go back and find Caroline.

We walk through the cold house as I make a few more notes for adjustments to be made. I'm going to begin moving in this coming week. Back at the apartment, the few items I need are already packed and waiting for the moving van. I'm not taking any furniture or appliances with me except my bed. Everything else will be a shopping spree with Lana.

We lock up the house and head back to the city. As we park, I spot Lana's car at the other end of the lot. A grin splits my face.

"She's here."

Caroline laughs. "Down boy. I can feel your excitement. Now I *really* can't wait to meet her."

We head into the shop and I look around. Caroline turns to me with a smile.

"I know you're in love and all, but it's not too late for me to introduce you to that nice girl I met at the hairdressers a few weeks ago. She's right over there."

"I'm all set, Caroline."

"She's a real darling. Let me say hi really quick and you can check her out for yourself, okay?"

She walks ahead of me just as I spot Lana. She looks up and smiles as we approach. I smile back. Caroline walks almost up to Lana's table. I slip past her and lean down to give Lana a quick kiss on the cheek.

"I'll be right back, love."

I straighten up and turn to Caroline. She's standing still with a goofy smile on her face as she stares at Lana. I wave my hand in front of her.

"Earth to Caroline."

She looks at me then looks at Lana. She stretches out her hand.

"Hello, dear. I don't know if you remember me? We met at the salon?"

Lana looks up at her and smiles. "I do remember you."

I look at Caroline as she smiles back. "This is my little friend. But I guess she's your little friend too." She bursts out laughing as she takes a seat.

Lana looks at her, at me, then back at her. She points at me as she speaks to Caroline.

"You mean this is-"

By this time, Caroline is in peals of laughter. Then Lana grins, followed by a smothered chuckle. Before long, she has joined Caroline in her fit of laughter.

"So, if I had set you two-two-two," she goes off in another fit of laughter.

"You would have been back at square one times two!" Caroline has tears rolling down her cheeks by this time.

I stand looking at them puzzled. "Would someone care to tell me what's going on here? Have you two already met?"

"We have! Have a seat, Ace. This is one for the record books." Caroline tugs at the hem of my jacket and I sit.

In between giggles and chuckles they fill me in on Lana's plight of being pursued by someone she wanted to avoid, and Caroline's offer to set her up with me. And then I had mentioned my pursuit of a young lady and Caroline had offered Lana as an alternative. With all the pieces together, it's hard not to see the humor in the situation.

When we are able to finally regain some decorum, we order a few sandwiches and juice as it's almost lunch time.

Caroline gives us her blessings and leaves after we eat. Lana and I sit a little bit longer.

"So, you wanted to have nothing to do with me, huh."

"You have to admit, Ace, you were quite obnoxious."

"Imagine if you had taken Caroline up on her offer."

"Or if you had allowed her to set you up with the 'nice girl from the salon'. What a shock it would have been on both ends."

I reach across and intertwine my fingers with hers. "It simply means we were meant for each other. Even in trying to walk away we would have been brought back together. I'm grateful you decided to give me a chance, Lana."

She reaches over with her free hand and caresses my cheek. "So am I. Ace, you make me happy. I love you so much."

I smile as I rub my thumb across her knuckles. "I love you too, Lana."

We sit smiling at each other for a few moments more, lost in each other's eyes. The waitress interrupts with our bill and we're brought back to the present. I settle the bill and help her with her jacket.

I hold her hand as I walk her to her car. As we stand facing each other in the lot, I pull her into my arms. Automatically, her arms go around my neck as I lower my head and take possession of her lips. The kiss is soft and sweet with an underlying hunger. I release her and see to it that she is seated and secure. I watch as she drives out and sigh. This is the life. This is love.

I complete a few more tasks around the city and make it to a meeting at four. That one ends just in time for me to shower and change and head to another meeting at dinner. Work never ends.

As I head home, I begin to think of how I can scale back on these obligations. As a single man living alone, it's not a difficult task to hop from meeting to meeting. But with Lana in the picture, there's no way I'm going to be heading home at one in the morning, nor will I have her out until that time just to sit through a meeting with me. I think long and hard about handing over some of the reins in some areas. I already know that as soon as Lana and I are married, I will step down as CEO of McEachron. If she wishes, she will continue working. But she doesn't have to as she will be financially secure with me as her husband. Married. Husband. As I think about the ring in the safe in the apartment, I know I will be asking her that ultimate question any day now.

I get home and fix myself a drink. As I look around, I feel a sense of coldness and emptiness. The walls are bare and the few things I wish to take with me are packed and waiting in boxes. My clothes are also packed and waiting. Yes. By the end of this week, I should be in the new house. Then hopefully by the week after, Lana will be with me.

As I get ready for bed, I text her, but get no response. I figure that she's sleeping and text a heart emoji. As I fall asleep, her image is seared on my mind.

My dreams are vivid that night as I see Lana and me, hand in hand walking through the house. She waves her hands excitedly as she discusses what she wants where. I smile and walk along with her.

There's a constant buzzing that rouses me from sleep and I'm surprised to see that it's light outside. I frown as the buzzing continues. I turn to the nightstand and see my phone vibrating. Lana's name is on the screen. I dive for it.

"Hello?"

"Ace?"

"Yeah, love?"

"Have you seen the papers this morning?"

"No. I'm just waking up. What's up?"

"Take a look at this."

While I wait for the message to come in, I rub the sleep out of my eyes. I peer at the photograph. There is a picture of Lana and me in the parking lot kissing. The headline reads: *Who's Channing's sweetheart?*

What the hell!?

CHAPTER 27

LANA

My heart feels as though it is going to beat out of my chest as I sit staring at the picture that Kyla had sent me a few minutes ago.

"Ace? Are you there?"

"I'm here. Where did you get this?"

"Kyla sent it to me. Who took this?"

He clears his throat. "Clearly someone who's looking for a quick buck or a quick story. I can track it down if you'd like."

I shake my head. "No. Are you okay with it?"

He sighs. "It's the story of my life. I should be asking you if you're okay with it."

"It's not that important to me."

"This is the sort of thing that makes up my life, though, Lana. Do you think you can get used to our picture in the media? I mean, this is just the beginning. And with this there will be even more attention focused on finding out who you are. The tabloids love this sort of thing."

I swallow hard. "I guess it was a matter of time, right?" I look at the picture once more. "There isn't even a story with it or anything. Just the headline and a caption: *Billionaire businessman Ace Channing caught smooching girlfriend in a coffee shop parking lot*. They could have at least gotten the name of the place."

He laughs. "They could have been a little more creative."

I can't help but laugh. "I know, right? They could have perhaps given a backstory or something and lead up to this."

"That's the editor in you talking, you know that right?"

I smile. "Guilty. Anyway, I was just wondering if you'd seen it and what you think about it."

"I'm just waking up actually. I messaged you when I got home last night but I guess you were knocked out."

"I saw your messages and was about to respond when Kyla sent that to me."

"Okay. What are you doing today?"

We chat for a moment and he decides to come over for lunch and dinner. We enjoy a rather cozy evening watching movies until he leaves reluctantly. The next morning when I wake up, I feel a bit under the weather which is typical for this time of year. I make myself some peppermint tea and get ready for work.

As I step into the office, I feel eyes on me. Here we go again. Clearly, the news has hit the office. I hold my head high and head to my office. Strangely enough, there's no feeling of intimidation or shame. Ace and I are in a relationship and it is not going to end. Folks will just have to deal with it.

I'm halfway through the manuscript in front of me as I suck on a mint to keep my mouth feeling fresh when there's a knock on my door.

"Come in!"

I look up and go still as Avery steps into the office. I feel as though I've not seen her in months though we have passed each other a few times since our last run-in. I brace myself for a few seconds as she comes closer. But as she approaches, I see that her face is wet as tears roll down her cheeks.

"Lana! I swear it wasn't me! I know what I said before. And, yes, I did go to the board. But please, Lana, you have to believe me! I have nothing to do with that picture! I swear!"

She sinks into the nearest chair and wraps her arms around herself, rocking back and forth as she continues to sob.

"I didn't do it. I didn't do it. I didn't do it."

I leave my seat and go over to kneel before her. I use the back of my hand to wipe at her face.

"Avery, get a hold of yourself. Calm down."

She looks at me with red, puffy eyes. She seems to have been crying for hours.

"I didn't mean for any of this to happen. I was just jealous and stupid. You got the job I wanted, and then when Ace came and he had eyes for only you. It was stupid of me to be so jealous and say the things I did. I'm so sorry, Lana! And now I'm going to lose my job, and I'll never get a recommendation, and-"

"Avery, Avery, calm down. Please. You're working yourself into a panic for nothing."

"Please! You have to tell Ace I didn't do it! Please, Lana! You do believe me, don't you?"

Before I can respond, my door opens. Ace steps in and I feel Avery recoil. I stand as he walks towards us. Avery jumps up and dodges behind me.

"Ace! I didn't do it! I didn't!"

He frowns as he looks at Avery. "Didn't do what?"

"The whole office is talking. They're saying I'll be gone by the end of the day and I've gone too far this time. But I swear I didn't!"

"Didn't do what?" Ace measures his words carefully with a hint of annoyance.

"She thinks you're going to fire her because you think she leaked our relationship to the press."

"Please, Ace! I didn't. I've done some mean and rotten things but I didn't do it."

Ace folds his arms and stares at Avery with a frown. "Why should I believe you? You threatened Lana that you would start spreading rumors and you did. You threatened to tell the board and you did. You threatened to go to the press. Why should I believe you didn't?"

Avery bursts into a fresh set of tears and I put my arm around her shoulder.

"*I* don't believe she did, Ace. And you know she didn't either. Don't you think she's suffered enough? She's beside herself."

"After the hell she put you through, Lana?"

"I think she regrets it. Right, Avery?"

"I'm so, so sorry!" she wraps her arms around her trembling torso once more. "Please don't fire me!"

"You won't be fired. Right, Ace?" I look at Ace and catch a hint of a twitch at the corner of his lips. The brute! He's enjoying Avery's meltdown. I turn to Avery.

"Dry your eyes and go wash your face. Go back to your desk and relax. There will be no firing. But I do hope you've learned to stop meddling, Avery."

"I have. I have. Thank you, Lana. I don't deserve it after what I've done to you. Thank you!" she hugs me awkwardly before hurrying out of the office.

"That was very nice of you." Ace smirks.

"You were being quite mean. You know she had nothing to do with it."

"Well, hopefully, as you've said, she has learned her lesson."

"I think she has. What brings you to my office, by the way?" I go back to my desk and take a seat. He sits on the edge.

"I'm just checking to see if you're okay with the latest developments."

"I'm fine."

"The entire office is talking, you know. Those who did not believe the rumor now have facts to confirm that we are in a relationship."

I shrug. "I'm fine. It is what it is. Besides, it was bound to come out sooner or later."

"True. Publicity is the story of my life. I, for one, am a little surprised we haven't been exposed before now. Anyway, I had the photo tracked down and Monica is in dialogue with the paper that printed the picture. I will take legal action against the violation of my privacy if it comes to that."

I raise my eyebrows. "Is it that serious?"

"It is. These tabloids do need to learn discretion and that we are people who deserve privacy too."

"Wow."

"Welcome to my world."

"And what a world."

"Will you be able to handle it?"

I look at him searchingly. "Do I have a choice? I don't intend to leave you. Do you intend to leave me?"

"Not even when I'm cold in the grave, babe. I'll haunt you every night."

"Likewise. So, I guess we'll just weather the storm and roll with the punches as they come."

He smiles and leans over to brush his lips against mine. "Love you. Dinner later?"

"Love you too. Yes."

He stands and I stand and walk around the desk to hug him.

"What do you feel like eating tonight?"

"Surprise me."

He arches his eyebrows. "Look at you asking for surprises. How far you have come!"

We kiss once more and he leaves the office.

There are no further interruptions for the rest of the day. I skip lunch as my appetite feels low. The changing of the season is doing a real number on me this year. I've always had an allergy issue or the flu once the temperatures drop, but by the end of the day, I feel as though I'm going to pass out.

When I get home, my skin is cold and clammy and my head hurts. I know that a part of the reason for the headache is my skipped lunch. But I still don't have much of an appetite. I call Ace.

"Hey, sweetheart. I was about to call for take-out. I'll be over in about thirty or so."

"I don't feel very well, Ace. I'm not sure I can eat anything."

"Is it your allergies again? I can stop by the pharmacy."

"I'm not sneezing. But my head feels woozy and my stomach feels queasy."

"Okay. I'll get you some broth as well."

"Thanks, hon."

"No problem. Go wrap up and keep warm. I'll be there in a few."

He hangs up and I head to the shower. I'm in my pajamas and robe and curled up on the couch when he comes into the apartment. He places the parcels on the kitchen counter and comes over to me immediately. He kneels and peers into my face, placing his hand on my forehead.

"You don't seem flushed or seem to have a fever. Still feeling woozy?"

"I am. I didn't have lunch so that could be it. Come to think of it, I didn't have much of a breakfast this morning either."

"Lana! You need to take care of yourself, sweetie. We may have to move in together so I can see to it that you're eating right. Come. Let's get some food into you."

I follow him to the table and watch as he opens the containers. I take one whiff and feel my stomach roll. Almost instantly my mouth is filled with that sudden surge of water that acts as a prelude to vomit. I clap my hand on my mouth and make a mad dash for the bathroom. I get there just in time to retch violently. But as my stomach is empty, nothing comes up but water. I feel the perspiration on my brow as I breathe deeply.

I look up as Ace rubs my back. He looks at me with concern as he helps me to my feet. I sway slightly and he holds me. I close my eyes and lean against him weakly. He strokes my hair and I sigh.

"I'll be fine in a week or two. My system just needs time to adjust to the weather change. That's all."

"Okay, love. Let's get you cleaned up and try to get something into you, okay?"

I nod. I manage to wash my face and rinse my mouth. I wrinkle my nose at the food as we head back to the kitchen. He hastens me to the couch and I sit obediently, watching as he bustles around the kitchen. The kettle is on as he rummages through the cupboards. He places a mug with a teabag on a tray along with a packet of crackers. He takes forkfuls of his meal while he waits. But as soon as the kettle is ready, his attention turns back to me.

He brings the tray over to me and places it across my lap.

"Try to get a few sips down before you try the crackers."

I do as I'm told, sighing as the hot, minty liquid slides down my throat. My stomach feels as though it wants to rebel again, but the mint soothes it instantly. I manage to drink about three- quarters of the tea along with some crackers. A loud belch escapes and he chuckles.

"That sounds like your stomach is saying thank you for being fed. Don't let another day go by that you don't eat, Lana."

"I won't."

"I won't try to force you to eat now, but I'll put the broth in the refrigerator and you can have it another time."

"Okay."

He takes the tray and I lie on the couch for a bit while he finishes his meal. By the time he's through, my eyelids are heavy and I'm barely holding back my yawns. It's just eight but I feel as though I haven't slept in days and need to catch up. He comes to stand over me.

"I'm going to let you get some sleep. You do look out of it tonight. Come. Let's get you into bed."

He scoops me into his arms and walks to the bedroom. I rest my head against his shoulder and sigh at the warmth of his body. All too soon, he places me on the bed. Gently he removes my robe and tucks me beneath the covers. He sits on the side and smooths the hair away from my brow.

"If you don't feel well tomorrow, stay home and ride it out. Okay?"

I nod obediently. "Okay."

"Good girl." He kisses my brow then stands. "I'm going to let you get some rest."

"Stay with me." I look up at him and he smiles.

"Okay. But only until you fall asleep."

"Okay." I watch as he slips beneath the covers with me and I roll into his arms. I snuggle into his chest and sigh. My eyes flutter close as another yawn comes out of nowhere. He strokes my back slowly and my eyes grow heavier.

The next morning when I awake, I'm alone. I open my eyes and take a deep breath. I attempt to sit up and groan softly as nausea overtakes me. It's a repeat of the evening before as I feel the warning signs. I make it to the bathroom just in time. This time there is no Ace to comfort me and help me to my feet. I stand on wobbly feet and rinse my mouth. I use the wall for support as I walk back to the bedroom slowly. I sink into bed and pull the covers around me. I don't feel feverish nor cold as I would with the flu. But my stomach just refuses to settle. With these unpredictable runs to the bathroom, there will be no going to the office today.

I fumble on the nightstand for my phone and manage to find Charles' number. I send a brief text before tossing the phone aside. I pull the covers up over my head and close my eyes.

CHAPTER 28

ACE

I stop by Lana's office the next morning only to find her absent. I think about calling but don't want to wake her in case she's asleep. Nevertheless, she's on my mind all morning. As soon as my last meeting ends at one, I hightail it over to her place. I use my key to enter as quietly as possible but my caution is unnecessary. I find her up and seated at the kitchen table. She looks up from the plate of leftovers she hadn't eaten the night before. I raise my brows.

"I heard you were out sick."

"I wasn't feeling well this morning, but I'm okay now."

"Clearly."

"I think it might be a twenty-four-hour bug or something."

"It's good to see you eating."

"I got up around eleven and didn't feel so bad after all but it would have been too late to come in anyway. What are you doing here?"

"I came to check on you."

She smiles at me and my heart melts. "That's so sweet of you. Have you had lunch? I have more than enough to share."

"Sure, I'll have some."

"Great. Have a seat."

She places a plate in the microwave and turns to look at me with a smile on her face. I smile back.

"What?"

"I'm just thinking about what everyone is going to say when we turn up on Christmas Eve. They aren't going to believe it's you. You're going to have to pull some memories out of storage, you know. There are things that I'm sure they know that only Chester could know."

"True. I am looking forward to seeing everyone again."

The microwave beeps and she removes the plate and brings it to me.

We finish eating and before I know it, I'm kissing her goodbye. I have a meeting with Reggie and barely make it to our usual coffee shop on time. She is already waiting.

"You're slipping, Ace. Usually, I'm the one running late and keeping you waiting."

"I was finishing lunch with Lana. What do you have for me?"

She raises her eyebrows. "How are things going with Miss Gray?"

I smile and wink. "You will soon see. But on to current business."

"Ah yes. We do need to talk about the former Mrs. Channing. Meredith has been a very naughty girl."

"You don't say."

"I do say. For one, she's been using your name and ring to get favors. The Channing name is quite powerful."

"What!"

"Don't worry. I've put the word out. It is especially troubling because some of these entities with whom she's been conducting business in your name are expecting returns on investments. I have informed them that Meredith has no authority to act on your behalf and that they may take it up with our lawyers. For others, I've asked them to continue to play along so that we can build enough evidence against Meredith and have her charged with fraud."

"Good. When will we have her behind bars?"

"At the rate she's been going, it's going to be a confined Christmas for Mer. This has been going on for some time, though, and she has been pretty slick about it. But she's put her hat where she can't reach it and the noose is closing. That visit she paid you was out of desperation to keep up appearances. It turns out she has been telling some of her creditors that you two are still together but you're just going through a rough patch. I'm sure she had hoped to somehow seduce you that morning and somehow find a way to sink her claws into you again."

"There is no chance in hell of that happening. Meredith needs to be dealt with once and for all. I'm very serious about Lana and I don't want anything messing it up for me."

"I agree she needs to be dealt with, and soon. The past few weeks that I've been shadowing her and getting intel on her movements and conversations, she sounds and behaves as if she's one nut away from the madhouse. I wouldn't trust her."

"It's that serious?"

"Ace. Meredith is borderline crazy. You don't think she feels the walls closing in on her? If she knows about Lana, there's no telling what she might do. It would be even more detrimental as she would see Lana as an obstacle to her goal of getting back together with you."

"She knows about Lana. Lana was at the apartment when Meredith came."

"Mmm. Just be careful. Please."

"I will. Do what you have to do to take her down as soon as possible. Like I said, I don't want anything standing in the way with Lana."

"Will do."

She updates me on a few other investigations. By the time we leave, it's evening. I head back to my apartment. As I fix myself a drink, I think about what Reggie has told me about Meredith. I don't doubt that Meredith is crazy. But I don't think she's crazy enough to harm someone. Nevertheless, I will take Reggie's advice and tread cautiously.

I look around the apartment. Tomorrow is moving day for the bed and boxes. There are a few loose ends I need to tie up so I won't officially move until Saturday. And hopefully I can make my move with Lana then and propose.

At the thought of proposing, my heart skips a beat. My life seems to have come together in a most remarkable way over the last few months, and I am grateful.

I walk into the bedroom and pick up the box from where I placed it this morning. I flip it open and the ring winks back at me from its velvet bed. I can't wait for it to be on Lana's finger where it belongs. And hopefully next week this time it will be there.

I put the ring back and spend the rest of the evening checking the items that will be moved in the morning. All my meetings are on hold as I want to supervise the process myself.

The weather the next day is remarkably warm and the move goes seamlessly. When I return to the apartment, I feel drained. I wasn't above pitching in and giving a hand where necessary, and muscles that haven't been used since my days of working as a packer in a factory, are protesting. I stand underneath a hot shower and allow the needles to penetrate every pore until I feel some relief. Finally, I towel myself dry and walk through the bare rooms. I check my phone and find a missed call from Lana. I dial her number as I put on the kettle to make some tea.

"Hello?"

"Hi, babe. How are you?"

"I'm good. How are you?"

"I'm a bit tired. But it's a good tired. How did your day go? Did you go to the office? How are you feeling today?"

"My day went well. I went in a little late as I still wasn't feeling so hot this morning. But I was able to muster some strength. I actually didn't feel too bad by the end of the day. What's making you tired?"

"I've been moving some heavy things." I don't want her to know anything about the move yet so I keep my response vague.

"Oh. Okay."

"You owe me dinner, you know. And I still need to make up for that dinner where we ended up at Eddie's. Are you free on Friday night?"

"Ace, when am I not free these days? You know what I'm doing, when I'm doing it and where I'm doing it. Of course I'm free."

I laugh. "I still want to ask. You do have your girlfriends, salon appointments, and goodness knows whatever else you women do in your free time. But thank you for being available on Friday night. I want to do what I should have done weeks ago."

"Which is?"

"Feed you then take you dancing."

"Now *that* I won't pass up. My poor feet haven't seen a dance floor in months."

"Happy to oblige, my love."

We talk a little longer until I hear her stifle a yawn.

"I'm going to let you go to bed, sweetheart."

"I wish you were here to tuck me in like you did the other night."

"Your wish will soon be my command. That is a promise."

She laughs as we say goodnight.

The next day, I head to the office early. I have a meeting with HR and Accounts regarding Christmas bonus packages. I also need to speak to my replacement and make it official that I will step aside as CEO on December thirty-first. I'm caught up in these meetings all morning and it's not until lunchtime that I check in with Lana. To my surprise, she's out of the office. When I go back to my office, I text her.

Where are you, love?

A minute or so later, her response comes.

I had to run out on an errand. I'm heading back to the office now. Did you want to see me?

When do I not want to see you? LOL. Come to my office when you get back, please.

Okay.

I send out for a couple of sandwiches while I wait for Lana. As I wait, I use the time to go through my email and respond to a few. I've just closed the last one when there's a knock on the door. Before I can speak it opens and Lana pushes her head inside. My face lights up when I see her. She smiles back and steps inside, closing the door behind her. I roll my chair away from the desk and stand. Like a homing pigeon, she comes into my arms. This is a feeling that will never get old for as long as I live.

I hold her for a few moments, inhaling the delicate scent of her shampoo. I sigh as I nuzzle her temple. She giggles.

"That tickles."

"Oh yeah? There are other places I want to tickle." My hand drifts down her back and I cup her buttocks. As I do, I feel my body begin to stir. "Do you remember the last time you were in this office and we were in this position?"

"Do I ever!"

"Care to finish what we started then?"

"Nope! We're past that now you know."

"You'd better make use of the chance while you can. How many people can say they've done it with the CEO in his office? Besides, the window for that is closing. I made it official with HR that I'm stepping down at the end of the year."

"What!?"

I nod. "I'll retain my ownership. But I don't need to be here on a daily basis. Besides, my mission for being here has been accomplished. I've got you."

She laughs and holds my gaze. "What a story that will be to tell our children. The time their father bought a company to get closer to their mother."

Her gaze penetrates me and I smile. "And that's not all we will tell them."

"So, you're not averse to us having children?"

"Not at all. I anticipate it with all my heart. What could be more thrilling than seeing the physical manifestation of our love in a flesh and blood being?"

She smiles and bows her head slightly. I kiss her forehead.

"I think I'll be getting back to my desk."

"Awww! What about doing it with the CEO in his office?"

She winks. "I'll take a rain check on that. But do it we shall."

I pump my fist victoriously. "Yes!"

Her laugh echoes as she leaves the office. I sit looking at the door for a few moments before I snap back to the present. I may not be CEO as of January first, but for now I am, and there are things to do.

Before I know it, it's Friday evening. I dress carefully. This is my last night in the apartment. Tomorrow morning, I'll move the few things that remain. And tomorrow afternoon I'll take Lana to the house.

I pick up my keys and head to Lana's to pick her up. As I wait on her doorstep rather than use my key to enter, I think about the next twenty-four hours. My birthday is in a week, and her 'yes' will be the only gift I need.

The door opens and I'm rendered speechless. Lana's wearing a midnight blue shift dress made of crushed velvet. It swirls around her calves with each step. Her hair is slicked back into a ponytail that curves over her shoulder. The low-heeled boots she wears are the perfect footwear for dancing and I smile.

"No stilettos?"

She winks and laughs as she caresses my cheek. "Nope. Shall we?"

"We shall."

We head to the parking lot. I think I see a light flash but it's only vehicles on the street passing. When we get to the restaurant and are ushered to our table, heads turn in our wake. I hold my head high as I catch some staring blatantly. Look at my woman, and know that she's mine. I can't take my eyes off Lana tonight. There's something extra special about her tonight. The thought of proposing makes her seem to glow in my eyes. Several times I catch her staring at me with a small smile, the same way I stare at her with a small smile.

We break away from staring at each other long enough to place our order. I slide my hand across the table and take her hand.

"You look beautiful tonight. You're always beautiful, but tonight you just seem to be-"

I blink as a camera flash goes off and microphones are shoved in my face.

"Mr. Channing, is there any truth to the fact that you're cheating on Meredith Channing?"

"Mr. Channing, is this the girl from the coffee shop?"

"Mr. Channing, when will you and Meredith be getting back together?"

"You bastard! How dare you humiliate me like this in public, with this-this-this gold digger!?"

The questions fly fast and the cameras don't stop flashing. Lana sits there staring and I try to shield her from the paparazzi. I feel a sting on my cheek and turn to find Meredith with her hand raised to strike me again. I grab her wrist and she stumbles as I stand.

"What the hell do you think you're doing, Meredith?"

"What am I doing? What are you doing here with *her* when we're supposed to be reconciling?"

I look around at the reporters who are eating up every word. The restaurant is eerily silent.

"Darling, I forgive you. We all make mistakes-"

"Save it for court, Meredith. I don't know what you're trying to do, but it's not going to work." I turn to Lana and pull her to her feet. I turn to the reporters. "You came for a story, but you're not going to get the one you were told you would get. This woman," I point at Meredith, "is a fraud and adulterer. You will see her name in the scandal pages not too long from now. And this," I pull Lana closer, "is the love of my life. Who she is, is none of your business. My life is none of your business unless I choose to call a press conference. So, mark my words, if I see any story written up about me after tonight, consider your jobs obsolete. I will find every last one of you and make you regret the moment you walked into this restaurant and disturbed my dinner."

There's a buzz of activity as security arrives. Meredith looks around wildly.

"Ace! Please! Just hear-"

I turn my back on her and the reporters, take Lana's hand and walk out of the restaurant. We get into the car and head back to Lana's. I am furious. Lana seems to understand my mood and is silent apart from a comforting hand on my knee. I don't take a calming breath until I'm safely in her apartment. I pull her into my arms and bury my face in her hair.

“I’m so sorry. I don’t want you exposed to this side of my life.”

She holds me tightly, rubbing my back in circular motions. “It’s okay,honey. It’s okay. I just have to get used to the fact that we’re bound to be news.”

“I just wanted one night out with you. And that bitch ruined it. I’m going to tell Reggie to make sure they throw the book at her. I’m sorry, Lana. I’ll make it up to you. I promise.”

“That’s okay, baby. We did say we will roll with the punches right? This doesn’t change how I feel about you. I love you, Ace.”

I hold her tightly as I breathe deeply. My heart feels full at her words. “I love you too, Lana.”

As we remain wrapped in each other’s arms, I know we can face anything together.

CHAPTER 29

LANA

As I sit waiting for Ace to pick me up, my hand rests lightly on my stomach. It's strange to believe that there's a baby in there. After the third day of feeling under the weather, I had stopped at the pharmacy on my way home. Then the next day I had slipped out of the office and gone to the doctor to confirm what the little stick had indicated. I'm six weeks pregnant.

As I replay the scene in the restaurant from the night before, I realize the extent to which every part of Ace's life is under scrutiny. I know I love Ace, and I know he loves me. But when I remember what Meredith did, it makes me hesitate. How do I tell Ace I'm carrying his child? Suppose he views it as my trying to trap him in a relationship? I saw how agitated he had become last night. I don't want to be another Meredith. So, for now, I will gauge his demeanor. But I can't hesitate indefinitely. By January I'll start to show. I rub my stomach once more. The doctor had prescribed something for the morning sickness and it's working wonders.

I look up as I hear the door open and Ace enters. He rubs his hands together.

"It's pretty nippy out there. You're going to need your mittens and a scarf with your jacket."

I go to the closet and retrieve the articles before heading downstairs with him. I sigh with relief as I enter the warm car. As he pulls into traffic, I turn to look at him.

"You took off so suddenly this morning."

"I had some things to take care of first thing today."

"Okay. Where are we going?"

He smiles. "That's for me to know and for you to stop being nosy."

"Another surprise?"

"Oh yeah!"

I lean back and laugh. "Strangely enough, I'm starting to like your surprises."

"I hope you love this one in more ways than one."

"I love you. I'm sure I'll love whatever it is."

He reaches for my hand and kisses the back before placing it on his knee. I turn to look out the window and am surprised to see some flurries. I smile.

"It's going to be a white Christmas."

"It sure seems that way."

"Do you have any plans for your birthday next week?"

"That depends on you."

"Oh?"

He smiles mysteriously. "Never mind. Have you told your folks which day we're arriving?"

Just like that he changes the topic and I allow it. At the mention of my parents, I realize that they, too, will need to know that they will be grandparents in another seven and a half months.

The rest of the drive passes and before long, we're in the hills. I look at the houses as we pass. I wonder which of his friends we are going to visit this time.

We turn in at a gateway and wait for the mechanized gate to open. As we drive up the driveway, I'm taken aback by the massive home. It seems to dwarf us as we step out of the car. He comes around and takes my hand.

"Close your eyes."

"What! Why?"

"Do as you're told," he pinches my nose and I smile and obey.

I grip his hand tightly as he walks me slowly into the house.

"Keep them closed."

I feel the change in temperature as we step into the warm interior.

"Almost there."

I shuffle forward a few more steps. He tilts my head back slightly. I feel him move away and I hear the door close behind us. He removes my scarf and mittens then moves away.

"Open."

My eyes flutter and the first thing I do is blink away the haze that comes when one has one's eyes closed for a while. As things come into focus, I see two people floating in mid-air. Floating? I blink again and I find myself staring at a life-sized picture. My mouth drops open as I look at a blown-up version of the picture Ace and I took ten years ago.

"Ace I-" I turn to find him behind me on one knee, his gaze fixed on me.

In his hand, there's a tiny box. My knees go weak as I grab my stomach and my mouth simultaneously. He reaches for my hand and I extend it, trembling as I do.

"Lana, I've loved you from the day I met you. And I vowed to one day find you and make you mine. You have brought so much light, joy, encouragement and stability to my life. And I want to make that a constant for the rest of my life. I will give you the world if you'll let me. Lana, will you marry me?"

I watch almost in slow motion as he flicks the top of the box open. I stare in amazement at the ring nestled in the black velvet. Tears fill my eyes as I think about my misgivings a few moments ago. I should never have doubted him. I nod.

"Yes, Ace, I will marry you. Yes! Yes!"

He jumps to his feet and pulls me into his arms. His lips find mine and I melt into his embrace. He kisses me long and hard until I feel dizzy. He pulls back and laughs softly.

"Let's make this official, why don't we."

I watch as he pulls the ring out of the box and holds my hand. He slides it onto my finger and I stare as it sparkles in the light. I look up at him and pull his head down to meet mine once more. After a few more moments, he raises his head.

“And there’s another surprise. This is our new home.”

“What!?”

“I bought it a few months ago. And yes, it was bought with you in mind.”

“A company, a car *and* a house!?”

He laughs. “And this is only the beginning, my love. So, what do you say Mrs. Channing? Would you like to look at your new home?”

Hand in hand, we explore the rooms. I’m rendered speechless at the vastness of the house. Most of the rooms are empty and I begin to think of how they can be furnished. I scream in delight when I see the pool through the French doors leading out to the deck. He laughs.

“That was the major selling point. It’s Olympic-sized too. I can’t wait until the weather is warmer and we get to try it out. Especially at night.”

He pulls me into his arms and kisses me once more. I run my hands up and down his back as I return it fervently. He raises his head.

“Enough of this floor. Care to take a look upstairs?”

I walk ahead of him, giggling as he caresses my bottom. As we get to the top, he hugs me from behind.

"There's one room in particular, I can't wait to show you."

He shuffles me down the corridor and opens a door at the end. We're in the master suite. His bedroom has been transported from the city to the hills. He turns me in his arms and kisses me hungrily. As we undress each other, kissing each inch of exposed flesh, my heart feels light. There will be no interruption, no wondering, no worrying that we have an expiration date. Ace and I will be together for the rest of our lives.

As we fall in a tangled heap on the bed, we strain hungrily against each other. I sigh blissfully as our bodies become one. There's a new fervor as we thrust with one rhythm, caressing and teasing spots that elicit the most pleasure for the other. And when we reach that peak, we cross over together, our hearts beating to the same rhythm.

As we relax in the aftermath of our lovemaking, our heads rest on one pillow. He strokes my arm gently with his forefinger, trailing a path upward to the curve of my breast. He kneads it gently as his thumb brushes my nipple. His eyes hold mine and I smile.

"So, this story that I'm going to tell our children, you know it's going to include the fact that you gave me a house and ring when you proposed, right?"

"What can I say? I've set the bar very high for my future daughters."

"Daughters?"

"And sons too."

"Which would you want first?"

"As long as it's with you, my love, anything goes." He moves his hand down to my stomach. "I can't wait to see your body stretching with our child."

I smile at him. "You may not have very long to wait."

He blinks at me and I keep smiling.

"What do you mean by that, Lana?"

I take a deep breath and entwine my fingers with his over my stomach. I look deep into his eyes.

"I mean, that in seven months or so, we will have a son or a daughter or both."

"You mean you're-" His mouth falls open as he gazes at me. I nod.

"I'm pregnant."

He stares at me for a few moments and I see his eyes mist over. He swallows hard. "I'm going to be a *father*." His voice breaks on the last word as he scoots down to place his head on my stomach. I feel the warmth of his tears and I try to hold back mine. I know that this is a tender moment for him as he never knew his father. I feel his lips nuzzle my still-flat stomach. His fingers drift between my legs and I feel desire rise within me again.

Our lovemaking this time is gentler as he takes extra care with me. As we lay wrapped in each other's arms once more, his hand rubs my stomach.

"So, will you be showing in time for my birthday next week?"

I laugh. "I'm only six weeks, Ace. You're so impatient."

"I've been patient all my life. I deserve to not have to wait, don't you think?"

"Well, I have no control over this. You're just going to have to wait and see."

"As long as you're by my side, Lana, I'll wait forever."

I smile and reach up to caress his cheek. "Only seven months, my love. Only seven months."

EPILOGUE

LANA

I take a deep breath as we come to yet another stoplight.

"Will these lights never end?" I groan.

Ace looks over at me and pats my hand. "Almost there, sweetie. Almost there. Just hold on a little longer."

"Don't tell me. Tell your son. Ahhhhhh!" I groan as another contraction rips through me. I grip Ace's knee and hear him grunt as my fingers bite into his flesh. When the contraction passes, my fingers relax.

"Just one more block, my love."

"Dr. Dawes-"

"-will meet us there. Your room is prepped and ready."

I lean back in the seat and breathe evenly. "Okay. I'm sorry, babe."

"For what?"

"We'll have to apologize to everyone for rushing out the way we did."

Ace laughs. "I don't think any apologies are necessary. You're nine months pregnant. Just this morning we were all saying you're ready to pop any day now. You've been a real trouper, Lana. I love you so much and my love has grown even stronger these past months watching our child grow inside you."

"Awww! Babe! I love aaaaaaaaahhhhhhhh!" Out of nowhere, another contraction rips through me. My fingers dig into Ace's leg once again as my toes curl and I grunt through the pain. I squeeze my eyes closed as I wait for the pain to pass.

"Breathe, sweetheart. Breathe."

"I can't! Ace!"

"You can. We're here. Relax and breathe."

I open my eyes and find that we are at the emergency entrance of the hospital. There's a wheelchair waiting on the ramp and I see Dr. Dawes smiling at us through the windshield. Ace comes around to help me out of the car and into the wheelchair.

"I see this young man is finally ready to see the world. I was wondering if I was going to have to bring you in for an induction."

I look at the doctor but I can't think of anything to say in response as another contraction rips through me. I can barely keep track of anything as I'm rushed through the corridors and into the delivery room. I'm now in constant pain and everything around me is a blur.

I feel my body being hooked up to all kinds of devices. I try to focus and start to cry.

"I'm here, honey. I'm here."

"It hurts."

"It'll soon be over." He brushes some strands of hair away from my face.

And in a few hours, it indeed is. I feel as though my body has been ripped into pieces and is hanging by a mere thread. But our baby has come into the world, and the pain seems to melt away the second I hold him in my arms. Through my tears, I feel for his little fingers and toes and smile up at Ace.

"He's adorable!"

Ace places a trembling hand on his son's head and smiles through his misty eyes.

"He gets it from his mother."

Wordlessly, I hold the baby up for Ace to take him. His hands tremble slightly as his emotions get the better of him and the tears roll down his cheeks. I watch as he rocks him slightly.

"Welcome to the world, Chase Abraham Channing. You are wanted. You are loved. You are desired." He chokes each affirmation out on a sob. "Our baby. Our son. Our beloved child."

A nurse taps him on the shoulder and whispers something in his ear. Ace nods and hands the baby to her then takes a seat in the chair beside my bed. I watch in surprise as he unbuttons his shirt and bares his chest. The nurse returns with the baby who is now naked save for a diaper. She gently lays him on Ace's chest then tucks a blanket around them both. It's now my turn to be misty-eyed as I look at my husband bonding with our son.

The past year seems to be a vague memory as I think about missing all of this had Ace not been determined to have me in his life. My family had been ecstatic to find that Chester was alive and well. Their delight had known no bounds when they were showered with news of the engagement and pregnancy. It had been a grand affair in March as Ace and I exchanged our vows. And now, one week after my birthday, my heart is complete.

Over the next couple days, visitors come and go. I'm especially delighted to receive a basket from McEachron. I had taken maternity leave. But after taking one look at Chase, I know I will be taking up the offer of working on contract from home. There's no way I'm missing out on any of these moments with my son.

I sit in the newly decorated nursery, rocking Chase to sleep after nursing him. As I stand to place him in his cradle, I turn to find Ace standing in the doorway watching us. I smile and place a finger on my lips as I tiptoe out of the room. He takes my hand and we sit on the love seat in our bedroom. I curl up in his lap as he nuzzles my neck. I gaze out the window at the view of the city below. The pool reflects the full moon which is high in the night sky. I sigh blissfully as Ace kisses me.

I am the luckiest woman in the world. I have life, I have family, I have health and I have love. Yes, the luckiest woman in the world and I dare anyone to disagree.

The End

COMING NEXT - SAMPLE CHAPTERS

ON HIS TERMS

Prologue

Olivia

(Eight Years Ago)

There were very few things that made me nervous.

Or rather, there were very few things I allowed myself to feel nervous about, especially given how particularly ungracious life has been to me so far.

However, standing close to the men's locker room at Emerson High makes my palms sweat.

For the better part of the last half hour, I had been waiting a little distance away, hoping my best friend would remember we agreed to meet up here after school so I could retrieve my biology notebook back.

I tried calling him once again, antsy, especially because I was running late for my volunteer gig at the animal shelter. He was well aware of this commitment and I was beyond aggravated.

He still didn't pick up. I frowned down at my phone. Perhaps his battery died again and he left it charging somewhere and isn't able to hear it ringing. I looked towards the door and imagined he's probably engaged in some sort of conversation with his teammates and had completely forgotten about our agreement.

"Don't ever ask me for my notes again!" I angrily typed out yet another message to him, anger simmered in the pit of my stomach.

The door swung open once again with a few of the guys heading out, but of course he wasn't amongst them.

My heart sunk when I moved a bit further toward the door. Maybe one of them would help me find him.

I truly hoped I wouldn't have to talk to any of the guys, but it became apparent now it's my only option. I began to inch closer, but made sure to stop a few steps away so it wouldn't appear as though I was outright trying to ogle them or something. The accusation, and the subsequent infamy it would bestow on me, is not particularly one I had any interest whatsoever in.

Another few minutes passed and the door swung open again.

My heart lurched into my throat when I stepped forward, ready to plead for some assistance in locating Danny, however, when I saw who it was my plan was immediately aborted. Because there was no way in hell I was going to speak to Xander King. He's super popular and for all the right reasons... smart, handsome, easy going, athletic, and so much more. I raised him up on such a pedestal that speaking to him was out of the question.

I turned to walk away, my eyes clenched shut as I cursed underneath my breath.

A few seconds later, I found the courage to open my eyes again, swearing to murder Danny, and turned back toward the locker room praying I had waited long enough for Xander to have moved on.

I'm not that lucky though and freeze because Xander hadn't moved and is staring right at me.

"Hey," he smiled over at me.

There was no hope of a response coming from me as my brain short circuited and I'm frozen in place staring back at him.

His smile widens to show his perfect white teeth. I could only imagine what he thought of me standing there. I tried to smile back but it came as more of a grimace.

He jerked his head toward the locker room door. "Do you need something?"

I opened my mouth and nothing came out. Could I be anymore lame? I'm tempted to look behind me to see if he was actually speaking to me or if someone walked up behind me.

But my brain slowly started working, reminding me the only thing behind me was a wall.

I'm tempted to turn once more to face it just so he'll hopefully walk away. Granted he would probably forever label me as mental but I could live with that. Anything was better than just staring at him like I'm mute.

At my continued stupor he held his perfect smile and a gleam in his icy blue eyes. They were usually cold... he has always seemed cold. He's never even looked in my direction, which makes it all the more jarring he's smiling at me now.

His hair's all over the place... raven black, thick, wavy, unruly. I'd fantasized about what it would feel like to run my fingers through it more times than I would ever admit, and now that I'm this close to it, the fantasies returned.

His gaze once again returned to the locker room door as it swung open.

"Are you looking for your friend?" he asked, looking back at me.

This startled me. *Friend? What friend?*

At my widened gaze, he responded. "I've seen you both around together."

I wondered if I would ever be able to speak again. He'd seen us around. I mean, it made sense he knew Danny, they played on the same team... but he knew *I* existed?

"Hello?" he waved again, and my throat had closed up. What in the hell is wrong with

Me?

My lips parted again as I tried to remember how to speak. At some point I backed up against the wall and I leaned more of my weight onto it.

An apology for my silence was on the tip of my tongue, but suddenly I heard my name.

"Olivia?”

I turned instantly to see Danny coming out the door, his phone pressed to his ear.

Just then mine began to ring and I looked down at my hand still clutching my phone.

Before I could stop myself the curse shot out of my mouth. “You piece of shit!”

The shock that followed from everyone, including myself, seemed to turn the entire corridor into a graveyard.

I’m not shocked I exploded, and neither is Danny, but the over six foot tall Adonis before me I had previously appeared mute to, is startled.

My gaze swept back over to him and met his widened eyes.

My lips parted again, but this time around it’s with the intention to explain my outburst.

He however began to laugh, softly and shook his head.

“At least I know your name now,” he chuckled and with a salute to Danny turned around to continue on his way, a satchel slung over his shoulder. “See you around... Olivia.”

I couldn’t breathe... I almost forgot all about Danny still standing there.

At least I know your name now? What did he mean? Why did he want to know my name?

"Livvy I'm so sorry, I completely forgot," I heard the aforementioned piece of shit say as he hurried over to me.

"Here," he held out my notebook but I couldn't look away from Xander King as he strolled confidently and unhurriedly away from us.

Just like every other girl in Emerson High who crushes on Xander my heart raced away in my chest, and I knew without a shadow of a doubt I would be replaying this scene in my heart and mind forever.

And his words- *see you around, Olivia?* What on earth could he possibly mean?

Chapter One
Olivia
Present Day

My palms were sweaty again.

On my drive here my steering wheel had received the brunt of my anxiety, but now it was the woven strap of my purse.

I looked down to inspect it as the elevator began to climb the floors. I loved this purse, it was a gift from my mother about two years ago when I had gotten my first job ever at Charter Middle School. The strap was woven in red and blue while the purse itself was a creamy, textured leather.

The last thing I wanted was for it to be sweat soaked so I considered unhooking it and instead use the short handle attached to the top.

I'd just gotten used to wearing it with the strap.

My gaze lifted to the floor display as the elevator stopped to let out and let in a few people.

It was a few seconds of shuffling about to make room, and then the car resumed its ascent.

My mind returned to the strap as my eyes glanced back to the display ahead showing we were now passing the 52nd floor.

My heart was racing, and I reckon it was going to be the case for the next hour or longer. Just as we reached the 58th floor, with three floors more to go, I began to unhook the strap from the corners.

It all came off just as the elevator came to a stop again. I lifted my gaze and watched as the entire car emptied out. However, I still had one more floor to go, the final floor.

I tried, but failed to swallow the lump in my throat so I gave up altogether and tucked the strap into the purse.

I arrived with a ding, the shiny steel doors parted but it took a few seconds for my legs to work.

I'm not exactly sure the exact moment life returned to them, but soon enough I'm heading into his reception area.

I was expected since I was already cleared from the ground floor, which gave me a bit of hope that perhaps this trip wouldn't be completely futile.

I hoped this meeting would produce the result I'm hoping for, otherwise my heart would be broken. This was my last resort, and one I would have never even seen as an option if my entire family's life wasn't hanging in the balance.

So although I wasn't expecting much, I needed to at least try so no matter what I could live with myself.

"Miss Rose?" the gorgeous receptionist called and I nodded in response.

"Please take a seat. Mr. King is on a conference call right now. He'll be with you shortly."

"Alright" I replied and headed over to one of the space's leather sofas.

Afterwards, I watched her leave, my gaze on her tasteful dark pumps and tailored pink pantsuit. She was gorgeous... hair blonde, slicked back into a neat bun at the back of her head. Behind the desk, was a man also dressed sharply in a suit and as our eyes met, he sent me a polite smile.

I settled in to wait, and once again assessed my appearance.

I wasn't over dressed, although I had been quite tempted to go that route but the last thing I wanted was to impress him. So I had chosen a simple pair of dark jeans, a lacy camisole underneath and a tailored camel blazer.

My wavy brown hair was arranged into a neat half up and half down style, my makeup simple, and on my feet were my usual low heeled work pumps.

I look decent, pretty even but I didn't expect him to think that.

In fact, I didn't expect him to think about me in any positive light whatsoever but still I had to try.

This is for your conscience, I had managed to convince myself before making the ultimate decision to come over.

The call was made almost two weeks prior but it was just the previous day I had received a response, relaying his approval and available meeting time.

And so here I was, in the midst of his extreme wealth and success.

I wasn't surprised... at his animosity towards me or his success so far. He was just twenty four, and as far as I'd heard, King Industries was now worth a billion dollars. The ultimate unicorn. Everyone in the media called him an ultimate success but only I knew how long he'd had this dream of developing the smartphone his company produced, and how he had begun working on it right from high school.

He deserved every ounce of his victory, and even though I was slightly jealous I had reminded myself time and time again I too was in the exact place I wanted to be. I'd always wanted to be a teacher, and I'd worked towards it from the time we'd both left high school.

That was one of the things I'd so loved about us... how clear we'd been about where we wanted to go. And how we both strived to achieve it. However the downside to knowing the exact directions we wanted had led to paths that had taken us away from each other. He had gone to San Francisco, while I'd remained here in LA.

But he had returned as expected, but it was too late. A lot of things were now too late but I had no regrets.

In the present I waited another half hour before I was called.

"Mr. King's ready for you," the receptionist said, and I rose to my feet.

I went with her down the elegant hallway, which was lined on both sides with what I was certain were original pieces of gorgeous art.

Soon we arrived at the wide double doors to his office and she turned to me with a smile.

"What would you like to drink?"

"Um… "

"Water? Tea? Coffee?"

I smiled because this wasn't that kind of meeting.

"Nothing," I replied. "Thank you."

She nodded and went on her way.

I stood before the heavy mahogany doors and took several deep breaths. And my hand rose to knock. I hesitated for a little bit because it wasn't too late. I mean I could turn back right now.

Squaring my shoulders I knocked on it, and heard the response from within.

"Come in."

With my heart in my throat, I turned the handle down and walked in.

Chapter Two
Xander

I couldn't believe she was here.

It had been two weeks and I still couldn't believe she had contacted me.

The first time Laura had informed me of the call, I'd been in the middle of a meeting in my office.

It had taken a little while for the name to register, and all the blood drained from my face.

"She wants to speak to me?" I'd asked.

"Yes sir."

My immediate response had been a no.

"Tell her to book an appointment and come in."

The call had ended, but my silence had continued on. It was such a contrast to my much more lighthearted mood from the minutes prior, and so the men before me were quite taken aback.

They allowed me the time to recover… to think… and to make a decision. And then I'd call Laura back.

"Wait to call her back for at least two week to make the appointment."

"Yes sir." had been Laura's quick reply.

It should have been more, I should make her wait forever… if possible. But I had no clue about what she wanted, and dragging things out any longer might have resulted in her not needing to contact me again.

I didn't necessarily want to see her but I needed the confrontation. I'd waited for it and almost even hoped for it for too long.

And now she was here, and it was a hard pill to swallow.

A part of me had imagined she wouldn't show up. That she would find an excuse at the last minute and cancel the appointment but she had made it. I was truly surprised. It made me all the more curious now as to what she needed.

I knew her, and was aware she wouldn't be here if it wasn't a matter of importance. It made me just a little worried. *Was she alright?*

I pointed to one of the seats before me and with a nod, she headed over, her head lowered to watch her steps.

I was glad because it meant I could watch her.

And what surprised me the most was not much had changed about her.

She was no longer the same fifteen year old teenager that had kept to herself back in Emerson. She was a woman now, a bit taller, a bit more curvaceous. My gaze couldn't help going to the lacy camisole that covered her chest and how it stretched across her breasts.

I felt the immediate and responding tug in my groin.

It had been so long, but I remembered. My heart remembered… as well as my body.

I suddenly began to feel heated, but didn't even bother examining the ventilation of the room. Because the air conditioner was running and all the heat was emanating from the pit of my stomach and spreading out to the rest of my body.

I watched as she took her seat, cautiously and she was arranging her purse on her lap. She took her time, but I watched and waited until she was finally ready to look up at me.

She soon did, a soft smile on her face but her gaze… was guarded.

What stunned me the most was she had become even more beautiful. Sixteen-year old me wouldn't have thought it was possible but yet here we were.

I gazed unashamedly at her brown eyes, warm and beguiling… the gentle slope of her nose and down to her full peachy lips.

I had kissed them, more times than I could remember but at the time was sure it would never be enough. That I would never get enough. I wondered now if it would be the case if I tasted her once again.

Perhaps we had outgrown each other or perhaps it was all still the same as back then. I felt like a moth drawn to a flame when it came to her.

"It's been a while," she spoke, and I didn't miss the slight tremble of her voice. She was nervous and it showed. I was too, somewhat, but I was able to conceal it well. I was already liking the direction of things.

She looked around the office when I didn't give a response. "You've done really great, Xander. I'm so proud of you."

I straightened in my seat. "Why are you here?"

I could no longer wait. I needed to know why she had set aside her pride and come all the way here to see me. She wasn't shameless as far as I knew, or perhaps she was or had become so? It had been almost four years now since we had been separated.

More than enough time for people to change, especially for her.

Bile instantly rose up in my throat at the reminder.

"Straight to the point," she smiled, nervous once again. "I won't waste your time. I just… I wanted to at least try."

Her gaze lifted to mine, and I didn't miss the slight sheen in them.

"My mom, um… she was diagnosed with breast cancer, about two years ago," she began. "She got treatment for it… a mastectomy, and then chemo. She started getting better, but we found out a few weeks ago it's back."

She smiled, but my heart squeezed at her words.

"We're still in debt from bearing all the costs from the first time around but now…" she sighed, smiling again.

"I couldn't help but come to you… to ask if perhaps you could help us out. It's alright if you refuse. I would understand. You have no obligation to help me out or anything. It was just… right now… it's a sort of last resort. Maybe another way will open up in the future soon. We're hopeful."

I looked at her, and had absolutely no idea of what to say.

I knew her mother, Linda. The sweetest woman to probably ever exist, she took me in like I was a part of her family for years. So hearing this hurt me deeply. But I couldn't let it show because her daughter on the other hand was a thorn in my side. A thorn I was still unable to pull out. And as I stared at her now, I wondered if I would ever want to.

A long silence ensued between us, and that was because I didn't particularly know what to say. Simply handing over whatever funds she needed for the surgery was no particular hardship for me, but as I looked at her I wondered if I was willing to just simply do this for her. I was willing to help her mother but her…

"I understand if you're not willing to do this, or if you need a bit more time to process it," she suddenly began to rise to her feet. "I'm grateful already that you were willing to have a meeting with me."

At this and without a second look at me, or even waiting for my response she turned around and began to walk away. I knew then what I wanted to say.

"What are you willing to… exchange?" I leaned back in my chair. "For these needed funds."

She stopped in her tracks.

ABOUT THE AUTHOR

Thank you so much for reading!
If you have enjoyed the book and would like to leave a precious review for me, please kindly do so here:

Resisting The CEO

Please click on the link below to receive info about my latest releases and giveaways.
NEVER MISS A THING

Or
come and say hello here:

ALSO BY IONA ROSE

anny Wanted

CEO's Secret Baby

New Boss, Old Enemy

Craving The CEO

Forbidden Touch

Crushing On My Doctor

Reckless Entanglement

Untangle My Heart

Tangled With The CEO

Tempted By The CEO

CEO's Assistant

Trouble With The CEO

It's Only Temporary

Charming The Enemy

Keeping Secrets

On His Terms

CPSIA information can be obtained
at www.ICGtesting.com
Printed in the USA
LVHW110354061222
734671LV00017B/251